To Nanette
Very best wishes
from Alice

BEYOND THE PURPLE SHADOW

In this, the final book of
THE MAGDALENE CONNECTION TRILOGY,
Beyond The Purple Shadow, Madeleine Manning gives an account of her part in preserving the connection between the two families generated in 1954 by the two original characters, Cecily and Bridie. The book takes a swipe at the celebrity culture as well as at deeply entrenched religious beliefs, attitudes and male-dominated prejudices, particularly in the Roman Catholic Church.

Other books by Alice Lee Thornton

ANGEL, SINNER, MERMAID, SAINT

In 1954, two unmarried girls, one Cornish, one Irish, give birth to babies within the harsh confines of a Magdalene Home. This book traces Cecily's life-long love affair; a story later taken up by a mysterious grandchild, Madeleine, arriving from the United States. Madeleine tells also the story of two boys adopted in Ireland; their incarceration in a notorious Industrial school, their subsequent involvement in the Northern Ireland troubles and their search for their birth-mothers. Set between London, Cornwall and Ireland, the story tells of the inextricable link between two families, leading to another story:

THE MAGDALENE CONNECTION

The second book of the eponymous trilogy, in which Madeleine invites contributions from some of the characters in the first book. The main story, however, is that of 'the other mother', Bridie O'Shaughnessy, a tale of innocence, misplaced trust, rape, and the legalised cruelty committed in the name of religion in the 1950s.

Beyond The Purple Shadow

The third book of

THE MAGDALENE CONNECTION

trilogy

Alice Lee Thornton

Matador
9 Priory Business Park,
Wistow Road, Kibworth Beauchamp,
Leicestershire, LE8 0RX
Tel: 0116 279 2299
Email: books@troubador.co.uk
Web: www.troubador.co.uk/matador
Twitter: @matadorbooks

ISBN 978 1838590 413

British Library Cataloguing in Publication Data.
A catalogue record for this book is available from the British Library.

Printed and bound in Great Britain by 4edge Limited
Typeset in 11pt Sabon by Troubador Publishing Ltd, Leicester, UK

Matador is an imprint of Troubador Publishing Ltd

For my children,
Thomas, Alicia and Charles, and for Isaac

DRAMATIS PERSONAE

CECILIA'S FAMILY
Cecily Rose James, b. 1936 m. Bruno Sabra b.1910
Dominic Cornelius Manning, their son, b. 1954; adopted by the Mannings of Limerick, Ireland
Madeleine Grace Manning, his daughter, b.1980

CECILIA'S STEP FAMILY
Edmund Knight
Agnes Knight m.Thomas Metcalfe
Elizabeth Knight m. Ross Penberthy
Petroc Penberthy b. 1992, their son
Isobel Sargent, their maternal Aunt

THE MANNING FAMILY
Dr Cornelius Manning ob.1968
Una Manning ob. 1968
Adopted Donal and Dominic 1954
Katherine Manning m.Will Sullivan
Cornelius (Con) and Jude, their sons
Theresa (Tess) Manning

BRIDIE'S FAMILY
Brigid O'Shaughnessy b.1934 m. Charles O'Malley
Donal Declan Manning b. 1954 (*adopted by the Mannings*) m. 1. Frances Harrington of Dublin

Grainne O'Malley b.1960 m. Colm O'Riordan
Rosaleen O'Malley b. 1964 m. Henry Kennedy
Bridget and Liam their children
Aoife and Tomas, their grandchildren
Constance O'Malley b.1967 m. Patrick Logan
Niamh and Jack , their children
(Sebastian Charles O'Malley b. / ob. 1969)

PRONUNCIATION OF THE IRISH NAMES

NAME	PRONOUNCED	ENGLISH EQUIVALENT
Aisling:	Ashling	
Aoife:	Ee-fa	Eva/Eve
Dearbhla:	Dervla	
Fearghal	Fergal	
Grainne:	Grawn-ya	Grace
Niamh:	Neave	
Oirbsean:	Orribshen. (This was the original name of Lough Corrib, Co Galway).	
Oughterard:	Ochter-ard	

BEYOND THE PURPLE SHADOW

"Your obsession with your family is beginning to piss me off," he said. "You're lucky enough to be the girlfriend of an international celebrity, and you choose to go chasing off to some remote, uncivilised place in Ireland, instead of coming to the U.S. with me, all expenses paid, and providing me with the support I need. Who is going to protect me from all those raving fans?"

He started to pick up the articles of clothing I had just packed in my case and threw them into the corners of the bedroom; a pair of panties here, a tee-shirt there. Pendragon growled softly at him when I protested, his lips drawn back to expose wolfish teeth. I guess it was then that I decided that I would never consider this guy to be a suitable mate, and father to my children.

PART ONE

ONE

As you may recall, spring came late into April in 2013. The long, long winter loosened its icy grip suddenly, and leaves began to emerge, shyly at first, as if expecting to be, literally, nipped in the bud. On a rare, sunny Saturday afternoon, I heard horses' hooves on the drive approaching Foxgloves, my cottage on the Cornish coast, when I was pottering around the garden. I went round the corner of the cottage to find Petroc Penberthy (my grandmother's step-grandson) and a pretty blonde girl reining in their steeds outside the side door.

"Hey, Maddie," Petroc said. "I brought Sophie to meet you. Sophie Boscawen, Madeleine Manning."

I took off my gardening glove and reached up my hand, which the girl took in cool, slim fingers.

"Good to meet you, Sophie," I said. "Why don't you two dismount and I'll make some coffee or tea. It's warm enough to sit outside on the other side of the house."

Sophie was a farmer's daughter from a village a few miles inland. She told me she was studying Accountancy at the local college and hoped to set up her own business, specialising in farmers' and landowners' accounts. The pair stayed for a short while until Petroc explained that they needed to get ready for a Young Farmers' Ball that evening.

"We met at the Valentine's dance," he explained proudly, reaching his large capable, farmer's hand to clasp hers fondly.

*

So that solves the problem of his crush on me, I thought, without regret, as they rode away. I was happy for him that he had found someone nearer his own age – still a teenager at nineteen.

And here am I, I thought, *at thirty three, my biological clock ticking away, as they say, waiting to be swept off my feet by someone I could love enough to be the father of the child, or children, whom I feel it my family duty to produce.*

I knew that I expected too much of life and love, my grandmother's, Cecilia's, memoir having led me to believe that there was one special person in the world who would be my soul-mate, lover, husband, best friend and father of my children. Cecilia's love for my grandfather, the renowned conductor, Bruno Sabra, never faltered from the day of their first meeting. It even survived a loveless marriage to another and, eventually, after nearly twenty years she realised her dream and the lovers were reunited at last.

Here at Foxgloves, the cliff-top cottage in which Cecilia and Bruno lived and loved, there is a bureau still full of their love letters and the poems she wrote when she thought that all was lost. As well as being, physically, the image of my grandmother, I thought that I too would be capable of such outpourings if I found *that person* . . . and the feeling was reciprocated.

*

Petroc had told me that the Gypsies were back on the common between Polburran and Porthwenna so, remembering Cecilia's account of Bruno's purchase of the second Nimrod, I decided that it was time for another dog. Cecilia's old Labrador had just survived the ceremony of the scattering of her ashes in June the previous year, broken-hearted though he was, only to suffer a severe stroke soon afterwards. Lizzie Penberthy,

Cecilia's stepdaughter and Petroc's mother, a vet in the local practice, had advised that he should be put out of his misery and made the necessary arrangements. His ashes, too, were scattered in the same place as those of his beloved mistress.

Taking some money and Dickon's old collar and lead, I left the house on the Sunday afternoon after Petroc's and Sophie's visit, walked up to the road and turned up the green lane leading to the common. The high hedges on either side were banked with flowers. There were primroses still, and violets nestling among the cow parsley and wild parsnip, with bluebells and deep pink campion striving to be seen among the tall blades of grass. The furze atop the banks bore the most profuse blossom that I had ever seen in all the dozen or so years I had lived in these parts. Its blaze of intense gold was breathtaking. I was reminded of one of my grandmother's sayings: *when gorse is out of bloom, kissing's out of fashion.*

As I approached the Gypsy camp, there was a little barking from the dogs, though I could not see any about. A few children were playing a game with sticks and stones around a muddy puddle.

"Hello," I said, walking up to them. "Do you think your dads have any good dogs for sale?"

"Hey lady," one of the boys replied. "D'you want one to match your hair,'cos I don't think we got one?"

"Cheeky lad!" I said, laughing. "It's just that my gran bought one from here once, long ago."

"They're tied up round the back." said one of the girls. "I'll get me Dad."

She disappeared into the nearest van and I heard her voice pipe, "Dad, there's a pretty lady with funny red hair come about a dog."

"She better be fucking pretty if she disturbs my Sunday afternoon nap," I heard, and a heavily-built, coarse-looking man appeared at the door, dressed in greasy-looking levis and a grubby singlet that had seen much whiter days. He looked me up and down and raised bushy eyebrows.

"So?" he inquired.

"My grandmother bought a dog at a camp here, years ago." I explained. "The man's wife was called Lavendi. She read her palm … and was very accurate."

"She always was, the wife's great-nan." He looked at his daughter. "Not so much funny hair as a funny voice, Roxy. The lady sounds like a Yank to me. You'll be wantin' a dog as can swim the pond, then?"

"I live over here now," I said. "But yes, I *was* born and raised in the United States." *(And here I should perhaps point out that, though I have made every effort to alter my spelling to the British way, my accent and certain different words still give me away).*

"Well, come with me and we'll see what we can find," he invited.

I followed him round the largest van, a little procession of curious children in my wake. Among the group of dogs, I met the eyes of a young lurcher, the image of the two Nimrods I had seen in photographs. He put his head on one side appealingly and I was immediately won over.

"That's the one," I stated.

"The best of the whole bunch," the man said grudgingly. "He'll cost ya."

"Then I shall expect a palm-reading as a bonus."

"I ain't got the gift, not being a real Romany – but my girl here . . . reckon it passed on to her. Look at the lady's hand, Roxy."

The girl, who I reckoned to be about nine or ten years old, grabbed my left hand in her grimy one but, before studying it, she looked searchingly at me with large brown eyes which bore signs of recent tears. Neither her eyes nor her lips answered my smile. Glancing nervously at her father, she lowered pink, swollen eyelids to examine my hand.

"There's love-trouble ahead, pretty lady," she said after a few moments . . . "like in *Eastenders*. You're a nice, kind lady as well as being pretty. There will be children before very long. . . and another thing: one day your lovely hair's gonna be as gray as that *jookel.*"

"Jookel?" I queried.

"Romany for 'dog'," said the girl's father.

He and I haggled over the price for a while and came to an agreement, once I had pointed out the extra costs I would have to bear for castration, injections and micro-chipping.

"Never bothered with any o' that," he observed, scowling.

I handed over the agreed sum and pressed a two pound coin into the girl's hand, closing her fingers over it and giving her a reassuring smile

"Thank you, Roxy. One day I'll come back and tell you how things work out for me."

Then I fitted the collar and lead to the dog, bade them goodbye and led my new friend towards home, aware of that troubled little face watching until we were out of sight.

TWO

THE NEXT FEW DAYS WERE TAKEN UP WITH VISITS TO the veterinary surgery with Pendragon and some basic training as to what was – and was not – acceptable behaviour on the domestic front. Lizzie Penberthy was full of admiration for my new companion and exclaimed at the similarity between him and both of Cecilia's 'Nimrods'. He was a sweet, gentle creature, very laid-back in temperament, obedient and anxious to please. We bonded immediately, he and I, and I soon realised that he was a real treasure of a dog: a best friend and a loyal guardian.

It was on a fine Saturday afternoon at the end of our first week together, that we returned from a long walk inland from home and noted a flamboyant purple cabriolet parked where my long lane of a drive met the road. Thinking my nearest neighbour must have visitors, I walked past without paying it too much attention, telling Pendragon that I was going to take him to a very special place before going in for tea.

We walked past the house and across the lawn and turned down the grassy path to the dell where the ashes of my grandparents lie scattered among the wild flowers and the waiting foxgloves, one of which was nearly in flower already. Pendragon was quick to discover the spring well and drank long and deep of its waters.

"This is St Elowen's Well," I told him. "Cecilia, my grandmother, named it after her stillborn daughter. Their spirits are here in this sacred place. Always be quiet and respectful here, there's a good boy."

Pendragon looked thoughtfully at me as if he understood every word that I spoke.

Suddenly I realised that we were not alone. A handsome young guy had appeared from behind the hawthorn tree and stopped for a moment, observing us and listening to my words. His blond (bleached) hair was cropped close to his head, upon which he sported a pair of over-sized Dolce and Gabana shades. He wore a loose shirt in pale blue, banded with mauve, over designer-distressed jeans and Nike Airmax Olympic Limited Edition trainers of multi-coloured effect. (I congratulated myself on my recognition of a very pricey and desirable fashion item I had seen in a Sunday magazine).

"I have to tell you that you are trespassing on private property," I said clearly.

"That is because I came looking for you and you weren't home," he said. "So I had a good look round till you returned. This is a really cool site and I'd like to buy it and build a home."

"Let me make myself quite clear. There is absolutely *no way* that I would consider that idea. It is not – *and never will be* – for sale."

"Wow! That's, like, a real no-no, Ms Manning."

"Perhaps you had better explain just who you are and exactly what you are doing here," I said loftily.

"I can't believe you don't recognise me, lady."

"Should I? And if so, why?"

"It's like, where have you *been*, angel, that you don't recognise the hottest dude on the planet? Take me down to the village and watch all the girls start raving and screaming. I'm like, totally gutted." (This last was spoken in an estuary accent, glottal stop and all; though otherwise his voice was devoid of regional accent).

"So identify yourself then, please."

"Thane Richmond . . . super-celeb, at your service."

"Oh really?" I said. "Yes, I suppose I *have* heard the name somewhere. Footballer, or pop-star, perhaps? I'm not familiar with either scene."

"Singer – songwriter: Glastonbury's hottest new-talent discovery, twenty-ten."

"Should I bow, curtsey or fall on my knees?" I asked, laying the sarcasm on thick.

"All three, I guess . . . the knees thing would be best."

"On the other hand, let me show you the only way back to your car, which I assume is the flash chariot at the top of my driveway."

"Thought you'd be impressed by Purple Petunia. I'll give you a spin in her whenever you like."

"That won't be necessary; I have my own car. It's just big enough for Pendragon, and he's still getting used to being driven around."

"Pendragon your boyfriend, Ms Madeleine?"

"No," I said, laughing. "It's my dog. Anyway, how is it that you know my name and have come trespassing on my land?"

"I asked at the hotel about building land or suitable residences for sale and they told me about an American lady who works at a local estate agent's. Said you might be prepared to sell your place. Give it a try they said."

"Absolutely no chance! I may *sound* like an American, but I assure you that I *am* fifty percent English and fifty percent Irish. I was born in the US, but I've lived here for years with my English grandmother who died eighteen months ago and left the house to me. I will, however, give you details of suitable properties in West Cornwall if you leave me your email address."

We had reached the back door of Foxgloves by now and I said, "Excuse me for a moment while I fetch a notebook, Mr Richmond."

"Call me Thane . . . or TR."

"It has a Shakespearean ring to it, your name; 'The Scottish Play', as the profession superstitiously calls it," I observed. "Apparently it's unlucky to call it 'Macbeth'."

"Yeah; Thane of Cawdor and stuff," he agreed. "My life-coach said I should adopt a trendier name than Martin – more manly and romantic. It's done me proud. My fan base is epic – includes royalty, I'm told."

I opened the back door and went into the kitchen, Pendragon pushing past me and, behind him, my uninvited visitor.

"I don't recall asking you to come in," I said, in an unwelcoming tone.

"But surely this is the time of day English ladies serve up Earl Grey tea and cucumber sarnis and stuff."

"Not today, I'm afraid. I'll just take down your email address and then I can let you know if I find something to suit you."

"Here, let me." he reached for the pad and wrote at some length with a messy ballpoint. *(Here's someone who could probably afford a good Parker fountain-pen,* I thought).

"I'll give you my website address, my email address and the number of my personal smart-phone as well; but you tell anyone *on pain of death*, especially your colleagues on the West Kernow Gazette. I understand you write a column for them, as well."

"Yes indeed – I enthuse about the more desirable properties on the market, on account of my part-time job at Tregowan and Hayworth. In my spare time, I am a peripatetic music teacher in two local upper schools. Jack-of–all-trades, you might say."

"Could be useful to me. What's your instrument?"

"Clarinet, piano and voice: strictly classical, I have to say; though I do quite like jazz."

"Shit! I *thought* you had issues around the pop scene. No wonder you didn't know me from Adam Faith. Maybe when you know me better, I can persuade you to do some, like, crossover stuff."

"I doubt it very much. If I *do* get to know you better," I said firmly, "it will be in a purely professional capacity. Now if you'll excuse me, I must bid you good bye."

"Okay, okay. I can take a hint," he said as I held open the door for him. "Good bye, fanciable lady. I can't wait to hear from you again; in fact I think I feel a song coming on . . ."

THREE

WHEN I GOOGLED OUR POTENTIAL NEW CLIENT AT the office, I was directed to a choice between his website and his Face Book and Twitter accounts. He did appear to be famous: a poser, to be sure, but nevertheless, a celebrated pop star. He had tweeted that he was house-hunting on the Cornish coast, seeking an established property or a site on which he could build a house ensuring sea views, south west coast preferred. The price was clearly no object so I gathered details of all the properties of seven figures and more, put them in a large folder and texted him that I would leave it at the Trevelyan Arms Hotel addressed to Mr T. Richmond on my way home. The boss, Penrose Tregowan, welcomed the news that the potential for a big sale might come our way. I did not divulge the name; . . . 'some pop star or other', I hinted. 'No upper price limit, it would seem'.

"Great, Maddie," he said. "I'll leave it to you to follow it up then. He can phone you at home, can he?"

I agreed to add my personal numbers, landline and cell phone, which I wrote on the top page of the property details.

*

WEST KERNOW GAZETTE

May 25, 2013-05-21

GOSSIP CORNER with Pandora Bennett

Guess who's been seen around Porthwenna / Polburran.

Put on your glad-rags, girls: there's a mega-celeb in town! OK, he's been hiding under a purple baseball cap and Dolce & Gabbana shades, but if you've clapped eyes on a sleek purple Porsche convertible racing around the country lanes, you can be sure that the driver is ... Sorry to disappoint you, ladies, but he's been seen around with glamorous redhead, Madeleine Manning, 30+, part-time journalist on this paper. Rumour has it that they're looking for a property together. . . or maybe she's just doing her estate agent stuff . . . but she *is usually* in that passenger seat.

Wait for it . . . it's **Thane Richmond**, girls – upcoming event at Glasto this year, at which, his website has hinted, he'll present his new single, *Madeleine*, inspired by the lady herself.

I read the article with mounting indignation. True, I had been several times in the passenger seat of TR's car. He preferred me to accompany him to the various properties on his short-list, rather than be driven in my much less ostentatious station wagon.

I tackled Pandora about her Gossip Corner snippet, observing that she was well-named indeed for acting in the manner of her classical namesake, who released all the troubles of the world from the box she had been told not to open.

"How did you know my age, anyway?" I asked. "And why should that be of any relevance?"

"It always *is* in journalism," she giggled. "Why – is he shocked? Have I spoilt your prospects? He must be a good deal younger; only twenty four, I read somewhere. My mum used to call it cradle-snatching."

Pandora lives with one of the partners in Tregowan and Hayworth, so I was not overly surprised that she had this knowledge at her fingertips. Application forms usually ask for DOB and it would be filed away somewhere in either of the two offices.

Next time TR picked me up for a viewing, I noticed the said W. Kernow Gazette lying on the front seat, folded back to the Gossip Corner article.

"So-o-o," he said, as I picked it up before seating myself, "We're an item, are we? And I've fallen for an older woman, it appears. There are heartbroken tweets from teenage fans all over my Face Book page."

"Well, perhaps I'd better post a disclaimer," I said, acerbically. "Something to put them out of their misery, since it's all journalistic conjecture. Take a right when you get to the T-junction."

As we drew up at the junction, he stopped the car, put the stick-shift into neutral, applied the handbrake and turned to give me a swift, firm kiss on the lips. I should have slapped his face; for weeks I reproached myself that I was too shocked to do so.

Instead, I protested feebly, "How *dare* you?" reluctantly aware of the delicious and seductive scent of his aftershave lingering on my skin.

"Oh, I dare all right", he said. "I could park up right here and kiss you all afternoon . . . and you'd *love* it."

As I turned towards him indignantly, he did it again, to the accompaniment of a furious hooting from a car which had drawn up behind. TR put the car into gear and drove away with a rude hand sign to the driver.

"This guy's following us," he said as we turned along a slightly wider road. "I'll pull in here and let him pass."

He drew into a passing bay, but the other car passed and stopped in the road ahead, blocking our way. The driver got out and walked towards my side of the car. Immediately I realised it was Pandora's boyfriend, Jack Hayworth, the junior partner in the estate agent's, dangling a set of keys in his hand. TR lowered the window.

"You took the wrong keys with you, Maddie, so I've been tearing after you to catch you up. Not that it was that difficult when you threatened to camp out at the junction. I don't think canoodling is to be recommended in mid-manoeuvre." He bent to look directly at TR.

"Sorry, mate. I suddenly came over all emotional," my driver explained.

"Hmmm," muttered Jack. "Don't forget, Maddie, the owners of Casa Blanca are away abroad on holiday, so you wouldn't have got in, anyway. Remember to double-lock everything when leaving. Perhaps I'd better come with you."

"That won't be necessary," TR said, very firmly. "I can deal with any difficult locks. I've got brains as well as looks and talent, man."

I fished in my bag for the keys I had mistakenly taken, and handed them to Jack.

"Thanks," he said. "I think you'll be impressed with that property, sir," he added, looking at TR.

"You *hope*," Thane returned, rather rudely, I thought.

After a mile or so, we turned in between showy white pillars topped by stone dolphins painted blue, and drove down a tarmac drive from which there was a panorama of the whole bay. Casa Blanca was as brilliant white as its name suggested; a house of quirky architectural features typical of the nineteen thirties. We walked round the outside first. There was a view of the sea, even from beside the large swimming pool. Two gardeners were trimming back the leaves of magnificent rhododendron bushes, so I called to identify myself and said that I had brought a client to view the house.

Once inside, I kept well clear of TR, in case he wanted to follow up on his earlier advances. We moved swiftly from room to room, assessing the potential of each space, in the light of his expectations of a part-time dwelling. As the house was newly on the market, I made notes for my property column so that I could enthuse about it in the next edition. TR raved about the lavish fittings, especially the bar in the huge living room.

"Quite a retro feature nowadays," I observed, "but it would have been just the thing when the house was built."

"Pretty cool, all the same," said TR. "I could see some wicked parties going on here."

I kept even further away from him when we moved upstairs, lest the sumptuously dressed beds gave him ideas. The eight bedrooms were light and airy, all the front-facing windows commanding extensive views of the sea. This was by far the most promising viewing I had attended on his behalf, it seemed.

"How would you like to live here *yourself,* Maddie?" he suddenly asked

"Oh, I am totally content where I am at Foxgloves," I said. "My job is only to stimulate other people's interest, not to envy their ability to afford the purchase and upkeep of such places. Give me the simple and not the grandiose."

"Well, Ms Modesty; I could see myself here with a lovely flame-haired lady . . . my 'thane-ess' – or whatever Lady Macbeth's status would have been."

I ignored what amounted to a proposal of a partnership of some kind, and told him that I had another appointment in half-an-hour's time and that I had better be getting back to the office.

"Actually," he said as we drove back along the lanes, "the place I *really* like is the part of your land where we first met. What would it take for you to agree to sell it to me?"

"My answer will be the same, however many times you ask. That is consecrated ground: the remembrance place of my forebears, the place where their spirits will linger forever. That is my final word on the matter."

FOUR

THERE WAS AN EXCITED PHONE CALL FROM LIZZIE Penberthy the following day. To begin with she asked how Pendragon was settling in and how he was taking to living in a house, rather than being tied up outside. I detected an excitement in her voice that told me that she would far rather be asking about something else. She soon cut through my assurances about Pendragon's welfare.

"What's all this I read in the WKG?" she gasped. "Everybody but *everybody*'s talking about your new boyfriend. Petroc's girl is already asking me for an introduction. *He's* getting quite jealous. Would you like to bring TR to dinner here?"

"I assure you that it really is all gossip, Lizzie," I said, quickly. "Just tell the star-struck girlfriend to watch out for next week's thrilling instalment. I have already taken issue with Pandora over this."

"Do I just have to believe there's nothing going on between you? It sounds ideal: a rich, famous beau for you; a celebrity wedding in the near future. What would Ma have said? Wouldn't she have been thrilled for you?"

"She would have been horrified," I protested. "Thane and I have absolutely *nothing* in common. All I am doing is trying to sell him a house and make some commission."

"Yeah, yeah, yeah," said Lizzie. "Must go. Speak to you again soon. Bye-ee."

My instrumental pupils clamoured round me when I returned to lessons after half term.

"Is it really true, Miss, – all that stuff about you and Thane Richmond in *Gossip Corner?*" Everyone's like dead jealous of you. Can you get tickets for us for his concerts – get his autograph on my CD cover – bring him into school?"

"Sorry to disappoint you, girls," I replied. "It's just journalistic licence. As you may know, I have another job as an estate agent and have been helping him with his house-hunting. Just keep reading *Gossip Corner* and you'll find out a whole lot more that isn't true. To tell the actual truth, I think it piqued his vanity when I first met him that I hadn't a clue who he was and what he did."

There was a stunned silence for a few moments: eyes widened and mouths fell open.

"But *Miss*! He's like all over the internet, telly and radio – like, the whole media – *all* the time," exclaimed one of my most promising clarinet pupils.

"Not where I've been viewing and listening," I assured her. "Now we'd better do some work."

"Well, if you don't introduce me to him, like tomorrow, I shall like, *die* of a broken heart," she threatened dramatically, her hand on her chest.

"I shall tell him there's a danger of that," I promised, laughing. "But I shan't actually be seeing him tomorrow. It might have to wait a little longer, Poppy."

"Okay, okay, Miss – but I'm like totally in love with him."

"You and a few million others, I daresay. Now, *work!*"

Two days later, there was a text from TR asking me to join him for dinner at The Trevelyan Arms that night. I texted him back to say that I was sorry, but I went to Choir on Wednesday evenings and Orchestra on Thursdays.

'Sht,' came the texted reply. "What's with all this clssicl stuff? Friday, then . . . and no excuses, OK? Pick u up

7.30. Wear yr best dress, plz. Will show you new lyric to *Madeleine*.

XX TR XX.'

My best dress, indeed! I opted for the plain black, scoop-neck maxi-dress that I wore for choral and orchestral concerts, swept my hair into a chignon and fastened a string of pale amber beads around my neck. As I made up my face, I tried to affect nonchalance about TR's attentions, telling myself that he viewed me merely as a decorative accessory. However, I had to admit to a certain excitement at the prospect of a date with him, even if he was a vain, arrogant control-freak. It was a long time since someone had taken me to dinner. In the car he handed me a piece of paper on which was a single verse, entitled *Madeleine*.

Lady with hair like a flame /
you've burnt a great hole in my heart
It's there that you branded your name /
now save me, I'm falling apart.
Madeleine, save me
Save me from all this emotion
Put out the fire that consumes me
Take my undying devotion

"I'm flattered. It sounds more like a poem than a pop song," I commented. "Whatever does the melody sound like?"

He proceeded to belt out a loud, passionate series of notes which swamped the words altogether. There was something highly amusing about being driven around the country lanes to such a deafening serenade. TR stopped singing as we drew into the hotel parking lot.

"Of course," he said, "there'd be a backing group and a band to give it support. I was only singing with half of my voice. Just wait till you hear it at Glasto! In fact, you could come with me. Think how famous you could be!"

"I *do* have a problem with modern pop-music," I admitted as we sat at the dinner table. "If I could *see* it written down, I could discover why it appears to have no direction, no modulation, no memorable musical phrases or melodic line, most of the time. I confess to having watched that ITV program *The Voice* recently and thinking that the participants just seem to make as much noise as possible at the expense of the lyrics and the emotions that they are trying to express."

"Oh ye of little faith! I have no clue about *writing down* the music: It's driven by emotion alone. Someone else has to *write* it, once I've recorded it. It's for the band to read the musical version. I s'pose if you play an instrument, you've got to understand it when it's written down."

"Right enough," I said. "I studied it at college and we had to compose and take down musical dictation in all sorts of different keys, as well as learning to improve our instrumental technique and studying musical scores."

"Perhaps you'd better give *me* a few lessons," TR said, eagerly. "All those notes on the page are a mystery to me; I just feel the music in my head and fit it to the words."

I agreed to give him a few lessons in basic notation, modulation and harmony as thanks for taking me out to dinner, suggesting that reading musical notation was like reading a map, in a way: "The musical line tells you where to go and what values to give to the notes, "I explained, "which is what gives the music its rhythm."

He drove me home after we had finished our dinner with excellent, freshly-ground coffee in the hotel lounge. To my relief, he did not suggest that we should start the musical instruction right away . . . or that he should come into the house for any other purpose – nor did I invite him to do so.

When I turned to thank him, he planted a swift kiss on my lips and said good night.

"I will call on you on Sunday," he said as I climbed out of the car.

"Make it the afternoon, then," I said. "I usually go to Mass in the morning."

"Oh my God!" he exclaimed. "You got religion then?"

"Yes; I was brought up by my Irish mother to be a good Catholic girl."

"That explains all this holy music you like then; right?"

"Exactly," I agreed. "I make no apology for it."

"Shame you're missing out on the real thing, Maddie."

"On the contrary, TR, this *is* the real thing. Next weekend I'm taking part in a performance of *Spem in Alium,* a forty-part motet by the sixteenth century English composer, Thomas Tallis. We're doing it in the cathedral."

"*Forty parts*? That'll take forever," he protested.

"Just a few minutes, actually. Forty parts means forty different vocal parts being sung simultaneously."

"Tell me more when we have our first lesson," he said, preparing to drive away

FIVE

THANE CALLED AT THE HOUSE AROUND THREE O'CLOCK on the Sunday afternoon.

"I've come for my music lesson," he lisped in a little-boy voice. "And after that I hope you'll invite me to stay to tea."

"We shall have to see how attentive you are," I said in a teacherish voice, "and how much you learn."

"I promise to be very attentive, Miss. I'm sure you could teach me *all sorts* of things."

In the music room, I found some blank manuscript paper and explained the principle of the staves and how the treble and bass clefs are linked by 'Middle C'. With the help of the harpsichord keyboard, by the end of half an hour, he had both played and written a simple ascending scale passage: the first six notes of the *Eastender*s theme-tune. The next obvious choice was *Doe, a deer, a female deer,* from *The Sound of Music.* This led us on to intervals as well as scale passages. When we 'got back to doh' at the top of the scale, I suggested that we had done enough for one lesson and invited him to stay for afternoon tea, for which I had baked, filled and iced a chocolate cake *and* made the essential cucumber sandwiches.

"I am well impressed," he said. "You did all this for me?"

"Maybe I did," I replied, noncommittally, "I thought you might deserve a reward for your attention to my teaching. I'm surprised you didn't learn the basics of notation at school."

"I wasn't interested enough to give it my attention. Our old music mistress couldn't explain it as simply as you did. She didn't look like you, either, or it would have been, like, *wow! Is she hot, or what?*"

"Well, methods change and keep on changing. I'm probably getting rather out of date, myself, now, in my teaching methods."

"Maddie, you'll never be out of date," TR protested. "When *Madeleine* gets to Number One, you'll be famous. Everyone will colour their hair red and want to be just like you. You'll never be forgotten."

"I shall only be famous as long as you are," I pointed out. "Even *you* will be old one day; even *your* songs will be forgotten. I hope you won't be like some of these sad has-beens who try to make a come-back when they really should realize that they're well past it. . . Excuse me now; it's time for Pendragon's dinner."

He followed me into the kitchen and observed the process closely as I mixed biscuit and tinned meat in Pendragon's bowl, talking all the while to the dog about what a good and lucky boy he was.

"Why do you say all of that, as if he can, like, understand every word, when of course he can't?"

"On the contrary, Thane, of course he *can*. Communicating with animals is a mixture of language and telepathy. He knows he is loved and cared for and, in return, he gives me his undivided loyalty and affection."

I put the bowl of food on the floor next to the water-bowl and Pendragon wolfed the lot in a few seconds.

"You have *my* undivided loyalty and affection, too, Maddie. Like it says in the song: *my undying devotion.*"

He spun me around suddenly and held me against him, causing Pendragon to growl softly at the abrupt movement.

"I want to make love to you, Madeleine," he said hoarsely, pulling my hips towards him and making sure that I could feel his rising desire. "Is that bloody dog going to act as your chaperone and protector? God! It's never taken me so long to get a girl into bed."

"Well, aren't you the lucky one, then? But I'm afraid this girl is old-fashioned enough not to hop into bed with someone she hardly knows. In spite of her own mixed parentage, she believes in sex *after*, rather than *before*, marriage."

"O – M – G! Are you saying that you've never . . . ?"

"No, I'm not saying that. But I've never been promiscuous and would never risk bringing a child into the world without a stable relationship to support it."

"But you can control these things. Don't tell me that you've never heard of the pill."

"Thane, I'm a Catholic and it's against the rules."

"So you'll just have to marry me then, if there's no other way of staking my claim on your favours."

"If that is a proposal, I shall need a few weeks to consider it."

"A few *weeks*? I want you *now*. Can you feel it, Maddie, can you *feel* it?"

I could feel it only too well: so much so that I felt the first stirrings of response, to my shame and disgust. I twisted away from him. Pendragon was sitting at my side, eyeing TR threateningly. I laid a hand on his head, telling him silently, 'Relax. I can take care of this, but thank you for watching out for me.'

The next edition of Gossip Corner began:

> 'He's still around, girls, and guess what I heard. . . I have it on good authority, from an eye witness, no less, that Thane and his lady-love were in a clinch at a T-junction on the St Breaca road. It was clear that the driver did not have his mind on the job – not on the job of driving, anyway! He only moved off when there was a long line of traffic behind him.

'You won't see him around for a while because he's off to the Isle of Wight Festival this coming weekend. At the end of the month it's Glasto, so those lucky enough to be going may catch a glimpse of him there. It remains to be seen whether the lady accompanies him on his travels. . .'

The article went on in the same vein for a while until Pandora had run out of conjecture on that subject and turned the spotlight on some other unfortunates.

*

TR had, in fact, asked me if I would go with him to both festivals. "You wouldn't have to rough it with the crowd; you'd have the full VIP treatment." He explained something I had often wondered about: how do the performers and other VIPs manage their own accommodation? Do they have to rough it in the mud like the rest of the campers? It turns out that they are separated from the campers in posh tents a mile or so away. They call it 'glamping'. I declined, however, explaining that some of my instrumental pupils had examinations coming up and I could not leave them at such short notice.

"I have some holiday booked in August," I had said. "There is no school anyway and I have asked for four weeks' leave from the estate agents then."

"Good," he had answered. "You can come to The States with me."

"I had planned to go to Ireland, actually," I'd explained.

"Well, I shall have to change your mind about that plan. We might even be married by then."

I had ignored this remark and wished him well for the two festivals, promising to keep searching for suitable properties, meanwhile, to show him in July when he returned to Cornwall.

SIX

LIFE RETURNED TO NORMAL WHILE TR WAS AWAY. An artist friend who sang in the same consort of voices invited me to supper one balmy evening in early June.

"I never see you these days," she grumbled. "You're so taken up with this pop-idol of yours. Please don't tell me you're going to marry someone who bats for the other side ... musically speaking, that is."

Mistletoe Masters, an artist in her early sixties, is as eccentric as her name might suggest. She changed her first name when she set up her studio in St Ives.

"I mean, darling, who was even going to look at paintings by *Mildred* Masters? I had to restyle my persona to something much more intriguing. I'm still MM, like you, dear one, so my initials haven't changed."

Her paintings are mainly, though not always, abstracts, inspired by the coast of Cornwall and textured with sand, granite dust and crushed leaves, mixed with the oils to great visual and tactile effect. She makes an adequate living from her 'bits of sand-paper' as she calls her work.

Mistletoe is firmly against the institution of marriage. "I tried it twice," she told me once. "There are two discarded husbands knocking about somewhere, but I'm free of all that now and can be my own person. Never subject yourself to a man, my pet. They are simply not worth all the time and love that women invest in them. Even if the sex is great at first, it never stays that way. Which reminds me … I read somewhere recently that men think about sex once in *every three seconds* – or was it minutes? Can you imagine a greater waste of time and energy than that?"

"But Mistletoe," I had protested. "I want a child or children one day and am old-fashioned enough to be a firm believer in a stable, two-parent family. Is that possible without marriage? Does not Nature decree that a woman looks for a suitable mate with whom to reproduce and that a child needs the support and guidance of two loving and committed parents?"

On the night of my visit, however, she did not quiz me immediately about my romantic attachment or intentions, but was full of a certain murder trial taking place in the High Court.

"Now tell me," she said, handing me a glass of Champagne on her small, flower-bedecked terrace overlooking the sea, and still bathed in sunlight. "This guy – the judge – who was shot dead, wasn't he related to you in some way?"

"No relation of mine," I shuddered, "but there is a connection, unfortunately. It did cross my mind that that my once father – now uncle – Donal, may have committed patricide – and with very good reason. But he had the perfect alibi, being back in Australia by that time. Bridie herself was back in Ireland and would have had to hire a hit-man to do the dreadful deed to her rapist. Fortunately, neither she nor Donal came under any suspicion because only our family – and you – and the wife – knew that there was any connection."

"The man on trial appears to be the father of one of the teenagers raped by a man the judge had previously acquitted of the same offence," Mistletoe said, "but the prosecution's case doesn't seem to be very strong. He may well get off. What a mercy that the deed is done anyway and the world is rid of that unjust judge."

I agreed with her. "At last he got what he deserved for raping Bridie; and yet ... discovering her long-lost son has brought her so much pleasure and comfort that one can't really regret its having happened to her. By the way, I'm hoping to go over to Ireland in August and discuss plans for Bridie's eightieth birthday next year, when we hope to have a massive family reunion."

The doorbell sounded with a confident ring.

"That'll be Alexander," said Mistletoe, rising from her chair. "I hope you don't mind: he's recently moved into the flat upstairs. Rather an intriguing character and a very good sculptor."

She swept through the French windows, an imposing, statuesque figure in the emerald green, ankle-length caftan she referred to as her loose cover. Her long, dark, greying hair, usually worn in a single plait, was swept up in a tidy chignon. I wondered whether she fancied the newcomer herself or was engaging in a little match-making on my behalf. She ushered in a striking-looking, thirty-something young man and made introductions.

"Alexander Temple," he supplied. "But call me Alex, or I sound like a sacred building." I liked his humorous mouth and guessed that he would see the funny side of many a situation. Indeed, there was a great deal of laughter throughout the meal, beginning with his accusation that Mistletoe was 'currying favour' with her new neighbour when she bore in a great casserole dish of delicious Prawn Vindaloo with numerous fragrant side dishes to accompany it.

"Good job I checked with said neighbour that he was a curry fan," she laughed.

Both Mistletoe and I tried to draw him out and encourage him to talk about himself and his work; but, unlike TR, whose favourite topic of conversation *was* himself, Alex was more interested in our lives and work, only occasionally referring to his own commissions and the prospect of new work. Hitherto, it transpired, he had been teaching Art at an upper school in Wiltshire, but the threat of cuts in arts funding had made him give up teaching and set up on his own amongst other artists, something he had always wanted to do.

"Oh, the Philistines and their cuts on arts funding!" I exclaimed. "When I can afford it, I'll ask you to do a sculpture of my wolfhound-lurcher, Pendragon."

"What a wonderful name!" he replied. "When I can afford it, I'll do it gladly for a nominal fee. I look forward to meeting the canine subject."

The evening ended with the promise of a 'return match' as soon as Alex had settled in sufficiently to entertain.

"Chilli-con carne is my speciality," he said. "Some like it hot, some even hotter. If you can take it like that, then be my guests."

When I phoned to thank Mistletoe next day, she remarked, "I'm glad you two young things got on so well. Don't worry – I don't have any designs on Alex myself ... though he is rather dishy; I just wanted to make sure that my dear friend has plenty of choice in the matrimonial market-place, since she's so determined to prolong the family line."

SEVEN

"I HEAR YOU'VE BEEN TWO-TIMING ME WITH ANOTHER man," TR said when he returned to Polburran from Glastonbury.

"And where, pray, did you hear that?"

"Oh, word gets around when you're in the public eye," he replied. "Living in my shadow, as you do, you're bound to be noticed. You were seen on the cliff path with some dark-haired guy holding the lead of your dog."

"Excuse me? I live in *nobody's shadow*," I said, huffily. "In any case, I have to take great care of Pendragon on the cliffs. If he was off the lead and chased after a rabbit, he could fall onto the rocks below, or into the sea."

"Okay, no need for a hissy-fit. I'm not talking about the *dog* – I'm talking about the other *guy*," TR said irritably.

"He's an artist friend of mine – not that I have to explain."

"Oh yes you do! You're my girlfriend – almost my fiancée, in fact. I expect absolute devotion and faithfulness."

"Huh!" I scoffed. "I will not be *owned* – or controlled by anyone."

"That reminds me," TR said. "I have to go to London next week for a couple of recording sessions and I'd like you to come with me. You could be my Plus One at a showbiz party and I have two tickets for the Men's Wimbledon Finals on Sunday".

That was enough to twist my arm. "I will come," I said "as long as you have a spare room for me. I shall not share your bed."

"Shame!" he said resignedly. "What's not to love about the idea of me making you the happiest woman in the world? Okay, I promise you can sleep unmolested, though I don't understand how you can resist me for so long."

He told me that he would like to leave on the Thursday as he had appointments on Friday, so I arranged to take leave of absence from then until the following Tuesday.

*

His serviced apartment was in a brand new block in Chelsea, ultra-modern in every detail and a far cry from the cosy Cornishness of Foxgloves. The furniture and décor were beyond modern, with the impersonal aspect typical of the rich client who waves his hand airily at a trendy designer, and gives him or her free rein. Nothing, from the cream leather sofas to the paintings on the walls, reflected the personal taste of the owner of the apartment. If I was impressed at all, it was merely by the sumptuousness of TR's dwelling, certainly not by any feeling of comfort and sense of home.

*

The Friday morning appointment turned out to be one for us both at his private dentist's in Harley Street. "I'm having my smile whitened and re-enameled and you may as well have yours done as well. The cameras are sure to pan in on us at Wimbledon and we need to dazzle."

After this procedure, TR had to go to a recording session, but first we went shopping.

"There's this party for a crowd of showbiz people tomorrow night and, as my plus-one, you'll need something to wow the other celebs. Money no object: just put it on my account. Anything up to a five figure sum. Try to steer clear of six," he laughed.

"I certainly will," I gasped. "But I do have something suitable with me."

"We don't do *suitable,* baby. We only do the ultimate wow-factor."

He dropped me outside an exclusive-looking boutique in Mayfair, saying he would park the car and come back for me, and that he had an account there. This confirmed my conviction that he regarded me merely as a decorative accessory and, looking back, I regret the way in which I went along with it. But go along with it I did, choosing an ankle-length dress in a vibrant blue made popular by the Duchess of Cambridge, with high stiletto-heeled patent leather shoes to match. The dress fell straight from under the bust in the front and was slightly flared from the hip. I felt good in it and walked confidently across the deeply carpeted floor, applauded by the manageress and two assistants.

"The dress shows Madam's bosom and derriere to great advantage," the senior woman commented. "How about a matching silk clutch to go with it?"

TR was favourably impressed by the new outfit, it seemed, and encouraged me to choose another of several beautiful frocks to grace my presence in the Royal Box at Wimbledon on Sunday.

"I hope it goes with my sparkling smile," I joked, flashing my teeth at my reflection in the full-length mirror.

*

The party was in a large house in Chelsea, though I never did discover who our host and hostess were. I recognised several people from films and television, though I could not put names to them all. They roll the credits so fast nowadays that it is impossible to follow them. Many greeted TR fondly and said, "So this is the famous Madeleine?" and shook my hand or air-kissed me in 'mwa-mwa' mode. I was delighted to encounter a few tennis stars, though not, of course, the two finalists whom I would see the following day at Wimbledon.

Eventually, TR and I were separated in the throng and I found myself cornered by a very well-known, ageing actor who shall remain nameless, though he may well remember me. He is very tall and was wearing a scarlet, tunic-style jacket with a Nehru collar, elaborate braiding and black, frogged fastenings, over skinny black velvet trousers. Oddly, his bare feet were clad in rather posh, gold-braided flip-flops.

"So you are TR's crumpet, the Madeleine of his number one song?" he said, lifting my hand and kissing it. "I was admiring your butt when you were standing with him. Some men are boob men, some are leg men ... but I'm definitely a bottom man." So saying, he ran his hand down the back of my dress and probed a finger into the crease between my buttocks. Furious, I stepped away quickly, saying, "I am nobody's *crumpet* – simply TR's Plus One; and that does not give you the right to grope me, *whoever* you are." Before retreating, I took one step sideways towards him and ensured that one of my sharp stiletto heels found the gap between two of his bare toes, with all the weight that I could muster driving it.

"What the fuck? You *bitch*!" I heard him shout as I walked away. But his words were lost in the buzz of conversation and the high-pitched, brittle laughter of the luvvies. A female soap-star grinned at me as I made my way back to TR.

"I saw that little sequence," she said. "Congratulations! The great man was obviously up to his usual tricks. He thinks he can take liberties wherever he pleases."

"Yes," I smiled. "I guess it's much better to deal with gropers immediately than to come out of the woodwork thirty years later when there's a court case."

"Absolutely! You can dine out on that episode for the rest of your natural," she laughed. "Good thing you're not an impressionable teenager. Love the dress, by the way. So good with that gorgeous hair."

I accepted the compliment as graciously as I could and fought my way back to Thane – though I did not tell him what had occurred on the far side of the room.

"Ah, there you are, my darling," TR said proprietorially. "Let me introduce some of my fellow pop-stars; not that she'll recognise any of you," he added to the group surrounding him. "Maddie's a *classical* musician, unfortunately – Bach, Mozart and holy music and stuff – and I don't mean Gospel. Christ! She didn't even know who *I* was when we first met."

There were the usual gasps of incredulity as I flashed my now dazzling smile at them in greeting and tried to feed their vanity by feigning interest in their latest hits. I listened with half an ear, and imagined a discussion dealing with the question: when is a celebrity not a celebrity? Answer: when nobody recognises them. Somewhere in this room, I thought, there must be somebody who is not driven entirely by vanity and self-acclaim; someone who is capable of discussing a subject other than celebrity and fame.

Leaving TR and his cronies, I made my way across the room again in search of a bathroom. Seeing a slightly open door with a marble floor and tiled walls beyond, I entered quietly, only to find two young guys at the counter top next to the wash-basin, doing a line of cocaine from a sheet of tinfoil.

"Oh, excuse me," I said." I was looking for the loo."

"Hey Madeleine," said the boy who may have been our host's son. "This is really good quality stuff. Will you join us? Not too much, mind, or you could get knocked out."

"No thanks, I don't do drugs," I said firmly.

"What! Never?" the other boy said. "I thought you Americans were really into this stuff."

“The only thing I’ve ever touched was the odd joint when I was a student. You guys take care; I’ll find somewhere else. ’Bye,” I said, before departing swiftly.

*

By contrast, the Wimbledon final next day held much greater fascination for me. Before the match we were treated to strawberries and champagne in a hospitality suite for VIPs, where I met more interesting people than had been present at the previous night’s party. Having long been a fan of Novak Djokovic, I was disappointed that he played less than his spectacular best and lost to Andy Murray. Tennis is such an individual game that one can be excused for supporting one’s favourite in preference to the player representing one’s country.

EIGHT

When I returned to Foxgloves, I found amongst my mail a letter with an Irish postmark, and recognised, much to my pleasure, Bridie O'Malley's hand-writing:

Oirbsean Lodge
July 2nd, 2013

Dear Maddie,
We are so looking forward to your visit next month and to welcoming you to Killogan for the first time. I have to tell you that, unfortunately, Declan (Donal) and I will not be returning from a visit to your mother and father (Dominic) until August 15th. We have planned the three week trip to the US this year because I feel that I may not be up to it in future years on account of my advanced age!

But do please come over at the beginning of the month as you planned. Grainne has said that you'd be welcome to stay with her at first but then again you'd be very welcome to stay here too and I would be thrilled to know that the house was occupied. Please feel free to bring your new dog, Pendragon, if he can tolerate a friendly cat. I'm sure he would love the grounds of Oirbsean House and my garden here. There are many places of interest for you both to explore, on foot, by car or by boat on the lough. Have you introduced him to rowing boats yet?

Declan has sold up his IT business in Australia and is coming back to Ireland for good next week. It will be wonderful to have him home permanently and to have his company on our visit to California. I hope he will be tolerant of the fact that your mother and Dominic are together now— actually married, I understand.

I will telephone you shortly before we leave on the 24th.

With much love from us all over here,

Bridie.

Let me explain my own irregular parentage for those who have not read the two existing family archives, the first of which was my edition of my paternal grandmother's – Cecilia's – memoir. In the mid nineteen-fifties two girls in their late teens gave birth to sons in a Magdalene home for unmarried mothers in Kilburn, London. Cecilia's son, Dominic, had a twin sister who died at birth. He was rushed away from his mother as soon as he had drawn breath and was given to the other girl, Bridie, to nurse along with her own son. Both boys were adopted as twins soon after birth by an Irish couple from Limerick, who brought them up kindly and lovingly and educated them privately.

Unfortunately, these adoptive parents were killed in a traffic accident in Belfast at the start of the Northern Irish Troubles in 1968 and the two fourteen-year-old boys, being left to the mercies of a heartless grandmother, were sent to one of Dublin's infamous Industrial Schools. After their many sufferings there, they were helped to escape by IRA activists from Londonderry, in return for freedom-fighting against Protestant domination in Ulster.

It was eighteen years before Cecilia found out that one of her children had survived. However, as the registration of the births had either been omitted or falsified, no-one knew by this time which boy was which. The other mother, Bridie, had married by this time and had three daughters of her own. She discovered only in 2013, nearly fifty eight years after she had parted from him, that Donal was her son and that, although he was married to my mother, Frances, and her first two grandchildren were his, my own father was actually Dominic whom I had been brought up to call 'Uncle'. In fact, it was only my striking resemblance to Cecilia, my grandmother, that led my mother to admit that she had slept with her first love, Dominic. If it all sounds irregular and complicated, it is because it most certainly is!

Naturally, I knew Donal as my father, until at eighteen I learnt the truth about my conception. He always seemed hard and unloving towards me, even though I was the youngest child of the family. Because I grew to resemble Cecilia, my English, *Protestant* grandmother, so closely, Donal assumed that *he* must be her son, rather than Dominic. His anger, when he discovered my true parentage, turned eventually to relief and acceptance, and now we are the best of friends.

Donal's father was, of course, the judge referred to earlier, who raped Bridie when he was a schoolboy of fifteen and she was the family's maid. On learning of this, Donal decided to beard the lion in his den and called on the judge in his Oxfordshire home, leaving Bridie waiting in the car outside. Donal blackmailed Rupert Bairstow into renouncing his impending knighthood, by vowing to expose his teenage crime publicly unless he did so. The judge expelled him from the house at gunpoint and he and Bridie escaped with their lives – as well as with recorded evidence of the preceding conversation.

Perhaps the chequered pattern of my own personal history explained my desire to fall in love, marry and establish a soundly-based family life for my husband and children. Call me old-fashioned, but in these modern days when practically any domestic set-up is acceptable and so far removed from the social and moral opprobrium of my grandmother's youth, I feel within me a traditional responsibility towards future generations. I feel strongly that children should be raised in an atmosphere of love and commitment, free of acrimony and the insecurity caused by parental arguments, competitiveness and control.

Incidentally, sometime after the confrontation between father and son, the judge was fatally shot with a rifle while in a shooting party with his cronies. Owing to lack of evidence in the trial that followed, the jury returned a verdict of Not Guilty on the only suspect, the father of a young girl humiliated in court when she was giving evidence against the defendant who had raped her. He was acquitted, so the mystery still remains unsolved. Many people had a motive – not least Donal himself, but the assassin covered his or her tracks too well. The judge's estranged wife, Gloria Bairstow, clearly did not relate to the Press or the Law the episode that had caused the breakdown of her marriage.

NINE

HAVING FAILED TO FIND TR A SUITABLE HOUSE, I agreed to his request that he should rent Foxgloves for the month of August when I would be away, so that he could store some of his belongings there until he returned from his US tour.

"As you'll be away anyway," he said, "it's not as if I'm asking to move in with you – much as I would love it to be a permanent arrangement."

He walked into the house and up the stairs to my bedroom as I was packing a suitcase on the afternoon before my departure to Ireland.

"Your obsession with your family is beginning to piss me off," he said. "You're lucky enough to be the girlfriend of an international celebrity, and you choose to go chasing off to some remote, uncivilised place in Ireland, instead of coming to the US with me, all expenses paid, and providing me with the support I need. Who is going to protect me from all those raving fans?"

He started to pick the articles of clothing I had just packed in my case and threw them into the corners of the bedroom; a pair of panties here, a tee-shirt there. Pendragon growled softly at him when I protested, his lips drawn back to expose wolfish teeth. I guess it was then that I knew that I would never consider this man as a suitable mate and father to my children.

"Maybe when you come back, you'll have had a change of heart," he said. "You'll realise how much you miss me and suggest that I build a larger house for us both on your so-called *sacred* plot of land. We could call it 'Ash House' in honour of your family's remains."

I gave him a withering look and told him that his remark sank below the very nadir of bad taste.

"Maybe," he retorted, "but the building itself would be in the utmost good taste. I've already instructed a well-known architect to draw a preliminary design – one that would be suitable for any site with a sea-view."

"Well, forget this particular one, Thane. It is a hallowed memorial ground, and the spirits of the dead are not to be disturbed at the whim of a rich man, a celebrity, no less."

He shrugged. "You'll change your tune and see sense before the month is out."

We went downstairs and I made tea which we took into the garden.

"You see now," he said, "how it could be like this every afternoon of our lives. This is civilised England at its best."

"It is, of course," I agreed, "but we both lead busy lives and have no time for the niceties of country living, except on very few occasions."

Afternoon tea in the garden reminded me of Cecilia, and a June garden full of foxgloves; an ancient Labrador leaning against my legs, hoping for my last mouthful of cake.

TR talked about his 'deprived childhood'. An only child, he was a latchkey kid, he said, coming home from school to an empty house most days: no welcome from his working mother, no tea on the table, no dog to wag its tail in a frenzy of excitement at his return. His parents, he'd told me often, spent more energy in quarrelling with each other than in showing any affection for him. His dad expected him to do well and be a credit to him but never spared part of his evening or weekend to do any child-based activities with his only son. He preferred to be 'down the pub wi' me mates'.

"I shall be quite different when I'm a dad. And the kids will think it's really epic to have a world-famous dad and be in *HELLO* magazine and on telly like the Beckham boys. Perhaps they'll be really musical like their parents."

"Don't get ahead of yourself," I warned. "I reckon you have some issues around your emotional security . . . I mean *problems* of course. My grandmother would turn in her grave if she heard me utter 'that ghastly Americanism which has crept insidiously into our everyday dialogue'."

TR laughed loudly. "But she can't *turn* in her grave, can she? She's just a pile of ashes *on* the ground rather than *in* it."

"Bad taste again, Thane," I reproved him. "It was just a figure of speech." *(I did think, however, that Cecilia would have chalked up a 'Brownie' point on the scoreboard for him!).*

"Sorry, Ma'am." He stroked my hair and stood to help me take the tea-tray indoors.

Before he left, I handed him the duplicate keys to the house and the shed-cum-garage. We kissed briefly and he got into his car saying, "Goodbye, beautiful lady. I hope you will miss me as much as I'll miss you."

"Missing you already," I chanted in an exaggerated American accent.

PART TWO

THE LAKE ISLE OF INNISFREE

I will arise and go now, and go to Innisfree,
And a small cabin build there, of clay and wattles made;
Nine bean rows will I have there, a hive for the honey bee,
And live alone in the bee-loud glade.

And I shall have some peace there, for peace comes dropping slow,
Dropping from the veils of the morning to where the cricket sings;
There midnight's all a-glimmer and noon a purple glow
And evening full of the linnet's wings.

I will arise and go now, for always night and day
I hear lake water lapping with low sounds by the shore;
While I stand on the roadway, or on the pavement grey,
I hear it in the deep heart's core.

WILLIAM BUTLER YEATS 1865-1939

TEN

TWO DAYS LATER I DREW BACK THE PRETTY CURTAINS of my bedroom, opened the lower sash window and knelt on the floor to breathe in the perfect summer morning. A pearly mist hung over the newly-mown lawn which sloped down to the edge of the lake. Dew sparkled like diamonds in the grass, and the water, unruffled by any breeze, reflected the perfect blue of the sky and the distant mountain-tops. I was here! Here in this place, Oirbsean Lodge, about which I had read so much in Bridie's contribution to my family story, *The Magdalene Connection*. Pendragon arose from his bed, stretched his back legs and came to sit beside me.

"Good morning, milord," I greeted him. "I think you and I are going to go exploring, even if it is early in the morning. I am going to introduce you to a thing called a boat and we shall row out to one of those islands over there."

I was reminded at once of one of my favourite poems: W.B.Yeats's *The Lake Isle of Innisfree*. My grandfather, Bruno Sabra, had set it to music, and I sang a snatch of it now: . . . *nine bean rows will I have there and a hive for the honey bee/ and live alone in the bee-loud glade*. Would beans really grow on one of these small islands, I wondered; and did Yeats ever live out his poem?

I showered quickly and dressed in suitable boating gear. Although there was probably no need to do so, I locked the garden-room door behind us and we walked down the lawn, leaving our two sets of footprints in the dewy grass, and found the small jetty at which three rowing boats were moored. They were of varying sizes, each painted in green and white and named 'Rosaleen', 'Lydia' and 'Grainne'. I chose 'Rosaleen' as she was the largest and I had to consider Pendragon's size and weight. I drew her alongside, stepped in and sat down immediately so that Penn's entry would not pitch me overboard. The water was shallow here but I did not feel inclined to bathe, fully clothed as I was. The dog stepped in gingerly and settled where I indicated. I congratulated him as I engaged the oars in the rowlocks and untied the mooring rope. He seemed unperturbed as we pushed away from the jetty. He had been in the car and below decks when we took the ferry from England so can have had no sense that he was traveling by water then.

I rowed round the nearest island which had dense vegetation coming right to the water's edge. The next was similar, so I rowed further south towards a wider part of the lake and saw ahead of us a much larger island with fewer trees and a shoreline which would allow for landing. On the eastern side of it, I tied up at a short wooden jetty with an iron ring set into a large rock.

As we stepped ashore, I started on the second verse of the poem. This could have been the very isle, I thought as I sang: *And I shall have some peace there, for peace comes dropping slow. . .* Pendragon snuffled around as we walked through 'the bee-loud glade' and emerged into an open area of grassland, littered with large stones. I sat down on a large, flat rock and looked around, alarmed when I saw evidence of human habitation. Beyond a clump of hazel bushes there was a stone building, an ancient chapel or hermitage, against the wall of which were a pile of logs and a small stack of turf.

"Oh Lord!" I said to my companion, "I think we're trespassing. Perhaps there's some mad woodcutter here who'll come out and threaten us with an axe."

I had spoken quietly enough to my faithful hound, but from somewhere behind me came a gentle cough. "I would hate to frighten you, but I assure you that I am no mad axe-man," said a male voice. I swung round, startled, to confront the speaker.

"Oh, I am so sorry," I said, springing to my feet. *Here is history repeating itself*, I thought, my cheeks flaming in a blush inherited from my grandmother, along with most of my physical appearance. *Was not Cecilia herself guilty of early morning trespass? Did she not meet her lover thus?* Pendragon stood up and wagged his tail uncertainly, clearly aware that I was ill at ease.

"I heard you singing," the man said in his soft accent. "I thought maybe an angel had come to visit me. And I recognised the words: Yeats's *The Lake Isle of Innisfree,* if I am not mistaken. This island is actually Inishcoll, the isle of hazel trees."

"I did wonder if this could be Innisfree," I said. "That was my own grandfather's musical setting of the poem, in fact."

"I should like to hear more about that. Will you come inside and have something in the way of refreshment? I was just about to have breakfast."

The man before me was tall and pleasant-looking – handsome in an academic sort of way; in his late thirties, I estimated. He had an air of both gentleness and strength in equal measure and I sensed that we would get along well, or I should not have accepted his offer of hospitality.

"But first," he said, "I would like to take a photograph of you and your dog emerging from the shadow into the light. I am an artist and would like to paint the scene as I first saw it. Your hair will test my ability to mix such a colour, if I may be so personal." He produced a camera and Pendragon and I went back into the wooded area and re-emerged, hesitating a little as we met the bright light of the open ground.

"Thank you for that, Miss? Mrs? ______; I am Fearghal Tobias Gabriel."

"Madeleine Grace Manning – Miss," I supplied, offering my hand which he took in a firm grip. "And this is Pendragon." The dog offered our host a damp, hairy paw. The stranger smiled. "What a great name! Of Arthurian legend?"

"Indeed," I replied. "I hoped it was Cornish, but now find that it originated in Wales."

"And you yourself hail from the U.S.of A, I would guess."

"Only in that I happened to be born there," I explained. "I am in fact half Irish, half English …with traces of Russian-Jewish on my paternal grandfather's side."

"Hmm; an interesting mix."

We walked towards the stone chapel-like building at one end of which was a single-storey, single-roomed hut.

"Welcome to my temporary abode," Fearghal said as we stepped inside. His manner was rather formal and slightly self-conscious. "The usual offices, as they call them – of rudimentary convenience – are tagged on at the back and the round bit is a small oratory. Several of these islands have the remains of religious buildings."

"So you are a hermit-artist then? Have I invaded the sanctity of Inishcoll?" I asked.

"I have chosen to be a hermit, *pro tem*, whilst I get over a kind of breakdown caused by stress. This place belongs to a friend of a friend, who lives in Sligo, and I have come here to paint in peace. You are in no way invading my privacy – in fact, you are already the subject of my next painting; you and Pendragon." The dog thumped his tail on the stone floor and regarded Fearghal with approval.

"But before you tell me all about yourself," Fearghal continued, "let's have breakfast."

He put a kettle on to boil on a bottled-gas burner and fetched a loaf of soda-bread and a dish of butter from a cupboard, followed by two pottery mugs and plates and a pair of ancient, mismatched table-knives. I had worked up quite a thirst and an appetite from my morning exertions, and the simple meal was much appreciated.

"This soda-bread is so good," I declared. "My mother used to make it in California, though she couldn't replicate the exact texture and taste, she said, because the brown flour was not the same as in Ireland. How do you manage so far away from shops?"

"I make it myself," he said, "bringing the supplies back by boat from the village over there." He gestured towards the west of the island, which I had not yet explored. "Now tell me how you come to be here."

I gave him a brief explanation of the reason for my visit: how I had arrived at Killogan the previous night, when it was nearly dark, to be greeted by Bridie's daughter, Grainne. It had been a long car journey from Cornwall I explained and, although I was very weary, Grainne and I had eaten a light supper and shared a bottle of wine, after which I fell gratefully into bed and slept like a log, waking to find this beautiful morning beckoning me out onto the lough. Cornwall was beautiful, I said, but these surroundings beat anything I had ever seen.

"Now tell me about your grandfather," he invited. "He was a composer?"

"Both a composer and a world-famous orchestral and choral conductor," I assured him. "His name was Bruno Sabra, though sadly I never knew him – except through the memoir and recollections of my grandmother, his widow."

"*The* Bruno Sabra? How fantastic! I know of his work, of course, being familiar with his *Messe Solonelle* in E-flat. I am not especially musical, but I do have a certain taste in classical music. I have some of his CDs at home."

"And where is home?" I asked.

"Oh, a little place south of Limerick," he replied dismissively. "Nowhere you would ever have heard of."

"Actually, my father spent his early childhood in Limerick," I said. "But that leads me into complications with which I will not bore you at present. Perhaps when I know you better, if that is to be. It has much to do with the reason why I am staying in Killogan for a few weeks. If it's not an impertinent question, what is your line of business when you're not taking a sabbatical?"

"People, mostly," he answered without hesitation, "Their educational, mental, and emotional welfare."

"A psychiatrist or psychologist?" I queried. "Then is it not a case of 'Physician, heal thyself'?"

"Touché," he smiled. "Perhaps I could better be described as a Social Worker." He raised his shoulders in a sort of prolonged shrug and let them drop again. "And what about you, Madeleine? What do you do when you're not rowing around foreign lakes?"

"Oh, a bit of this and a bit of that: estate agency, journalism and instrumental teaching – but that, too, is a story for another time. I should get back to base now. Grainne said she would phone when she got to her office in Galway."

ELEVEN

Bridie had left Oirbsean Lodge well stocked with all the food and drink I might need for three or four days. All I needed to do was to explore my new surroundings on foot while the weather was so fine. I had missed Grainne's call during my early morning excursion so phoned her back to reassure her that all was well and tell her that I had had a wonderful night's sleep. I admitted taking a boat out to explore the lough, but stopped short of relating my encounter on Inishcoll. Fearghal had told me that, though certain people in the nearest village knew of his presence there, he thought that few others were aware of it.

"That was daring of you!" she commented. "Which boat did you take? Was it the *Grainne O'Malley?*"

"No, with Pendragon in mind, I chose *Rosaleen* because she's the biggest. He took to boating like a duck to water, so to speak."

"That's grand altogether," she said, laughing. "Well, you both come from a seafaring part of the world, I suppose."

"We do," I agreed, "but actually it was his first introduction to being afloat – apart from the ferry, of course. It was good not to be confronted by a heavy Atlantic swell."

"Well, have a grand day," she wished me. "I'll call round on my way back from work. I'll just phone Mam now to let her know of your safe arrival."

"Send her my fondest love," I said. "And tell her that I'll keep a very good eye on this lovely, lovely house."

"Will do," Grainne said. "We'd love you to come over for a meal on Saturday evening. Bring himself as well," she added, meaning Pendragon. "He'll command some respect from my two, being so much bigger. If you walk over, Colm will bring you back in the car so that you don't get lost."

I gladly accepted her invitation.

*

Much of the conversation on that Saturday evening centred round Bridie's forthcoming eightieth birthday celebrations the following August; the gathering of the clans that had been suggested and approved by many who had attended the ceremony of the scattering of Cecilia's ashes at Porthwenna the previous year. It was a date in the diaries of Bridie's entire family, and those of Cecilia's oldest friends; those who were still alive, that is. My Irish grandmother, Moira, was frail at over ninety, but was determined to make it. The hotel, Oirbsean House, formerly the family home of Bridie's late husband, Charles O'Malley, was already booked for the entire weekend of the celebrations.

The element of surprise would not be there for Bridie because she herself had suggested a grand family reunion; however, there were additional details which could be kept secret while we waited, and these were easier to discuss in her absence.

At one point Grainne asked: "Might there not be a grand wedding later this year? This celebrity guy of yours . . .?"

"Not *mine*," I interrupted her hastily. "I'm not sure that he would be a desirable addition to the family."

"But writing a song especially for you, Maddie. Wow! He must be keen."

"Keen, yes; but marriage material, no."

"Well," sighed Grainne, "if it were not for my beloved Colm here, I'd say send him this way."

Colm laughed. "Fame and fortune are not everything, it seems. Don't throw yourself away on someone who is not worthy of you, Madeleine. Some day your prince will come, as the song goes."

"I hope so," I said coyly. "I feel duty-bound to add another branch to the family tree before I'm too old. And, by the way, I'd like to attend Mass with you here tomorrow. Are local people likely to make the connection with Thane Richmond? Perhaps I could go by my second name, Grace, instead of Madeleine?"

"Good thinking," said Grainne. "It means the same as my name; Grace it shall be. Remember that, Colm."

TWELVE

TIME FOR ANOTHER VISIT TO *INISHCOLL*, I THOUGHT on the Monday morning, and I admit to you now that my heart gave a bit of a lurch when I thought of seeing Fearghal again. In the intervening days I had accused myself of being ridiculously romantic when I acknowledged to myself that I was undoubtedly attracted to this island hermit; that there had been a certain recognition at that first encounter – certainly on my part. Only time and future visits would tell if had been mutual.

So back we went, Penn and I, after an early breakfast, only to be disappointed, on reaching the hermitage, that the resident did not answer my knock at the slightly open door. I pushed the door wider diffidently and called his name, but there was no reply. On the table there were signs that breakfast had been taken: a still-warm teapot, half a loaf on a wooden board, a dish of butter and a pot of local honey. But this inspection I took in with only part of my mind, for on an easel at the far end of the room was an unfinished picture that was unmistakably of Pendragon and myself, the colour of the hair amazingly accurately reproduced. I was spellbound, though to spare my absent host's embarrassment, should he suddenly appear unclothed to find his privacy invaded, I called 'Hello-o' intermittently until it became quite clear to me that he was not there at all.

I explored a little, my eyes briefly taking in the little bedroom at the back, before entering the oratory at the end of the building and bowing my head to say a short prayer before the little wooden altar, behind which was a tiny, arched east window with stone mullions and leaded lights. A stone on the floor was carved with the name 'Tomas O'Faolain', with the other information on the memorial engraved in Irish. The small space was redolent of incense and seemed to speak of the sanctity of ages.

I rose and left the building, Pendragon at my heels, and walked down to the landing stage on the west side of the island where, to my joy and relief, I saw Fearghal tying his boat to the railing and bending to pick up two bags of provisions.

"Madeleine!" he exclaimed, a warm smile lighting up his features. "I felt very strongly that you might come again today; so much so that I nearly left you a note to explain my absence."

"So you will forgive me for invading your domain yet again?" I questioned demurely, a touch flirtatiously, I suppose.

"It is no *invasion,* Madeleine," he assured me. "You and the devoted Pendragon are most welcome, whenever you choose to grace me with your presence. Did you go inside? Did you see the picture?"

"I did, indeed, and was most impressed. You have great talent."

We walked across the green turf, picking our way between the small, rounded boulders until we reached the front door of his tiny abode.

"I'll make coffee and you can tell me more about yourself," he invited. "I want to make a painting which illustrates where you came from when you emerged from the tree-shade into the light ... and beyond that moment, where you will travel into the future."

"I am extremely flattered, sir," I said, aware that I was blushing with that tendency inherited from Cecilia, partly from embarrassment but equally, from intense pleasure because this man, whom I had permitted to occupy so much of my imagination of late, was showing so much interest in me.

"So tell me," he said later, as we sat at the table drinking freshly-brewed coffee, "Who have you left behind in England bemoaning your absence?"

So I told him about Thane Richmond: his persistent courting, his proposal of marriage, his wanting to build on my land, his composing and performance of the single, *Madeleine,* and the publicity the relationship (or rather, *non*-relationship) attracted locally. Fearghal had heard the name, he said, though he was not very knowledgeable about pop-music.

"And have you led him to believe that you will eventually capitulate?" he inquired.

"I very much hope NOT!" I declared passionately. "I do not love him and could not marry for any reason other than love. My child – or children – must have a father to whom I am totally committed."

"And that man, when you find him, will be the most fortunate man in the world." he said. "More coffee?"

Oh, but I think I have found him. I could not give voice to my thought but felt another blush rise to my cheeks as I passed my cup for him to refill.

*

"The rest of that picture is forming in my mind," said Fearghal, indicating the easel at the end of the room.

"The rest?" I queried.

"Yes. I have in mind that it should be more of a frieze, a sequence of events: past, present, future; a triptych."

"I am flattered," I said. "Past and present can be managed, but are you a clairvoyant as well as an artist?"

"The future is what we make it," he said mysteriously. "However, I am running short of canvases and paint," he continued, "especially of a very effective purple colour, made in Australia, for depicting deep shade. I read about it in an excellent publication called *International Artist* and they stock it in a brilliant art shop in Galway. I shall have to take the bus in to the city tomorrow and restock, before I can continue."

"Better still," I interrupted quickly, "I shall take you in by car. We could make a day of it. I'd love to get to know the city."

His face lit up. "Would you really? I would gladly show you around; and it would be a great help to bring back the supplies in a car, rather than risking them on the bus."

We arranged that I should pick him up in a lay-by opposite the Post Office and store in Derrybeg, where he would leave his boat on the quay below the road.

THIRTEEN

THE ANTICIPATION OF A WHOLE DAY SPENT IN THE company of this man was a pleasure in itself. Fate, Fortune had suddenly presented me with a gift I had unconsciously been searching for ever since the death of my beloved grandmother. Thane – Fearghal: they were not to be compared. When had any action, word or look of TR's ever made my pulse miss a beat, my heart melt, my knees grow weak? If what I felt for Fearghal was the magic of love, I was already bewitched.

That afternoon I drove on the Galway road as far as Derrybeg, to find out how long it would take me and to be sure of identifying the meeting place. The lay-by he had described was a little way on from the Post Office/shop. I was glad that it was out of the range of prying eyes, and resisted the impulse to go in and buy postage stamps or groceries. My red hair, even in Ireland, where such a colour is not so unusual, still makes me very recognisable.

*

Tuesday dawned bright and fair. There had not been a drop of rain since I had arrived the previous Wednesday so, after my shower, I put on my prettiest summer frock and white sandals and brushed and braided my hair. Hitherto, Fearghal had seen me only in tatty jeans, wellies and a waterproof jacket. Today

I wanted to display my femininity so that he might be aware of me as a woman . . . and a possible mate.

The thought had occurred to me that the reason for his 'breakdown' and need to get away from civilisation for a while could have been a broken relationship, with the resulting bereavement and heartbreak. I wondered if I could persuade him to speak of this; of his reasons for seeking solitude. At any rate, I thought, I could show him that 'there are as good fish in the sea . . .' so this particular fish glammed herself up as best she could to impress the object of her desire!

*

I made sure that I reached our meeting place five minutes early, and parked the station wagon in the lakeside lay-by in time to see Fearghal's boat approaching the landing stage below. I spoke to Pendragon as I waited for Fearghal's appearance at the top of the steps from the quay. "Now you have to be a good, patient boy today and wait in the car without making any fuss. I'll make sure we park in a multi-story lot so that the car doesn't get hot, and I've brought water and treats, so all your needs are taken care of. This could be a very important day for your mom."

And it did indeed turn out to be a momentous day for Pendragon's 'mom'.

Fearghal's only concession to the warm, fine weather was a red, checked, loose shirt worn over dark trousers and leather sandals.

"This is so kind of you, Madeleine," he said as he got into the car. "And you look like the very breath of summer." (So he *did* notice!).

"It is quite as much my pleasure," I assured him, letting my hand touch briefly on his shoulder before grasping the stick-shift and driving off.

Our conversation covered many topics on the way to the city. It was not the right time for confidences; maybe they would follow later, over lunch, or in a little teashop. I made up my mind to savour each moment of his company, knowing that I would want to recall every word and action at the end of the day, and beyond.

Arriving in the city, we found a multi-story parking-lot near enough to the art shop to come back and off-load the purchases. While Fearghal stocked up, I bought myself some Calligraphy equipment, with the idea that I would make a framed and illustrated manuscript of Yeats's *The Lake Isle of Innisfree* to present to him at the end of my visit to Killogan. Armed with everything we needed, we made our way back to the car.

"Time now for a little exploration before I buy you lunch." said Fearghal.

"Sounds good," I agreed, "but I insist on buying lunch. With that large bill in the art shop and having a sabbatical year, I imagine you could do without treating casual acquaintances."

He looked slightly pained. "I think of you as a close friend, not a 'casual acquaintance'," he protested.

"However, if you insist, I shall buy afternoon tea when we have finished our tour."

(How I loved 'close friend', though I wished it could be 'girlfriend' or 'partner').

*

As we were parked in Merchants Road, we walked first to the Spanish Arch on the riverside. It was here that the French and Spanish galleons would have docked with their cargoes of wines and silks in Elizabethan times. Legend has it, too, that the Spanish Arch was the last point of land contact for Christopher Columbus before his voyage to America. Nearby we saw the Columbus sculpture presented to the City of Galway by the City of Genoa on the five hundredth anniversary of Columbus's discovery of America.

Fearghal pointed out the Claddagh Village and the Cathedral of Our Lady Assumed into Heaven, on the other side of the river.

"Perhaps we could drive over there when we leave the car park," he said, "to save too much walking now. There's still the museum to do, and that's quite close, on this side; but let's find some lunch now and do that before we fetch the car."

We walked up Quay Street towards the pedestrianised streets of the city centre until we found an attractive-looking restaurant with waiter service. One thing that charmed me about Fearghal as we walked along was his courtly manners, now rather old-fashioned in men's behaviour towards women. Clearly, I thought, he was used to escorting ladies through city streets, walking on the outer edge of the sidewalk in traffic, ushering them safely across roads and holding open doors for them.

The menu looked promising and we both made successful choices of a main course, and ordered a carafe of red wine to accompany our meal. I decreed that he should drink the lion's share so that it would not affect my driving. *In vino veritas*, I thought; and was bold enough to ask, "I told you a great deal about myself yesterday. Is there, or has there been, someone special in your life? I'm sorry to ask such a personal question."

"You are forgiven for that," he answered. "Yes, there is someone very special, but I shall say no more than that at present."

"Okay," I said, my heart plummeting, "but if you feel the need to talk about it, I am a sympathetic listener."

"Not just now, but thanks; I'll remember that. Maybe we should decide what's next on the agenda for this afternoon. St Nicholas Collegiate Church is very interesting – and not far from here ..."

I felt shut-out by his swift change of subject. There was no way of going back to his previous statement, so I listened with only half an ear to what he had in mind for the rest of our day together.

When we had finished our meal, I excused myself to go to the rest-room and discreetly settled the bill with our waiter, so as not to embarrass Fearghal at the table. I added a good tip for the young man, whose name was Nathaniel and who was black and extremely handsome. "You looked after us very well," I said. "You obviously enjoy your job here."

"Oh, I do, ma'am. And I, like, know you from somewhere. I said to myself 'I seen that lovely lady on TV; you're a pop star, right?"

"Not exactly," I replied, "but I did have a song named after me. Madeleine is the name."

"O-M-G!" he exclaimed. "Wait till I tell the other guys. How cool is that?"

I smiled and went back to our table to join Fearghal, who rose from his seat as I approached.

*

Next on our tour was Eyre Square, part of which is Kennedy Park, with its sculpture of the bust of the eponymous president, after which we walked back the way we had come and visited St Nicholas Church, a Protestant church, very much in the centre of the shopping area. Fearghal was as attentive as ever as we walked along.

"I think we should make our way to the museum now," he said as we left the church. "Would you like to check on Pendragon in the car park, beforehand?"

"That's a good idea. I could just let him out for a quick wee and give him a drink," I replied.

Penn was pleased to see us after so long and did what was expected of him, while I explained that he would have to wait a little longer. I promised that we would take him for a walk when we crossed the river after our visit to the museum.

As we toured the exposition of Galway's rich history, I tried not to think about Fearghal's earlier admission and what it might mean for me. He himself was extremely informative about Irish history in general and impressed that I knew about the famous pirate, Grace O'Malley, from my editing of the second family archive. I told him about the two publications and said that I had copies of both with me for my hostess's family. They were still in the car and I told him that he was welcome to read them before Bridie's return.

"I would be most interested," he said, "from what you have told me already. Do you think a cup of tea would go down well, now?"

By now I was gasping for liquid refreshment so we found a convenient café and sat at one of a few tables outside, sharing a pot of tea.

"I have so enjoyed this day with you," he said, briefly touching my hand which was resting on the table. My heart lurched. *Maybe all is not lost because of his former attachment*, I thought. Little did I know at that moment of the faint hope that can turn into the most profound disappointment. At the edge of my vision, I was aware of a sharp-faced woman, sitting alone at a table not far away from ours, who seemed much too interested in us. As we got up to leave, she sprang to her feet as we were passing.

"Why, Father Gabriel, it *is* you, isn't it? I thought I recognised you over there, even without your clerical black. Are you having a good holiday? It's a fine city, isn't it?"

There was no warmth in Fearghal's tight smile and I could feel the tension as he replied. "Ah, Mrs Buckley, you are a long way from home too. May I introduce my cousin, Miss Manning?"

Two breathtaking shocks in a few seconds! "Hi," I squeaked faintly. "I just love this city, too. It's my very first visit." I laid on the American accent thickly.

An exchange of awkward conversation ensued until eventually the encounter ended and Fearghal and I walked back towards the parking lot. I could feel the woman's eyes boring into us as we retreated; imagine the thoughts buzzing around in her head as she rehearsed the hot gossip on her return home to 'somewhere south of Limerick'.

"I do apologise for all that," he said grimly. "Thank you for going along with it. My cover is blown, it would seem."

"Don't say any more," I begged. "I am in deep shock. Forget the rest of the tour. I think we should leave for home right now. I will let the dog out on the way back."

FOURTEEN

THE SILENCE THAT HAD FALLEN AS WE FOUND OUR WAY out of the parking lot and onto the Oughterard road was a million miles from that comfortable, companionable silence that can fall between true friends or lovers. Pendragon shifted about restlessly in the back of the car as if the seething thoughts of the two humans in the front were audible and the tension tangible: those unasked and unanswered questions that raced from one to the other and back again. The only actual words spoken were solely to do with finding the correct route back to Derrybeg.

Once we had left the city far behind, Fearghal spoke in a low and contrite voice.

"I feel I owe you an explanation . . . an apology, Maddie."

"You do," I replied shortly, the hurt I was feeling evident in the timbre of my voice. "Both for withholding information *and* lying about our relationship."

"Let me start at the beginning," he started, as I swung the car into a bay at the side of the highway, where a rough track led away into the hills.

"Just rehearse it in your mind for a while," I interrupted, getting out of the car. "I'm going to take Penn for a walk."

"Be careful on those stones in those delicate sandals," he warned solicitously. But I cared nothing about the 'delicate sandals' as I strode away, welcoming the discomfort of the stony ground to my vulnerable toes because it counteracted the numbness of my mind. I walked fast until I was out of sight of the car, inwardly shrieking with pain and rage. *And what was a priest doing, talking of 'a very special person'*, I screamed to myself? Around another bend in the track a flock of mountain sheep was grazing. I turned back lest Pendragon should give chase, perversely exultant at the sight of my bloodied toes. *I had better hear him out,* I thought, too impassioned for tears as I marched purposefully back towards the car.

Fearghal got out when he saw us approaching, opening the trunk and pouring water into a bowl for Penn, as he had observed me doing earlier.

"You have hurt your feet; there is blood," he exclaimed, his voice full of concern.

"No matter," I said, tersely. "Okay, I will listen to what you have to say now, before we drive on."

Clouds were gathering to the west of us and rain looked imminent. We got into the car and swung round to face each other, albeit avoiding eye-contact.

"I can make no excuses for myself, Maddie, and regret very much that you appear to be hurt by this afternoon's revelations. Indeed, I *am* a priest – *was* that woman's, Mrs. Buckley's, parish priest until April this year, when I was wrongly accused of a sexual assault on a teenage girl who had a crush on me. You will understand the seriousness of the sort of scandal that ensues, whether the accusations are true *or* false. The bishop was called in and it was decided after the hearing that I should leave the parish for a period of at least two years. He was very supportive and I know that he believed me when I protested my innocence. It was he who suggested the hermitage on Inishcoll; he who arranged my tenancy with the owner who is a friend of his. When I met you, I accounted for my presence there by saying that I'd had a kind of breakdown. Can you understand all this, Maddie? It's very important to me that you do."

I realised that I had not taken a breath since he started to speak so I took a huge draught of air, which cleared my lungs though not my head. I felt totally confused.

"So this girl – do you still have feelings for her? Is she the very special someone you spoke of at lunchtime?"

"Huh! Dearbhla Corcoran?" he shrugged, lifting his hands palms upwards in negation. "After the lies she told? When I spurned her advances, she went and got herself pregnant by some layabout, and laid the blame on me out of pure pique"

"Then *who?*" I queried, doggedly pursuing what must have seemed like an irrelevant line of inquiry. "God? The Blessed Virgin? You're a *priest*, Fearghal. There's no-one else you're *allowed* to venerate!"

"Madeleine," he said softly, looking deep into my eyes. "I did not say there *was* someone very special; I said there *is* ..."

"No, NO!" I shouted. "That cannot be, even if I feel the same, which I *do*. It is against the laws of God and the Church. Think of your vows. Now please fasten your seatbelt and we'll go back."

He sighed deeply as he obeyed my instruction and I drove away, faster than I should have done, unable to deal further with what had just taken place.

When we reached our former meeting place at Derrybeg, I helped him take his purchases out of the car and remembered that I had promised to lend him the two family archives I had compiled: Cecilia's Memoir and *The Magdalene Connection*.

"That should inform you further of the immorality of my forebears," I said. "I should warn you that there is some sexual content in both books which may offend your *priestly* sensibilities."

"Thank you, Maddie." He ignored my sarcasm. "I shall read them with interest. When shall I see you again?"

"I cannot answer that at present," I answered. "It will take me some time to come to terms with what I have heard today.

Bridie and my uncle return from America on Friday week, so things will be different then, in any case."

I watched the dejected, departing figure descend the steps to the quay, my eyes brimming with tears as my precious day, which might have ended with an exchange of thanks and even a kiss, disintegrated into disappointment and despair. There was nothing for it but to drive back to Oirbsean Lodge and try to make sense of the events of the day. The first drops of rain began to fall. *He will get wet in that open boat,* I thought. *What a good thing his purchases are in a strong plastic bag.*

FIFTEEN

On entering the house, I switched myself into automatic pilot mode and went about the business of feeding Pendragon and Pooka, the cat. The latter had been very wary of the canine invader at first, keeping well out of his way both indoors and out. On our return, however, he seemed genuinely pleased to see us, even rubbing against Pendragon's long legs as both animals waited to be fed.

I found some disinfectant and bathed my blood-stained feet and cleaned the narrow straps of the white sandals as best I could. There was tidying to be done and a little cleaning, after which I checked the emails on my laptop, reading them at least, though I had neither the will nor energy to reply to them. The longest of these was from Mistletoe, thanking me for my postcard and telling me the local news. Alex had been asking about me, she said. He seemed daunted by the fact that he had a rival in Thane Richmond and had asked her if he stood any chance of winning my affection. *No chance at all,* I thought, *after what has happened to my heart since I arrived here.* Had Mistletoe been present, I would probably have poured out my heart to her. As it was, I soaked myself in a warm, scented tub and retired to bed early, knowing that, once I was lying down, I should have to deal with all the stuff in my head, sorting it through like an untidy cupboard and deciding what to do with the contents.

I could not pray for guidance to a God against whom I railed because he had played such a cruel trick on me. Instead

I invoked the spirit of my beloved grandmother, Cecilia; she who had known what it meant to love and lose, to love and lose, and finally to love and be rewarded and recompensed for her loss by her beloved Bruno. Cecilia's spiritual presence was not confined to the sacred ground around St Elowen's Well where I had communed with her so often. Her angel wings brought her to me across the miles that divided me from my home. Our conversation went something like this:-

M. Darling Cecilia, you witnessed what happened today. What shall I do? Where do I go from here? How can I go on living?

C. Too many questions at a time. Let me ask *you* one. What do *you* want to come out of all this?

M. I want it not to be true. I love him. I want him to be an ordinary man, not a priest. I want to marry him and have children with him.

C. And what do you think *he* wants? Who do you think is this very special person to whom he refers?

M. I think I am that person.

C. Exactly. And how do you think *he* is feeling at this moment?

M. I think he is sad, despairing and wrestling with his conscience.

C. He is pacing around in the pouring rain outside, unable to sleep, wanting you, shouting your name into the storm; refusing to listen to the voice of his vocation.

M. Can you see him, Cecilia?

C. Dearest child, I cannot *see*; I can only *know* how it is with him.

M. So what shall I do right now?

C. Cry a little, if you must. Go to sleep; allow yourself to dream. Do not go to the island again until he calls you – and he *will* call. Give him time for his inner struggle. Meanwhile, occupy yourself. Explore Connemara without him. When it rains, do your Calligraphy. Make a beautiful, illuminated copy of Yeats's poem for him; frame it, wrap it.

M. How can I be sure that he will call me? How can I wait for that moment?

C. Pour your love into his heart and your courage into his soul at every moment. Remember his words: 'The future is what we make it' Together you will find a way.

And with a swish of her silken wings, my bright angel departed and I gave myself up to tears and eventually to sleep.

SIXTEEN

THE STORM RAGED ALL NIGHT AND WHEN I LOOKED out of the window in the grey dawn, the waters of the lake were whipped into a frenzy by the wind from the south west. I gazed bleakly across the smaller islands in the direction of Inishcoll, imagining Fearghal, asleep at last in his tiny room; asleep, but not at peace. As I gazed, concentrating the full strength of my mind, I tried to penetrate his dreams, to pour my love and courage into his heart as Cecilia had instructed; to bring him comfort and peace of mind, hope for the future. My despair of the previous night had given way to the faintest glimmer of hope. I would not only stand shoulder to shoulder with him in his struggle against his conscience, I would make sure that he could not bear to live without me. Cecilia had bequeathed to me the capacity for love that had been the mainstay of her life, as well as the tenacity to believe that, in the end, that same love would win against all the odds.

I showered and dressed with none of the care I had taken yesterday. My flowery, summer frock lay in a heap on the bedroom floor where I had stepped out of it, the ruined once-white sandals beside it. I simply put on clean jeans and tee-shirt and a sweater for warmth as the rain lashed spitefully against the windows.

It was all I could do to stomach any breakfast, but several cups of strong coffee were very welcome. When I had cleared away, I assembled my Calligraphy pens and paper on the kitchen table and started on my manuscript. At the top of the page I ruled a musical stave, drew a treble clef sign and key signature and added my grandfather's notation of the first line of the poem, resolving to dedicate as much time and care as it needed to produce a work of art worthy of the beloved recipient.

The foul weather persisted for two whole days, so I was able to work undisturbed until I had finished the task in hand, finding that it brought me a measure of comfort in my distress.

The intuitive Pendragon, ever perceptive to my state of mind, tolerated my absorption, keeping close to my side and attending only to calls of nature, making brief excursions not far beyond the back door when I remembered to let him out. I did not stop for food, unable to tolerate anything but soup and bread in the evenings. But there was always a drink of water within reach, if only to replace the fluid in my lachrymal glands. By the end of the second day I had finished the lettering, which I executed in the attractive Celtic script used so extensively in Ireland.

By the Friday, the thirty-six hour storm had passed, along with some of the storm within my soul. I needed to go to the village and buy supplies for the weekend and, once I came home, I started on the illumination of the margins of my work, making a design of trailing, emerald green shamrock and tiny golden harps. Beneath the poem I depicted the *nine bean rows will I have there; a hive for the honey bee.* In any artistic work it is essential to know when to stop: a piece can so easily be ruined by over-tweaking. I propped the finished work on the dresser for a while before putting it in the frame that I had bought in the Art shop. Now all that was needed was a dedication to the recipient. I made this in the form of a bookmark, upon which I wrote:

For Fearghal, with my love always, from Madeleine...

On the reverse I transcribed the Ovid quotation which Bruno had written in his dedication of a book of songs he gave to Cecilia and which was used thereafter as a code between them:

Littore quot conchae, tot sunt in amore Dolores.

(Literally, ...*As the shells on the seashore, so are the pains of love,* or, more loosely, ... *There are as many pains in love as there are shells on the seashore.)* I did not insult Fearghal's intelligence with the translation; he had told me that he read Classics at University, as well as doing some private tutoring in the subject.

*

The framed poem was still propped up on the kitchen dresser when Grainne called round on her way home from work on Friday.

"Oh, that is so beautiful," she exclaimed. "I can see how you have been passing these rainy days. Have you done it for yourself or as a present?"

"The latter," I answered, tempted to tell all, but instantly deciding against it. "It's for a dear friend of mine who loves that poem."

"Well, lucky them! If I could do anything like that, I'd keep it for myself. It's perfect. You've taken so much trouble."

"If the rains return, I'll do one for you," I promised. "If you tell me your favourite poem, prayer or passage from literature."

"That would be wonderful. I'll look something out. I have to warn you that it really does rain most of the time around here. That's why we're called The Emerald Isle."

"Well, you might be lucky then," I laughed.

"Come for Sunday lunch after Mass, will you," she invited. "And bring that with you to show the others. Rosie and Henry are coming tomorrow and staying overnight."

"I'd love that," I said, "and look forward to meeting them."

SEVENTEEN

AND SO THE DAYS DRAGGED PAST WHILE I WAITED FOR the summons from Fearghal, which Cecilia had promised me *would* happen. On Saturday I wrapped Fearghal's present in bubble-wrap and plain brown paper so that I should not be tempted to add anything or alter it in any way. On Sunday I 'forgot' to take it with me to Grainne's house, so her description of my work to the others had to suffice.

"Maddie is just too modest," she explained, "but her work would make you gasp, I assure you. Just pray for more rain because she's promised to do one for me if she has to spend more time indoors."

"Nobody needs to pray for rain round here," Connie said. "It *happens* without the Lord's intervention." We all laughed.

"So do you have a favourite passage in mind?" I asked Grainne. "No doubt it will rain again at some point before I go home at the end of the month."

"Another by himself," Grainne said, handing me an open book. "Or rather, a translation by Yeats of an old Celtic poem. Did you know it was his work?"

"Had I the heavens' embroidered cloths,
Enwrought with gold and silver light,
The blue and the dim and the dark cloths
Of night and light and the half light,
I would spread the cloths under your feet;

But I, being poor, have only my dreams;
I have spread my dreams under your feet;
Tread softly because you tread on my dreams.

"No, if ever I did know the words were by Yeats, I had forgotten," I said. Thinking of Fearghal as I read, I strove to hold back tears at the sentiments expressed. *How vulnerable one is in love,* I thought. *Two weeks ago I was perfectly normal and now the slightest reference to love can set me off.*

The rest of the afternoon passed pleasantly enough and the good company was a diversion, the frequent laughter a healing balm. Pendragon behaved impeccably whilst we were eating lunch and was rewarded with a plateful of meaty scraps afterwards. As we drank coffee in the garden room, he lay sprawled in the middle of the room where everyone could admire him.

*

The following day I decided to explore Connemara, wishing with every bone in my body that Fearghal could have come with me. Although the Derrybeg shop was out of my way, I decided to call in and buy a detailed map of the area I planned to explore. There was just the faint chance that Fearghal might be shopping there, I thought; though how I would have coped with 'bumping into him' I could not know. As it happened, there was no sign of him either on land or water, and I could hardly ask in the shop whether he had been in. There was a pleasant girl at the counter who did not show any undue interest in my visit, although she was friendly and courteous enough, and I walked out with a few postage stamps and a tourist leaflet on the attractions of the surrounding area which I studied for a few moments, sitting in the car in the lay- by where I had last seen Fearghal six days ago. I looked across the stretch of water which separated us and sent him insistent loving messages, willing him to contact me soon, soon, soon. *Telepathy is such an inexact science,* I thought; *such an inadequate means of communication.*

*

Fearghal's 'call' came on the following day, three days before Bridie's expected return. It came in the form of a letter addressed to Miss Madeleine Manning, c/o Mrs Bridie O'Malley, Oirbsean Lodge, Killogan. At the sight of the unfamiliar handwriting, I tore open the envelope with trembling fingers.

Inishcoll, Monday
My dear Maddie,
The last phrase of 'Innisfree' has been haunting me since our sad parting last Tuesday. 'I hear it in the deep heart's core'. But it is not the lake water's lapping that I hear, but your voice. There seems to have been a remarkable telepathic link between us these last few days and I am begging you to come to me once more before your friend and hostess comes home. Please come early on Wednesday and have breakfast with me. I have finished the painting and want you to see it. Also, now we have both had time to think things through, there is so much we need to discuss.

I have read both the family stories with great interest. The thing that most impresses me is the quality of the love which shines through those pages. 'Immorality', -- yes -- in the context of the attitudes of those earlier days; but chiefly, love in its purest form.

In case I omit to mention it when we meet, I would like to thank you for never questioning whether the accusations levelled against me by that wretched girl could conceivably have been true. They were not, of course, but bless you for accepting that.

Please, please come to me. I know that I hurt you and I want to make amends.

Yours with deepest affection,

Fearghal

EIGHTEEN

GRIEF YIELDED TO JOYFUL ANTICIPATION AS I LAY IN bed that night, planning my early morning response to Fearghal's summons. His letter, couched in more affectionate terms than I could have expected, gave me a measure of hope. It seemed strange to have as a rival, not a secret wife or lover, but the mystical bond of a spiritual vow demanded by his vocation. In many ways, the former would have been easier. I found it difficult to imagine how our meeting would proceed. It was not a dialogue that could be rehearsed or anticipated. Eventually I fell into a short but deep and dreamless sleep.

The dawn when it came was sunless and damp with the threat of more rain to come. I rose, showered, dressed warmly and brushed and tied back my hair, spritzing myself with fragrance to make up for the lack of allure in my dress.

I explained to Pendragon that on this occasion he must stay and guard the house. I needed my full attention for Fearghal, I told him, with no distractions. I let him out into the garden for a while and donned a waterproof and wellington boots, remembering to put my present for Fearghal into a waterproof carrier bag.

I left the house with a racing heart and a fluttery stomach and took the boat out onto the choppy water of the lake in time to see a skein of wild geese flying southwards, with their characteristic honking sound filling the air. This is, to my mind, one of the most beautiful sights and sounds in the world. I was thrilled by it on such an auspicious day and trusted that it boded well for me. A violent rain-storm raced over me, leaving me dripping and soaking. When I arrived at the landing place, in spite of the extra time it took me and the further soaking I had to endure, I drew the lightweight protective sheet over the boat and secured it well so that the interior should not fill with water in my absence.

Thus, it was a thoroughly bedraggled creature who presented herself at the door of the hermitage. Fearghal answered my knock promptly.

"Maddie, you're here – and so wet. Come in, come in. I'll take your waterproof and boots and put them in the back room. Will you be all right in stockinged feet? No, I'll fetch a pair of thick socks to keep your feet warm on this stone floor."

His solicitude was touching and eased any possible awkwardness there might have been in our meeting. When he brought the socks, I handed him the parcel I had concealed under my waterproof.

"I made this for you, Fearghal – something to remember me by." He unwrapped it while I drew on the thick, warm socks.

"Oh Maddie," he exclaimed. "How beautiful and what a wonderful gift! I shall treasure it always. Did you really do this especially for me?"

"Of course," I said, very quietly. "How else was I to pass those empty, rainy days of tortured thought?"

"I am honoured indeed. You have touched me, as always, 'in the deep heart's core'. And the Ovid quotation: so apposite" he said, having turned over the card of dedication. "Now, let me show you the painting I did of you and for you; how *I* passed those hours of tortured thought,"

He moved a screen to reveal his finished work. The painting was long, stretching right across the end of the room. It was somewhere between abstract and surrealist in style, in that it depicted recognizable figures and geographical features, yet demanded much of the viewer's subconscious in appraisal.

The eye is drawn at once to its dramatic centre: an arresting contrast of dark and light. A female figure with bright hair emerges from an area of intense purple shadow, stepping into dazzling brightness, a large, gray dog running ahead of her. As the eye travels to the right, it encounters mountains with sharp, rocky peaks. In the foreground, a river meanders through green lowlands towards the sea on the far side of the mountains, the furthest foothills of which are dotted with suggestions of chimney-like structures, tin mines perhaps; and, on the far right, in Dali-esque style, a rocking cradle stands on a golden beach.

Then it is time for the eye to travel back along the vibrant colour and leftwards from the centre through the dense, deep purple shadow of threatening, leafless trees, where it is drawn, eventually, to a spectral, male figure which seems to have stepped into the picture in pursuit of the female, though his whole bearing is one of hopelessness and defeat.

My eyes travelled slowly back along the painting before I turned to face the artist.

"The past, the present, I understand," I said. "But what of the future, the path *beyond* that purple shadow?"

And, without warning, a sense of utter desolation overcame me and huge tears welled from my eyes and rolled down my cheeks.

"That path starts here," he said as he gathered me in his arms, "When I drink from the chalice that holds your tears." And he kissed my eyes and then my mouth so that I tasted the saltiness of my own tears. We held each other tenderly close for several minutes, until our kisses became ever more passionate and he said," Come with me and we will make that future begin to happen." And he led me into the little bedroom and closed the door.

Dear reader, I cannot take you with me to the far side of that door. I will tell you only this: at one stage I murmured, "Fearghal, my dearest, this is breaking all the rules." To which he replied, "My beautiful girl, I have lost my battle with those rules and will face the consequences later. I love you, I love you. I *must* make love to you."

And moments later I felt the seeds of that future springing within me as we sighed and cried together in the bliss of fulfilment.

NINETEEN

BREAKFAST WAS TAKEN RATHER LATER IN THE DAY THAN Fearghal had planned. We were both too emotionally shaken to be hungry, devouring the sight of each other more avidly than the food on the table.

"I feel I am to blame for encouraging you to break your vow of celibacy," I said. "For myself, I cannot possibly regret what happened; but what have I done to *you*?"

"You have made me the happiest man in the world," he said, quietly and simply. "Yes, indeed I have broken my vows – or at least the discipline that was imposed by those vows – but I cannot at this moment regret it. It was an overwhelming force and I lost any power to resist it. I had long hours and days to wrestle with my conscience, but lost the fight as soon as I tasted your tears, knowing that they were the expression of your love, the love I have felt 'in the deep heart's core' since we parted so awkwardly last week."

"Oh, I was shocked – devastated – by those revelations. It seems we both had a miserable week. Is it that that has made our reconciliation so stupendous?"

"It must be that. I wanted you so much that I refused to listen to the voice of God. I heard only *your* voice and worked hard on the painting because it was for *you*. And at other times I read the two family stories in order to bring *you* closer. There are parallels between you and your grandmother: not just similarity in appearance, it seems – especially in view of what has just taken place."

"It has struck me all along. The circumstances of our meeting were so similar ... and now, of our coming together in a more intimate way."

"Oh Maddie," he sighed. "I realise now what a cruel discipline celibacy is, when a person is so profoundly moved by love and the need to express it in its fullest sense. Our coming together was so natural and spontaneous. How can it be a sin when it seems like a God-given gift? It was indeed a marriage of two souls and two bodies; a ceremony which had no need for words and vows. If the world would see it simply as an act of lust, I cannot believe that the Almighty would see it thus and condemn us. Wilt thou take this man to be thy lawful, wedded husband, my dearest one?"

"I will," I answered, "If thou wilt take this woman to be thy lawful wedded wife."

"Oh, indeed I will. I now pronounce us man and wife."

There were difficulties ahead, we knew; opposition, disapproval and seemingly impossible heights to scale. But these were considerations for another time. The breakfast things were left on the table and we went back into the little room to celebrate our union further. Later, as we lay so close on the narrow little bed, Fearghal said,

"Tomorrow is our last day before your friend Bridie comes home; after that you will be hers. Please can we spend the day together? We have so much to talk over . . . the future . . .."

"Ah, that future," I sighed. "Those sharp, rocky mountains in your painting; I see now what was in your mind. But at least you *saw* a future, whereas I could see nothing but impossibility, because of your profession."

"'Many waters cannot quench love" he quoted, "'neither can the floods drown it.' There must be a way over or through those mountains, my dearest; a way to the joys that lie beyond."

"Oh, there must, there must, there *must*," I sighed again, looking at his beautiful, artist's hands: the hands that had caressed my body so wonderingly and reverently, until increasing passion made his touch more demanding and insistent. I lifted one to my mouth, kissing the palm and the inside of the wrist and sucking each fingertip. It was his turn to sigh now.

"Oh Maddie., Maddie . . . I had no idea that love could hold so much pleasure, such heights of passion, such depths of tenderness, such intensity of fulfilment. We are entwined, interwoven, entangled, en ____"

"Enmeshed," I supplied. "And it's all so delicious and delightful. Let us never forget this day, Fearghal. Whatever happens, let it stay forever in our memory."

"Precious, hallowed consummation", he breathed, and kissed my eyes again, his tongue gently probing under the lashes. "No tears now," he smiled.

"Only of utter, utter happiness," I replied

*

Eventually I tore myself away and returned to Oirbsean Lodge and the longsuffering Pendragon, who was very pleased to see me after my absence of several hours. Although I was spaced out in a blissful trance, I passed the rest of the day preparing for Bridie's return: airing her bedroom and the second guestroom in which Declan would sleep, gathering flowers for the house and shopping for a welcoming meal. If I was to spend the entire day with Fearghal on the eve of their arrival, I was determined that everything should be in order before my early departure for Knock Airport to meet them from the plane on the Friday.

TWENTY

I PICKED FEARGHAL UP IN THE USUAL PLACE THE FOLLOWING day, having brought with me a picnic lunch and a half-bottle of wine, mainly for him though, mindful of my responsibility as driver, I would have the odd sip from his glass. Pubs and restaurants were, I imagined, few and far between in the wild reaches of Connemara, and we did not want to risk another encounter such as we had experienced on our outing to Galway. This was, after all, a popular holiday destination. In any case, we needed to talk seriously about the future . . . and needed also to touch and fondle and punctuate our discussion with kisses now and then.

Our broken vows preoccupied us: the incumbency of celibacy on his part; the self-imposed rule of marriage before sex and childbirth on mine.

"One day," he said, "priests will be allowed to marry. There is already a strong movement towards that. But it will not come soon enough for us, I fear. Before the Middle Ages, celibacy was not a pre-requisite of priesthood, even though it was for monks."

"What will happen to you as far as the priesthood is concerned?" I asked, handing Fearghal another sandwich.

"I shall be unfrocked, stripped of my position by the bishop, when I have refused to renounce you and put the sins of the flesh behind me. He will try to give me another chance, beg me to pray for the strength to resist temptation. He is a good man, a fair-minded man … which will make it more difficult than if he were stern and unforgiving."

"Oh, my love," I said, "I have ruined your life; yet I cannot wish our coming together had never happened."

"Nor I" he replied. "I want, more than anything, to travel with you on that journey beyond the purple shadow," he said, offering the wineglass to my lips.

I sighed and took a small sip, kissing the rim of the glass and turning it towards his mouth.

"And your family – your mother? How will she react?"

Fearghal groaned. "That I dread as much as telling the bishop. It is every Irish mother's dream to see a son enter the priesthood. She will be heartbroken."

"And will she want to meet the temptress who caused your fall from grace?" I asked.

"I cannot tell how she will deal with it, though I fear the worst," he said regretfully, biting his lip. "However, I shall go to her very soon and tell her what has happened. I plan to visit both her and the bishop before you return to England at the end of the month."

"Would you like me to come with you?" I asked him.

"I love your courage, my darling, but I think this is something I have to face alone – at least at first."

"I think I must tell Bridie and my uncle what happened while they were away," I said. "I cannot keep all this secret, whatever they think or say about it. When the time is right, I shall tell her, anyway. I think she would understand, though I scarcely know her yet."

*

We finished our picnic and tidied up after ourselves. Pendragon, who had stayed close to us, lying stretched out in the sun, rose to follow us back to the car. Before we reached it, Fearghal took my hand in his, turned towards me and said, "Maddie, my dearest one, this place is so quiet and secluded. From tomorrow we shall not be able to be together. I need to hold you as I did yesterday. It will help us to muster the courage to face what lies ahead for both of us in our different ways."

"Oh yes," I replied, "let's leave an imprint on this place so that our love and happiness blesses everyone who ever sets foot here."

We retraced our steps out of sight of Pendragon in the car, lay down on the short turf beside a large rock and made love delightedly, to the musical accompaniment of a small mountain stream falling between rocks to one side of us. Oh Connemara! How can we ever forget your generous hospitality in affording us this blissful place in which to celebrate our union?

"You know that what we have done carries risks, don't you?" I said, as we walked back to the car.

"Pregnancy, you mean?" returned Fearghal. "Especially if you take after your grandmother when Bruno first made love to her."

"And what would you do if it did happen?" I asked.

"I would have to marry you all the sooner," he said, gathering me to him more closely. "I mean it, Maddie; we are not meant to be apart now, after this."

"Oh Fearghal," I sighed. "You are the end of my search; the fulfilment of all I have ever desired; the answer to my unspoken prayer."

We held each other and kissed with all the passion we had shown earlier among the rocks and heather, then returned to the car and set off to explore more of that wonderful country, making each place special by our delight in each other's company.

*

Before we parted on that happiest of days, we discussed the problem of how we were going to communicate for the rest of the month. At this stage, Fearghal's only contact with the world beyond the island was his rowing boat and a *Poste Restante* address at the Post Office and village store.

"You must have a cell phone," I insisted. "I shall drag you into the twenty-first century and order one online this very evening. I'll have it sent to me at Oirbsean Lodge, and then I shall have to come to the island and set it up for you."

Fearghal agreed that this would make our separation more bearable, if anything in the world *could* make it more bearable.

"In some ways, these next few weeks will be the hardest," he said regretfully. "My greatest fear will be that you might change your mind and insist that the rules by which we lived before we met must be observed and respected."

"Never, my darling!" I reassured him. "The rules have been broken already . . . and the breaking of them was the most wonderful affirmation of love that I can imagine. On the other hand, it may be you who repents of your 'sin'." I gestured the quotation marks with my fingers. "The powers that be – and your mother – may convince you of the error of your ways."

"Fear not, my first, my last, my only love," he soothed. "They cannot sway me."

TWENTY-ONE

THEIR PLANE WAS FORTY MINUTES LATE. I HAD ARRIVED at the West Ireland Airport in good time and parked the car as close as possible, leaving Pendragon in the back and hoping that there would be room enough for my two passengers and their luggage. In contrast to the previous day – *our* day – a light rain was falling and there was little sign of a break in the cloud.

At last I saw them come through the barrier: the man I had called Daddy for over half of my life and the petite Bridie, his mother, beside him, looking travel-weary and glad to be nearing her journey's end. Warm hugs and kisses were exchanged and Bridie exclaimed, "Why, Maddie, you look so well; positively blooming … and even more beautiful than last year. Ireland must be suiting you!"

"Oh, it is, it is," I agreed fervently. "I am so happy to be here. Now, you must be dying to be home again. I'll run and get the car and bring it round to the drop-off, pick-up point, if you take your trolley through that door over there. Not much room to stow the luggage, I'm afraid, because Pendragon is occupying most of the space. However, I'm sure we shall manage."

*

The sky lightened as we drove southwards and, in the distance, the sun smiled gently upon the mountains, the Twelve Bens of Connemara, turning their purple into pale mauve. Half of my mind attended to my passengers'account of their journey; the other half dwelt upon my lover, rehearsing what I would tell Bridie when the time was appropriate; wondering whether I would be able to count on her support as Fearghal and I continued our journey beyond the purple shadow. Donal's support would be needed also, I realized, and the approval of the rest of the family … or, at least, the lack of *dis*approval.

Soon we were turning in through the gates of Oirbsean Lodge.

"Oh, how good to be home!" Bridie sighed. "Wonderful though our holiday was, there's no place like home." Whereupon Donal and I chimed in with the words of the old song.

*

"How welcoming you have made our homecoming, Maddie," Bridie exclaimed, as she and Donal stepped into the house. ('Declan' I shall call him from now on, since that was Bridie's original name for him). "Everything is so clean and fresh … and those lovely flowers!" She indicated the vase of lupins, delphiniums and greenery I had picked in an early morning raid on the garden of the hotel. The cat, Pooka, came from the kitchen to greet her mistress, heedless of Pendragon who was sniffing round the newcomers with great interest. I went ahead to put the kettle on to boil.

"What can I get you? Coffee, tea?" I asked.

"Oh, I'd die for a cup of good Irish tea!" Bridie cried. "It never tasted quite right over there."

"Me too, please, Maddie," said Declan. "It must be the water that makes it taste less authentic in a foreign country."

"Anything to eat?" I asked. "I have prepared a meal for later."

"Then I'll wait till then, thanks," Declan said. "We were well supplied with the usual plastic food on the plane."

"You should claim to be vegetarian," I advised. "That way you not only get served first but you get more palatable food – and no plastic meat."

We sat around the kitchen table drinking our tea until Bridie said, "I'm longing to tell you all about our visit and give you the news and messages from your family, but I think I shall have to lie down and have a sleep and come back refreshed later on. I want to hear all about your adventures here as well."

"Good idea," I agreed. "The jetlag is always worse travelling east because you miss a night. I'm longing to hear about your trip, too. Would you like me to call Grainne and tell her you've arrived safely? She said she'd call round this evening."

"That's a kind thought. Yes, if you would, I'd be most grateful. Just tell her that I'm having a bit of a rest to recharge my batteries."

*

"Ah! My beautiful sister!" Declan declared as Grainne walked in after our late tea or early supper. She hugged her mother fondly and kissed Declan on both cheeks. It was with constant amazement that I thought of the days when I had called him 'Daddy'; days when he had never known that he had a mother and three sisters in Ireland.

"It's wonderful to see you home, Mammy," Grainne said. "I've missed you so much, even though we were able to Skype a few times. Now, how was it really? Tell us all about it."

"Okay," said Bridie. "I've saved it for when you came round so that I don't have to tell it twice over. Poor Maddie has heard nothing yet because I took to my bed for a few hours."

I went to the fridge and took out a bottle of 'fizz' which I handed to Declan. I had found some Champagne flutes in the dining room sideboard and had laid them ready on a tray.

"I thought a celebration would be in order," I said, "Though, strictly speaking Bridie and Declan should be rehydrating with water after that long flight."

"Just water for me, then," Declan said, to my enormous surprise. When had he *ever* refused alcohol?

"Just have a wee sip, Ex-Daddy," I insisted, laughing." It is a celebration, after all."

"What a lovely idea!" Grainne said as I handed her a foaming, sparkling glass. "Don't tell me you bought *this* in the local shop."

"No: actually I brought it with me from England," I explained. "Not on Thane Richmond's account, I assure you!"

"You must tell us all about that," said Bridie. "But now I think Declan and I are ready to tell you all about our transatlantic visit."

At this, we clinked glasses all round ... and it was well past our usual bedtime by the time they ran out of things to say.

"And this was just a mini-reunion," Bridie finished. "A prelude to The Big One next year."

She yawned and stretched her arms upwards. "Time for the second night of the day," she laughed. "We shall have to wait until tomorrow to hear of Maddie's doings in Killogan."

"You must get her to show you her work of art, Mam. She has done some amazing calligraphy for a friend and has promised to do some for me when there's another rainy period."

She kissed us all in turn and insisted that we should come to lunch on Sunday. Declan helped her on with her raincoat. (*Helped her on with her raincoat!! Declan*?)

"I'll see you out to your car, Sis," said my newly chivalrous ex-father. I think my jaw must have been fixed in a dropped position!

TWENTY-TWO

THE OPPORTUNITY TO UNBURDEN MYSELF TO BRIDIE did not arise until six days after their arrival, when the parcel containing Fearghal's new cell phone arrived. I had ordered it online as soon as I arrived home after our day out together.

"It's a new cell phone," I explained to Bridie.

"I thought you already had a smart phone," she said.

"Well, this is for someone else. Look, Bridie, I'd better tell you that I have met somebody very special over here."

"How wonderful, Maddie dear. Tell me all. Whoever can it be? Someone I know?"

"No, I'm sure you don't know him," I said. "I met him on my first morning when I took one of the boats to explore the lake. He lives on Inishcoll – or rather, is living there temporarily and painting."

"An artist? How romantic! Tell me all, now."

"Oh Bridie. All is very complicated."

"In the name of all that's holy! Don't tell me he's gay or married, or something."

"Don't be too shocked, Bridie, when I tell you that he's a *priest*."

"Holy Mother! You poor darling. What a disappointment for you!"

"Not a disappointment. You see, he loves me too and wants to marry me. Let me tell you the whole story so far."

"Let me make us fresh coffee," Bridie said, "And then begin at the beginning."

Declan had gone for a walk with Pendragon, who seemed to have taken to him from the moment they first met.

So we sat down again, Bridie and I, at the kitchen table – that same table at which Bridie had discovered that her son of fifty-eight years was alive and well and staying close by and wanting to meet his mother – and I started on my story, not going into detail, but nevertheless, leaving nothing out. When I had finished my account, Bridie reached a hand across the table to clasp mine.

"No, I'm not shocked," she said softly. "Just so sorry for all the difficulties that lie ahead for you both. However, I must ask you this: are you quite certain that you really love each other; that it isn't the added excitement of 'forbidden fruit'? After all, you have only known each other for three weeks."

"Definitely not on my part," I protested. "I fell in love with him long before I learnt that he was a priest."

"You know, there is a strong feeling in the church that priests should be allowed to marry – among the lay people, that is, and some of the clergy themselves. How can a man know that he won't fall in love after he has taken his vows and been received into the priesthood? And if he does, how can he turn his back on it and deny himself the pleasure and comfort of a kindred spirit?"

"Fearghal will, of course, be unfrocked or excommunicated for this," I said. "This seems very unfair when you think of the blind eye that is often turned to priests who have interfered with children."

"Too true," she agreed. "It sometimes seems that natural, normal heterosexuality is less acceptable than perversion."

"Anyway, now you know why I bought another phone. Now I must take it to Fearghal and get it going for him. I only hope there's a reasonable signal on the island. I'll go this afternoon, if that's all right with you?"

"Grand with me. Will you be telling Declan about all this – or would you like me to?"

"Yes, I'll tell him, and say that I've already told you. Maybe we'll take Pendragon for a walk together tomorrow morning and I'll tell him then."

TWENTY-THREE

FERGAL AND I FELL INTO EACH OTHER'S ARMS AS SOON as he answered my tap on the door.

"Maddie! You cannot know how pleased I am to see you."

"Oh yes, I can," I insisted."It has been such a long, long week since we were last together."

"So you haven't had second thoughts and decided to renounce our unofficial marriage vows?"

"My only second thoughts are thoughts of you every second," I assured him, smiling into his loving eyes, lost for a moment in their depth. "And you, my honey-love? Must I acknowledge that I have a jealous God as a rival for your devotion?"

He lifted my hand to his mouth and ran his lips along the inside of my wrist.

"Is the Almighty a lady with beautiful red hair, sea-green eyes and a ravishing body?" he asked. "This is very irreverent, I know, but since I met you I have learned the true meaning of the words worship and reverence."

"Irreverent, sacrilegious, blasphemous," I agreed. "— but oh such music to my ears!" I confessed. "Nevertheless, I am only human and have many faults, however perfect I want to be for you, my love."

A few kisses later, I produced the cell phone and insisted that he should listen to the instructions for its use.

"We must do this first," I said. "It would be disastrous if we were unable to communicate."

"When you say 'first'," he asked, "what had you in mind for 'second'?"

"Whatever *you* have in mind," I replied, laughing, "And I think I know exactly what that will be."

"I am not at all sure that this was a safe time to do what we have just –so enjoyably- done," I said later as we sipped tea, sitting in warm sunshine outside on a rock just large enough for two. Fearghal called this his fair weather sitting room.

"Oh, I should have thought ..."

"*We* should have thought, perhaps, though it is asking too much of us to resist such delightful encounters."

"Suppose something *did* happen, what then?" he asked.

"We are married in all but the official certificate, aren't we? Perhaps it would strengthen your case," I said, hopefully.

"I cannot think it would," he said ruefully. "No, I have broken the rules and the vows, so I must face the music, whatever tunes it may play. Seriously though, how would you manage if you found there was a baby on the way?"

"I would be thrilled and honoured to bear your child, my love. And I *would* cope if I knew that eventually we could be together. There is still a long way to go, but we *are* living in the twenty-first century and attitudes towards unmarried mothers are not what they were in my grandmother's time. I should hold my head up and display my bump proudly until my husband and lover came to claim his wife and child."

We continued our conversation through the drinking of a second cup of tea until our shadows began to lengthen behind us and I had to take my reluctant leave and make my way back across the water for dinner at Oirbsean Lodge.

"Phone me when you reach the jetty, my darling girl," Fearghal said. "They say there are monsters in the Lough and I would hate you to meet one when I am not there to protect you."

I laughed. "I've not seen one yet; let's hope they're elusive like the one in Loch Ness. Yes, I will phone and again when I'm alone in my bedroom. I hope the reception will be really good and we can keep up to date on our future plans."

Our farewell kiss down where the boat was moored was long and lingering. It was so hard to part and we were both fully aware that the sharp, rocky mountains of our immediate future were ahead of us, as Fearghal had foretold in his painting.

Pendragon greeted me like a long-lost friend when I walked into the house. Declan had taken him for a long walk along the boreens of Killogan while I had been with Fearghal. They seemed to get along well together. My own relationship with the man I had known as my father for most of my life was now a great deal more comfortable than it had been in my childhood.

"You have a faraway look in your eyes," Bridie observed with a smile as I greeted her in the kitchen.

"With good reason," I said. "I'm away with the fairies after my blissful afternoon."

"The Pooka, we call them over here. They can be mischievous, you know, and make all kinds of trouble for folks."

"Such as?" I queried.

"Such as muddling up all the islands on the lough, for instance, so that you never find the one you're looking for, even though you know you've gone in the right direction."

"What with the monsters in the lake that Fearghal told me about … and now the leprechauns and fairies, there must be magic about here," I laughed.

"Oh, there is indeed," Bridie whispered. "And by the look of you, you've had a magical encounter this afternoon."

"Oh, I have indeed," I averred.

"My dear Maddie. I hope you are being *very* careful. Don't jump the gun when there is so much at stake, will you? Or am I too late with that advice?"

"Only time will tell," I said, enigmatically.

"Oh dear! I think I *am* too late with my grandmotherly advice."

"Have I time for a shower and a change of clothes before dinner?" I asked.

"Yes, fine," she answered. "It will be half-an-hour yet."

*

"So where did your row-boat take you this afternoon?" Declan asked as we ate the tasty casserole that Bridie had prepared.

"I shall tell you all about that when we walk Pendragon tomorrow," I promised. Then I swiftly changed the subject and asked where Declan had been for his afternoon walk with the dog. "You must have been a long way," I added. "He looks completely exhausted."

"Okay, *go* all mysterious on me," he said, not to be redirected in the conversation. Bridie looked at me and winked.

"She has her reasons," she said to her son.

"Even more mysterious," he said. "Is it secret, female stuff?"

"Not especially. All will be disclosed at the right time," she assured him.

TWENTY-FOUR

I WENT TO BED EARLIER THAN USUAL, LEAVING BRIDIE and Declan watching television. As soon as I closed the door of my bedroom, I phoned Fearghal. Reception was perfect, for which I offered a prayer of thanks. We had already spoken briefly when I rang from the landing stage confirming my safe arrival, as arranged.

"I've been thinking and planning," he told me. "When you leave for home next week, I shall pay a visit to my mother and try to make an appointment to see the bishop. I must do something positive if you are going to leave me and go so many miles away."

I thought quickly. "What if I were to drive you down on my way to the ferry? We could spend more time together and, if we timed it sensibly, I could take you right to your mother's door."

"My dearest Maddie, it would be well out of your way and would cost a day of your holiday."

"And do you think I wouldn't sacrifice that to be with the man I love for a few precious hours?"

"Yes, but you'd have to spend a night somewhere."

"Where will *you* stay?" I asked.

"With Mother, I suppose ... and anticipating the kind of reception I shall get, I could hardly ask her if *you* could stay."

"Suppose I were to find a dog-friendly B and B within a few miles – one where you could join me if you get thrown out on your ear?"

"Let's sleep on it and see what ideas we come up with in the morning," he suggested. "Shall I phone you in the morning? At what time before you get up?"

"I'm usually awake by six," I said. "I'll keep my phone under the pillow and turn down the volume of the ringtone."

*

"So this mystery ..." my father/ uncle began as we walked up a grassy track with Pendragon the following day. "You promised to enlighten me today, Maddie."

Confident that he would not be judgemental if I shared my secret, I launched into an account of my meeting with Fearghal, our day out in Galway and our subsequent reunion after days of misunderstanding. He listened attentively with the occasional 'Uh-huh' of encouragement or a prompting 'Hmm?'He was quick to read between the lines regarding the intimate details I had omitted from my narrative.

"I guess you're not going to admit that your reunion resulted in the breaking of his vow of celibacy?"

I felt myself blush. It was not the kind of matter that you discussed with close male relatives or friends.

"That tells me *everything*," he laughed, putting his hand to my cheek and whipping it away again as if burned."You're your grandmother's own granddaughter with your red hair and your blushes. Have you told my mother all of this?"

"All *what?*" I asked. "Actually, she knows as much as you do."

"And what did she have to say about it all?"

"She just told me to be careful," I said demurely.

"And have you been? Will you be?"

"Probably not," I said. "That is something I shall find out in a week or two."

"O-M-G! as they say; that would put the proverbial cat among the white-collared pigeons"

My blush had subsided; nevertheless, it was strange to be discussing such personal matters with the man I had once called 'Daddy'. I told him of my intention to leave a day earlier than planned and take Fearghal to see his mother.

"Hell hath no fury like a mother whose priestly son is about to be unfrocked," he misquoted. "I wish you both the very best of luck."

*

There followed a diversion because Pendragon decided he would like a romp with a lone ram yearling who was not about to have his grazing interrupted by a playful giant. The dog lowered his front legs and crouched in play-mode, but the ram ran a few steps towards him and stamped both his front feet defiantly. Pendragon, realising that his invitation to play had been refused, rose nonchalantly and turned away with his nose in the air, hoping his humans had not witnessed his loss of face at the hands (hooves?) of a stupid sheep!

Declan and I talked of other things, and the subject of my love affair was not mentioned again while we finished our long walk and returned, hungry, to a delicious lunch of ham, cheese and scallions with fresh soda bread and bottled beer.

*

The remaining days of my visit passed in a series of outings to places I had not explored already: more of Connemara, the stone Circle and abbey ruins at Cong on the northern edge of Lough Corrib, Kylemore Abbey, Clifden and the coast of Mayo and a visit to the foot of Croagh Patrick, if not a climb; that ascent would have to happen on a future date because that day the mountain had its head in the clouds. It would have been a pity to make the arduous climb up the stony track and not be rewarded by the spectacular views from the summit. Grainne and Colm accompanied us on that excursion. Both had made the ascent on a day of pilgrimage and spoke of looking over to Achill Island and other, smaller islands in the breath-taking ocean panorama, and, to the south, the vast expanse of Connemara and the Twelve Bens.

Back at Oirbsean Lodge the talk was all about the grand family reunion that was to take place the following August. It was decided that invitations should be sent out with Christmas cards so that the prospective guests could put the date in their 2014 diaries and plan their holidays accordingly. I was asked if I would kindly design the invitation cards and have them printed by November, to which request I agreed with great pleasure. *It will give me something to stop me agonising too much over how Fearghal is faring in his fight against the Church authorities,* I thought, *and ameliorate the pain of his absence.* I imagined him accompanying me to the great celebration, as my husband, or if not that, certainly as my lover. Only the future would tell.

"Of course, we may simply imprison Maddie and Pendragon," Bridie said at the end of one such discussion. "Not let them go home at all. They fit in so well here."

I laughed. "It will be a great wrench to leave on Thursday, I assure you. I shall miss you all so much and long for the great day next year when we can return."

"Thursday?" Grainne asked. "I thought you weren't going till Friday."

"She wants to call on friends near Fermoy on the way," Bridie said hastily. "She's arranged to spend the night with them."

I shot her a grateful glance and caught Declan's wink as I looked away again. To my relief, Colm followed her remark with an anecdote about someone who came from Fermoy, and the moment passed without further comment.

TWENTY-FIVE

FERGAL AND I HAD ARRANGED FOR HIM TO BE WAITING for me to pick him up in the usual place at ten o'clock on the morning of my departure from Oirbsean Lodge. By the time we had our last phone conversation, his cell phone was on its last pip of battery charge. Though I had fully charged it before taking it to him, I had overlooked the fact that there was no electricity on the island.

"We'll stop for lunch somewhere," I said, "and ask if we can charge it there while we eat. This is going to be a problem when we're apart. D'you think they would charge it for you at the post office?"

"I'm sure they will," he replied. "I'm a good customer and go nearly every day in case there's mail, and for milk and food, of course, because there's no refrigerator."

"I can't imagine not having electricity," I said, "though my grandmother was brought up in a house that had none, and remembered paraffin stoves and lamps with mantles and glass chimneys, and candles to light the way upstairs at bedtime."

"Yes, well, I know all about that; so would you if you'd stayed after dark, but you couldn't have done that because of the boat. I would never have let you loose on the lough by night, my darling. Think of all those monsters: they're always worse at night."

"Pendragon would have defended me," I laughed.

"But you might both have been mown down by a steamer returning from Galway,"

"I hadn't thought of that," I said. "That really *would* be a monster."

*

I said my goodbyes at Oirbsean Lodge with warm hugs and kisses for Bridie and Declan, promising to phone when we were safely home and at various stages on our journey. I had already said my farewells to Grainne and Colm the previous evening. I was touched to see tears in Bridie's eyes at my impending departure and was quick to reassure her that the year would pass quickly and that, anyway, I might well be back again before the family reunion, depending on the outcome of Fearghal's interviews with his mother and the Church authorities.

"I may have to come and take him away from the furore," I said. "Take him back to Cornwall with me till it's all sorted out."

"Well, whatever happens, you must include him in the party next year," Bridie said. "There won't have to be any explanations: he will be introduced as your partner or ____"

"Husband," Declan put in."And you'll bring Pendragon, won't you?"

"Sure I shall, if he's invited," I assured them.

"Of *course !*" said Bridie. "You can both stay here, rather than in the hotel. That would be lovely, really something to look forward to."

*

My heart leapt at the sight of Fearghal standing waiting for me. He had a small holdall with him and his entry into the car was witnessed by a woman on a bicycle, heading for the shop.

"No doubt my being picked up by a gorgeous redhead will be all over the village within the next hour," he laughed. "And with an overnight bag as well. How shocking is that?"

He had told the postmistress that he would be away for a day or two and asked that any mail should be held until his return.

"Well, they don't know who *you* are," I said. "They may, however, recognise her description of *me* from my attendance at church during the past month."

Fearghal's forthcoming encounter with his mother was very much on our minds as we set off on our journey south but we both tried to celebrate the fact that we were at last *together*, not only in a real sense but metaphorically, travelling together on our journey to a different life; heading for the mountains in his painting: those sharp peaks and stacks which represented the difficulties lying ahead of us on our way, the first to be scaled raising its jagged profile heavenwards in a neat house in a small town south of Limerick.

We stopped in the city for lunch, finding a welcoming Thai restaurant in a side-street off O'Connell Street with a convenient parking place right outside. Limerick must have changed a great deal in the nearly sixty years since Donal and Dominic were brought here in their infancy. The handsome Georgian houses in O'Connell Street, in past centuries elegant private dwellings, are now shops and offices and the street is the main traffic thoroughfare. I wondered about the location of Sheridan House where they had lived with my adoptive Manning grandparents, and also about Ormond House where their adoptive grandmother, Mrs. Leahy, had lived. If I had had more time and had not been concentrating on such a serious mission, I would have looked up my aunt and uncle, Katie and Will O'Sullivan who lived in the city now. I mentioned this to Fearghal, saying that, if we had had time to arrange it, they might have put us up for the night. He smiled and shook his head.

"I think we must keep it impersonal at this stage, my darling. Whilst I am undergoing the confession and inquisition, you can find us a pleasant, dog-friendly B and B. I *shall* spend the night with you, whatever my mother says."

"You're right of course, my love," I said. "Impersonal is best. Nowadays I imagine one does not even have to flash a wedding ring when booking a double-bedded room – even in Ireland."

"I cannot comment on that," he laughed. "My knowledge of that scene is not only limited, but non-existent."

"Quite right, too! I'm very relieved to hear it." I kissed my finger and leant over to place it on his lips, just at the moment that our food arrived. "I have a rather nervous stomach at the moment," Fearghal said, "but this smells so wonderful that I cannot resist it."

"It will fortify you for what is to come. The beer will help too. Drink as much as you can; it will give you Dutch courage."

"Dutch?" Fearghal exclaimed. "It's a strong dose of *Irish* courage I need!"

TWENTY-SIX

I DROPPED HIM RIGHT OUTSIDE HIS MOTHER'S HOUSE IN the small town where she lived and arranged that he should phone as soon as 'the interview' was over and I would pick him up at the end of the road.

"I shall come flying out of the house and land on my ear," he joked, "so you will, literally, be picking me up."

My own heart was beating hard as I drove away to find a B and B in which we could spend the night. I did not imagine that our first night together would be one of passion and delight: it would be more like camping on the perilous slopes of the first mountain peak that we must cross. I drove eastwards for a few miles through pleasant undulating countryside, until I came to a riverside hamlet where I saw a hopeful-looking sign outside a large stone farmhouse. I drove into the forecourt, which turned out to be a stable yard. Extending from the house was an L-shaped block of several loose-boxes, all of which contained horses of high quality, clearly race-horses. My knock at the front door, was answered by a woman of about the same age as myself.

"Would you have a double-bedded room for my partner and me – and a biggish, well-behaved dog?" I asked, after she had greeted me.

"Yes, indeed I would – and we do welcome dogs here as long as they're clean and well-behaved.

"I can understand how necessary that is, with all your precious tenants to consider," I said, indicating the horses.

"Well, come in and see if you like the room," she said.

"Look, I'm sure it will be okay," I said. "I was hoping to leave our overnight things and go back to pick up Fearghal who is visiting a relation."

We walked back to the car and I opened the trunk.

"O-M-G!" she exclaimed when Penn jumped out. "I thought you said a dog, not a pony."

"Shake hands with the lady, Pendragon," I commanded and he obediently lifted his right paw towards her."

"Hey there, Pendragon. I'm Deirdre. Oh, I love *you*. You can stay here as long as you like." she said, shaking his paw vigorously.

"He'll be curious about the horses, but won't bark or frighten them," I assured her.

"I think they'll be even more curious about him," she laughed. "Look; they're all staring at him. We'll introduce them later."

The room met with my full approval. It had its own well-appointed bathroom and the bed looked clean and comfortable. Downstairs I signed in and paid for one night, explaining that I was on my way back to England, while Fearghal would be returning to Galway.

"If you don't mind taking pot-luck, it's boiled ham, champ and cabbage for supper this evening."

"That sounds wonderful," I said. "Please book us in."

And with that, Penn and I departed to be nearer to Fearghal when his phone call came through.

*

The poor love looked exhausted when I picked him up outside the post office, as arranged.

"Did she give you a hard time?" I inquired. "You look as if you've been through the mill."

"I feel as though I've had several lashes from the cat-o'-nine-tails, rather than the never-ending lashings of her tongue. I'm glad you weren't there to hear that diatribe, darling, much as I would love to have had you holding my hand. I'm just after bumping into the biggest mouth in town, so don't hug me here. Just drive on a bit and stop when we're well past the last house. Then I need a really big hug."

We stopped in a lay by, just long enough for me to give him the comfort he needed.

"If we are blessed with children, you will be more of a mother to them than my mother ever was to me."

My heart bled for him. "I feel so sad about that, having known so much love from my own mother, both as a child and an adult – even as a stroppy teenager."

As we drove on I told him about the B and B I had found. "I think you'll like it. Before dinner, there's probably somewhere we can take Penn for a good walk and blow the cobwebs away."

"Good idea," he said. "And I must ask for a directory to find the phone number of the bishop's office and try to arrange an interview with him tomorrow or Monday. Also, I must find a means of getting to Limerick, and somewhere to spend tomorrow night, if necessary."

"I guess you can hardly ask your mother," I said, smiling.

"God forbid!" he agreed, squeezing my hand fondly.

Our first night together was much as I had expected: more about tenderness and comfort than desire and passion. We held each other close all night, knowing that this was the last time for several weeks that we should be able to do so. However, we did not allow ourselves to be sad; rather, we both agreed that this was the beginning of our future together. Certainly, there were all sorts of obstacles in our path, the mountain metaphor in Fearghal's painting being something of which we were both very aware; but those mountains were there to be scaled, and beyond them lay our future: the green pastures and the flowing streams of the lowlands, the rugged cliffs and the golden sands beneath them.

I had to make a quick getaway in the morning in order to get to the ferry by checking-in time, so we asked for an early breakfast. Fearghal had to wait until Monday for his appointment with the bishop so I took him as near to Limerick as I could on my way to the motorway east and dropped him at a bus stop. With one long hug and many kisses we said good bye for we knew not how long.

TWENTY-SEVEN

I HAD BEEN BACK FOR TEN DAYS WHEN THE PHONE CALL came. I picked up, expecting to hear a friend's voice.

"Am I speaking to Miss Madeleine Manning?" (A woman's voice, but not my friend's).

"Yes, that's correct. Could that perhaps be Mrs Gabriel?"

"Indeed it is; it seems that you were expecting my call"

"Fearghal did tell me that you would probably contact me."

"You would do well to remember that my son should be referred to as 'Father Gabriel'."

"Mrs Gabriel, if your son had introduced himself as such at our first meeting, events may well have turned out differently."

"I would rather say this directly to your face, Miss Manning: You have ruined two lives by your actions: my son's and my own."

"Mrs Gabriel, the word 'actions' suggests something deliberate and premeditated. The simple truth is that your son fell in love with me and I with him."

"Don't split hairs and try to deflect me with semantics, Miss. You know exactly what I mean. I intend to stay with a friend in London next week and should like to meet you while I am there."

"Had you thought of coming to meet me here in Cornwall – in which case I could arrange to meet on neutral ground?"

"I think the most neutral ground would be in London. My friend is a doctor in Harley Street and could arrange for us to meet in a room at her clinic."

"It is rather difficult for me to get away as I have a dog to look after."

"I do not care for dogs at all, so I hope you would not bring it with you. Also, as you must know, my son is highly allergic to both dogs and cats. Contact with them has caused severe asthma attacks in the past."

I ignored this lie. Fearghal had told me that the mere possibility of such a reaction was cited as an excuse every time he expressed a wish for a domestic pet.

"There would be no question of that, Mrs. Gabriel; Pendragon is a very large dog – almost as big as a Shetland pony." I laughed a little in a feeble attempt to melt the frost by a few degrees.

"Well, I think you will agree that a mere dog is of little importance when compared to the main concern: that of my son's future."

I sighed, audibly. "I shall make arrangements to have him looked after and come up by train on a day of your choosing. Perhaps we should leave further discussion until then."

"Very well; I shall phone you again when I have arrived in London. Meanwhile, just let me remind you that, if you really have feelings for my son, you will let him go and not persist in this sinful relationship. Good bye, Miss Manning."

I was not to be dismissed so easily. "I think you will find, Mrs Gabriel, that Fearghal's mind is quite made up and that matters have gone too far for us to backtrack now. Good bye now; I look forward to meeting you very soon."

"I cannot honestly say that *I* look forward to meeting *you*, unless you can tell me that you have come to your senses. However, it seems that such a meeting is a necessary evil. I bid you goodbye."

The phone went dead at the other end, whereupon I disconnected and stood for a few moments, shaking a little in the wake of the first of our confrontation. My future mother-in- law was every bit as formidable as Fearghal had warned she would be.

*

A week or so later, a brief phone call from Fearghal's mother sufficed to fix a date for our face-to -face meeting. Not feeling equal to doing the upward and return journey in the same day, I took Mistletoe up on her offer to arrange for me to spend the night with a friend of hers in her flat near 'Little Venice', close to a tube station. Zara was a successful freelance commercial artist, she told me, a staunch feminist who would, however, be sympathetic to my predicament and would be interested to hear the outcome of my difficult encounter with my lover's mother

"Zara was renowned in her younger days for falling for married men," she told me. "She found that, though they professed their undying love for her, they never had the courage to leave their wives and set up home with her. So she embraced feminism and swore never to get involved with another man. It will be a change for her to hear of one who is wedded to the Church rather than another woman! Will he? Won't he? Although she's long ago given up on men, she'll be agog to know the outcome."

"Oh well, I shall be pleased to provide some entertainment in exchange for a night's board and lodging," I laughed.

*

Harley Street seemed to be full of expensive-looking women alighting from taxis or chauffeur-driven cars. I decided to walk from Regents Park station, having previously downloaded a map of the area. As soon as I reached the street, I asked a taxi driver where I would find the appropriate number, to save myself a walk in the wrong direction. By not hurrying I made sure that I was at least eight minutes late.

A haughty receptionist in killer high-heels answered my ring and showed me into an elegant room of Georgian proportions in which my attention was at first drawn to the heavy scent of a vase of lilies and alstromeria on a round, polished table

My 'adversary' turned to face me from her position by the window as the receptionist announced me and withdrew from the room. I advanced across the deep-piled, pale blue carpet my hand outstretched, taking in the petite figure, neatly dressed in neutral shades, with her bright gold-coloured, curly hair and powdery face. I looked in vain for some likeness to my beloved Fearghal, but could see no hint in any of her features. She did not lift her hand to shake mine but kept it firmly by her side, fist loosely clenched.

"Miss Manning, I do not feel inclined to shake you by the hand until we have reached some sensible agreement." She looked at me with a frosty, critical eye.

"A red-haired siren," she observed. "I suppose I should expect no less of my innocent son's seductress."

"I assure you that there was no seduction involved, Mrs Gabriel. The attraction between your son and me was entirely mutual from the start."

"In that case, it was your bounden duty as a good Catholic woman to call a halt before matters went too far. Surely you were brought up to know that it is always up to the woman to put the brakes on a man's desires." She shuddered visibly. "You *knew* that he was a priest ."

"Indeed I did by the time that we acknowledged our love and attraction – but I must stress that I was ignorant of that fact when I first fell in love with him."

"Love indeed! He is a priest and as such should love only God and his congregation. He has vowed to renounce the sins of the flesh and to embrace self-denial and purity."

"I cannot acknowledge that our coming together was a 'sin of the flesh'. It has struck us both that it was pre-ordained, meant to be."

"Holy Mother! I cannot listen to this sacrilege. Have you confessed your sin to your own priest?"

I ignored her question. "At this point, Mrs Gabriel, I think I should tell you that it is highly likely that Fearghal and I are going to present you with a grandchild in a few months' time."

I had not told Fearghal himself this news yet.

The woman sat down suddenly on a nearby chair, a horrified expression on her face.

"Oh my God! I never expected to hear such a thing." She buried her face in her hands and her shoulders heaved with sobs, though I noticed that her eyes, when she revealed them again were tearless.

"It grieves me that my son seems to have taken after his father in that respect. I cannot say that I cared at all for that side of married life." She pursed her lips as she was forced to confront such an unpleasant memory. *No wonder Fearghal's father had pursued other women,* I thought. There was silence for a few moments. I realised afterwards that during that short time she was preparing to deliver her trump card.

"What you have told me makes it easier to believe that the accusations made against my son by a girl in his parish are in fact true." There was a note of triumph in her voice. "He probably left you in ignorance of the reason for his living in solitude on that island?"

"He did tell me, actually," I said quickly. "I gathered that a teenager accused him of seducing her."

Again her voice rose in pitch. "He *impregnated* a fourteen-year-old girl. Her mother tells me that there is DNA proof that my son is thc father of the baby born two or three months ago."

"I really cannot believe that that is true," I protested. "Fearghal told me that she had a crush on him and accused him of making sexual advances towards her because she wanted it to be true. I believe and trust Fearghal's word absolutely. There is, after all, a boyfriend. Perhaps she was already pregnant when she made those allegations."

"Well, think again, Miss. You may not be the first female to make him forget his solemn vows. I shall leave you with that thought. I bid you good day now."

She walked purposefully to the white, paneled door, turned the decorative porcelain handle and disappeared from view, closing the door firmly and loudly behind her. Shaken, I caught sight of my reflection in the gilt-framed mantel mirror. My expression was one of pain and shock: my face having the pallor of one who has received life-changing bad news. The heavy, cloying scent of the lilies sickened me and I ran to the door and made for the rest-room I had noticed on the way in.

TWENTY-EIGHT

THROWING UP IN THE POSH LOO OF THE HARLEY Street clinic, though triggered by my emotional response to Mrs Gabriel's parting shot, was the start of several weeks of sickness which confirmed the presence of a small new member of the next generation of Mannings . . . or Gabriels. Morning sickness, evening sickness; is there anything more miserable and debilitating? The joy I should have been feeling was noticeably absent and I found myself quite unable to share the news with Fearghal before I had missed another period, done a pregnancy test and had it confirmed by the doctor. I wondered whether Mrs Gabriel had deliberately embroidered the truth before delivering her *coup de grace*. Had she perhaps been blackmailed by the girl's mother into handing over a sum of money to keep the secret from being revealed? No doubt the parish had witnessed the girl's pregnancy, heard about the subsequent birth and drawn their own conclusions anyway, in the wake of the dismissal of their priest.

Eventually I realised that Fearghal must be told. Our recent conversations on the phone had been brief and rather formal. I had exaggerated the effects of a slight backache I had been suffering, attributing it to my having slipped on the steps of a granite stile on the cliff path. I had not gone into detail regarding my meeting with his mother, telling him that the interview had gone much as we had both expected.

Fearghal had told me about his interview with the provincial bishop who had requested that he should go back to his erstwhile hermitage to think and pray. This he had agreed to but assured me that he would not change his mind.

It was certainly time to tell him about the baby, I thought. Autumn was well advanced by now and nearly three of my nine months were already past. The sickness was infrequent now and I was beginning to lose what had once been a waistline. Mistletoe and several people in the choir told me that I looked blooming.

"Maybe it was all that gorgeous soda bread they make in Ireland," said one. "That little bit of extra weight really suits you. It's all very enviable being as slim as a wand, but your face has filled out a bit and you look really good. Sorry to be so personal."

"Nobody minds a compliment," I smiled. "Thanks, Carrie."

"They'll soon find out what's going on," Mistletoe muttered as she walked away. "It won't be long before you're as wide from back to front as you are from side to side."

"Thank goodness for loose, warm tunic tops and elastic-waisted trousers," I laughed.

"It's going to show by the time of the December concert. That black jersey dress of yours with be quite revealing, clinging to that little pod."

"And, by the way," she went on, "what does TR say about all this?"

"All *this*? TR? For Heaven's sake! I haven't even told Fearghal himself yet. Now I'm feeling so much better, I'm going to tell him the very next time I call. Our conversations have been rather constrained for weeks lately, on account of what his ma told me, I suppose. Try as I have to discount what she said, there was still an element of fear and mistrust which must be evident in my voice when we speak."

"You'd better explain that matter as well then when you tell him," she advised. "You'll feel better once he's denied the truth of it, of course you will. When you think of it, that wretched girl's mother would have to have a forensic scientist in her clutches to produce a DNA sample from Fearghal in his absence. They take a specimen of saliva, don't they? But think of it: no Fearghal, no mouth, no saliva . . . no DNA evidence!"

Mistletoe's words reassured me a little. I would be less reticent in my next exchange with my beloved.

*

At this same time, other doubts and anxieties began to trouble me. TR had been in London and on tour since the incident after my return from Ireland at the end of August. I realized now that, as soon as Pandora Bennett sniffed a possible scandal, she would assume that TR was 'the father' and Gossip Corner would be full of it. She was, she told me, rather peeved that she had had nothing to report on that subject for months because TR and I had gone our separate ways in August and had not been seen together since.

Up to this point I had managed to get my nausea out of the way before I went to the office. My aversion to coffee I managed to hide on the pretext that green tea was healthier. My craving for pink sugared almonds I satisfied at home or in the car and gave no hint of at work in either office. However, there would come a time when colleagues, especially Pandora, were going to notice my developing bump and know that it was too soon for middle-aged spread. I was, after all, only in my early thirties!

TWENTY-NINE

When Fearghal called I had just returned from a short walk with Pendragon. Summer seemed so far behind now. In the hedges the Old Man's Beard was already looking sadly bedraggled in a heavy mist of drizzle. Still feeling despondent, I entered the warm kitchen, took off my wet raincoat and patted the dog dry with an old towel before putting the kettle on to boil for a comforting cup of tea. I had missed a third period, yet had seemed to feel all the tension and discomfort that I would have felt in normal circumstances.

At the first ring of the phone I took a deep breath and picked up the handset, sadly aware of the unintentional *froideur* of my greeting.

"I'll call you back right away," I said.

"Darling Maddie," he said when he answered, "I miss you so much. You sounded so distant in our last conversation. My ma must have upset you more than you let on."

"I'm sure she did," I sighed. "I am sorry if my voice lacked warmth. I assure you that my feelings have in no way changed. I told her something which I must now tell you."

"Oh, my love; that sounds ominous. Please tell me you are not ill or suffering from some incurable disease."

"Fearghal darling, on the extreme contrary! That would have given her hope that this 'problem' might be solved by my likely demise. No, this is something far more predictable: I seem to be expecting your child." I said no more than that in order to hear his first reaction.

"Maddie? Did I hear aright? Are you sure? How do you know? Have you been to a doctor? I am shocked, but also delighted. Does this not, surely, strengthen our case with the powers that be? I must go outside and sit on the table rock to take this in."

I heard his footsteps on the stone floor, then the door opening and closing. After a few seconds he said, "Now tell me all. I'm sitting in the evening sun in a light breeze."

"Lucky you! I'm looking out at cloud and rain and a sea that is getting angrier by the minute. So yes, you did hear aright. We're expecting a baby in May next year. I don't need a doctor to tell me. A woman knows the signs: the physical and emotional changes that take place."

"Well, sweetheart, are you happy about this? Tell me that you don't regret it."

"Of course I don't regret it . . . but I have broken my own rules – not to mention the much stricter rules of the Church."

"Then we must be married as soon as possible so that our baby is born in wedlock. *Our baby!* I can hardly believe it. But are you absolutely happy about it, my darling? I sense some constraint on your part. Whatever did my mother say when you told her?"

"She was appalled, as you might expect. But she told me something deliberately designed to shock and upset me too. It's not anything I can discuss except face-to-face, but it may account for the 'constraint' you mentioned."

"Then I think we must be together as soon as possible, my darling. Would you be happy for me to come to England as soon as it can be arranged?"

"Happy? I should say! How soon can you come? How will this stand with your bosses?"

"I shall simply tell them that I intend to marry the mother of my child. There is absolutely no question now of a period of reflection and prayer, as was advised."

"Oh, dearest Fearghal, I can't wait to see you. Come as soon as you can. Fly to Bristol or Exeter and I'll come to meet you and bring you back in the car. Just give me a time scale and possible dates and I'll book you a ticket online."

I was flooded with relief at the idea of Fearghal's arrival. We could face the immediate and long-term future together and support each other in scaling the metaphorical mountains that lay ahead.

As soon as we finished our conversation, I explored the various travel websites and started to plan for the coming months. We had decided on arranging a civil marriage to begin with, followed, perhaps, by a religious ceremony if and when the time seemed right. Meanwhile, I was to make enquiries with the local registrar.

*

An anxious thought struck me as soon as I had hung up. I called Fearghal back immediately.

"Darling, have you got a valid passport? I wasn't asked to show one either when I was coming into Ireland or when I came home"

"Yes, my love, I checked that very early on in our relationship and collected it from my mother's house when I went there. I needed it for a visit to Rome in 2010 so it's well within its validity period."

I heaved a sigh of relief. "Thank God for that! You'll also need it for ID purposes when our civil marriage is arranged, no doubt."

"How about you? Will it be difficult for two foreign nationals to marry?"

"I obtained a British passport when I decided to stay over here with my grandmother, so that will be no problem. I'll go to see the registrar tomorrow and find out how we proceed from here. I hope there won't be any obstacles. At least we have a few months before that little person makes his or her appearance."

"How long exactly? I'm still having trouble getting my head around it"

"My own reckoning is that the birth should happen towards the end of May 2014. Must get onto the airline websites now and book you a flight."

"Good bye, my precious Maddie; I can't wait to see you, darling."

I found that there were flights available from Shannon or Knock to Bristol. The latter, serving a place of pilgrimage, was the nearer of the two. There would be the matter of his personal belongings to address, particularly his paintings. I would offer to go back with him again to his erstwhile hermitage and collect what could be carried in the car.

THIRTY

I LOOKED ONLINE TO SEE WHAT THE REQUIREMENTS would be for our civil marriage, expecting difficulties that might mean a long delay. I was relieved to find, however, that the rules were easier than I expected. Because Fearghal was a citizen of a country with European Union membership, therefore exempt from immigration control, all we had to do was to give at least twenty eight days' notice at a Designated Registry Office, the nearest being Truro. We would both need only proof of name, date of birth, nationality, address and a £35 fee. I decided to wait until he was safely in England before making any arrangements.

While I was scanning the site, an email popped up on my screen. I was not pleased to see that it was from sTaR1@richmond.co.uk (the vanity of the man!) On opening it, my unease turned to anxiety, though I had known this would have to happen sooner or later. He told me he would be back in Polburran on a day about three weeks hence, though he had to be back in London on the following Monday. He wanted to collect his stuff, he said; give me back the keys to house and shed and see plenty of me ... in fact, carry on where we left off at the end of July. He had lots of plans, he wrote, and would keep asking me 'the usual question', convinced that our long separation would have brought about a change of mind on my part. *Hell's bells! I thought: another mountain peak to negotiate ... and one I must tackle alone, without Fearghal's help. I want this one out of the way before he arrives. I've got to find a way to finish with TR and convince him that I really, really mean it.*

My head buzzed as I rehearsed scores of conversations in my mind. Thane's pride would be hurt more than his heart, I decided. I would have to tell him the truth about the pregnancy, if not about the fact that Fearghal was a priest. That was something I certainly did not want generally known because it was the very stuff of scandal. It had been bad enough to have been the subject of talk and conjecture on account of TR's celebrity, but how much more uncomfortable these disclosures could be! He was not going to write a song about this; but he was sure going to make a song and dance! One thing was certain: it was only fair to tell him first. Pandora and co. must get no wind of it until he himself had come to terms with it. It was unthinkable that he should find out through the local gossip column or on the grapevine. Only the previous week I had met a canny old country woman on a walk to the village. "Morning, Miss," she had said. "Saw you coming out of the doctor's t'other day, 'n' I thought to meself 'ope there's nothing wrong with 'er. She'm too bonny a maid to be poorly with anything."

"No, I'm fine, thank you, Mrs Penwithy," I'd replied. "Just needed something checked."

"Reckon there can't be nothing wrong with a maid who has a smile like yourn," she said, with a knowing look. "And, sure enough you look blooming. Wouldn' surprise me if you …"

Her voice tailed off so I ended the exchange swiftly.

"Well, anyone would smile on a day like this," I said firmly. "It's more like July than November, don't you think? See you, Mrs Penwithy." I turned around and walked quickly away from her, imagining the smirk and the raised eyebrows that followed my retreating figure. These country women could always tell!

*

The days passed, during which time I booked Fearghal's flight from Ireland West airport, Knock to Bristol ... so that he would arrive after Thane had left Cornwall for London. I explained briefly to him that one of the 'mountains' in his painting had suddenly loomed up in front of me and I had to negotiate it alone.

"You shouldn't be rock-climbing in your condition," he commented, laughing.

"Oh, it will be a gentle climb, my love," I replied, not feeling inclined to share his mirth. "Just understand that I'm considering damage limitation here. Because of the risk of gossip, I have to handle this particular interview with sensitivity. TR has to leave with at least some of his pride intact."

"Yes, of course," he agreed. "How hard it must be to live the life of a celebrity; almost as hard as living the life of a celibate." He laughed again, and this time I joined him, though not without that niggle of doubt that assailed me from time to time since my encounter with Aisling Gabriel.

"And I am a celebrity in my own right by association, so you don't know what you're letting yourself in for!"

*

At the office of the Kernow Gazette, just days before TR's impending arrival, Pandora asked me outright when TR was due to visit Polburran again. I replied without hesitation that he was expected any time soon, though he would not be staying for long.

"Not long enough to get married, then?" she asked.

"Not likely!" I smiled, "he's just collecting some stuff he left at mine and then heading back to London for a recording session." I thought it best to give her a little to write about because people were sure to see him around in the next few days.

"Well, when's this fantastic wedding going to take place, then?"

"He's far too busy to be thinking about that, I'm sure," I replied.

"Oh wow! When it does happen, it'll be such a *sensation*, she exclaimed "Just *imagine* – an event like that in our own little corner of Cornwall!"

"Steady on, Pandora. Don't jump the gun. You can't give even a hint of something that hasn't yet been arranged and may not even happen. That would be irresponsible journalism."

"What are you saying here, Maddie?" she asked quietly.

"I'm not saying anything except *hold your horses*. I'll tell you all you need to know, if and when the time comes, promise. But let's have no embarrassing conjecture before that, okay?"

"Okay," she said reluctantly, "as long as you give me sufficient notice for a ginormous build-up.

THIRTY-ONE

I HEARD THE SCRUNCH OF TYRES ON THE DRIVE OUTSIDE as I was drinking a late afternoon cup of tea at the kitchen table. Pendragon barked and growled softly so I knew it was the arrival that I dreaded. I opened the door and there, sure enough, stood the purple car. Thane got out of it, stretching his back and exercising each leg in turn.

"Maddie, my Maddie," he exclaimed. "I've driven non-stop from London, so anxious was I to see you again."

He flung the keys onto the table and tried to take me in his arms but, to my relief, Pendragon, sensing my reluctance, stood in the way, his teeth bared in warning. I turned quickly towards the table.

"You're just in time for a cup of tea," I said. "Would that be welcome?"

"Welcome indeed! I'm gasping, in spite of the fact that this bloody dog is not making me *feel* welcome."

"Come and sit down then," I invited, pushing a cup of tea across the table. "Help yourself to milk and sugar. I'll shut Penn in the other room for a while."

I was to regret this action, unaware as I was of what Thane's reaction would be to what I was about to reveal to him. I took a deep breath and delivered my bombshell without further delay.

"TR, I know you are not going to be happy about this but I have to tell you right away that when I was in Ireland

I met someone and fell in love with him and we plan to get married."

TR gasped. "Christ almighty! One of those fucking holiday romances? You *cannot* be serious!"

"I am very serious indeed," I assured him. "In fact, to prove how serious, I am about three months' pregnant with his baby."

His mouth fell open. "Whore! Slut!" he shouted. Pushing back his chair so that it fell backwards with a clatter onto the slate floor, he strode towards me, his expression thunderous. I got to my feet quickly, afraid of the expression of incredulous anger on his face.

"You filthy, fucking female!" he went on, not impressing me with his alliteration. "After all the holy, Catholic talk about marriage and responsible parenthood!"

He hit the left side of my face so hard with his closed fist that I fell back against the dresser, causing several pieces of Cornishware to fall and smash into pieces on the hard floor. I collapsed amongst them, groaning with pain and shock, fearing greatly for the safety of my precious little 'passenger'. There was a furious barking – almost a howling – from the next room and the sound of Penn's claws scraping urgently on the door.

"How dare you assault me like that?" I shouted, as soon as I could summon the energy. "Get out through that door and never show your face here again. If the dog comes after you he will surely kill you, you evil creature. As soon as I can get up from here I shall set him on you, so GO, NOW!!"

I struggled painfully to my feet and made my way slowly to the door which Pendragon was trying so desperately to break through. As soon as my hand reached for the handle, I heard the outside door slam and the car door open and close. Within micro-seconds TR was reversing up the drive as fast as he could.

"Find and kill!" I ordered Pen. It was the first and last time I have ever issued such a command. He set off in hot pursuit as soon as I opened the door but gave up the chase when he heard the car reach the road, engage a forward gear and roar away towards Polburran. Penn came running back to me, looking anxious, as if for reassurance that all was well with me in spite of TR's hostile treatment.

I immediately picked up the phone and rang the surgery, asking to speak to my doctor, who called me back very soon afterwards. I told her that I had had a fall in the kitchen and asked if the baby was likely to be harmed in any way.

"What caused the fall?" she asked. "Were you standing on a chair or anything silly, and reaching up?"

"No, no, nothing like that." I said hastily. "Listen, Sarah, please don't tell me I ought to report this. It's very sensitive information. Actually I was assaulted by a certain person, punched in the face, no less – on the cheekbone; it made me fall against the kitchen dresser and I sort of slithered to the ground amongst the broken plates, in pain and shock."

"Yes I think I understand what you're telling me and I realise who the certain person is likely to be. It's unlikely there's any damage to the baby but I advise you to take a warm drink and go to bed very early and try to think positive thoughts before you sleep. Don't dwell on what happened. And look, you've got my private number; if you're at all worried or have any sign that something's amiss, give me a call. If necessary, I'll come out to see you."

"Oh, bless you!" I sighed. "You've made me feel better already."

"Good luck, Maddie. And by the way, put some arnica cream or raw steak on that cheekbone. I'm afraid you'll have a black eye tomorrow – probably a real shiner."

"Okay, and thanks, Sarah. I shall have to decide what to do about my assailant . . . but not tonight."

"No – put it out of your mind at once. I'll say no more about it, rest assured. Oh, by the way, no alcohol in your hot drink."

"Yuk! Hate the stuff," I laughed.

Though it was only early evening, I did as Dr Sarah suggested and prepared for an early night, first making sure that the outside doors were double-locked and bolted on the inside. I could not imagine that he would try to come again, and risk a confrontation with Pendragon, one that would be sure to result in injury, even permanent damage or, at the worst, death. All the same, I felt more secure as I carefully mounted the stairs, carrying my mug of hot malted milk. Penn followed me and went to his bed on the landing outside the bedroom, a slightly puzzled expression on his face.

When I caught sight of my face in the bathroom mirror, I wondered whether it was that or the unaccustomed bedtime that had caused Pen's consternation. I was shocked myself. The arnica cream had not prevented the bruising: my left eye socket and brow were dark purple. No amount of make-up was going to mask it. Even large sun glasses were not going to cover the ravages. Tomorrow I would take a 'selfie', I resolved, just in case evidence of TR's assault was ever necessary.

As I sat up in bed sipping my comforting drink, my thoughts were anything but comforting. Quite apart from my anxiety about the baby, Fearghal was due to arrive in four days' time. Whatever would he say and think? What might he do? I had wanted so much to look my best for his arrival; had even planned what I would wear when I went to meet his flight. But Sarah had told me to think only *positive* thoughts so I banished my immediate worries and picked up a travel book by Bill Bryson which I kept by the bed and dipped into from time to time. A bit of his quirky humour would cheer me up, force me to think of something else and relax my mind, even if it did not improve my looks!

It was a wild evening outside. A fierce westerly wind was whipping the sea into a frenzy and sending the waves crashing against the cliff below. Huge raindrops slashed against my window as if trying to force entry. It was as I lay there, propped up snugly (smugly, perhaps?) on soft pillows, secure in the warmth and comfort of home that the most amazing, life-affirming event happened: I felt an unmistakable 'ripple' in my lower abdomen, a ripple that said, "I'm here and I'm okay, Mom. I've just discovered I can swim in here. There's plenty of room now but it may be a bit cramped later on. Just saying 'Hi'."

Imagine my relief! I waited, breathless, to see if there would be another sign of life but all was still again. I picked up my cell phone and texted Sarah: *All well here. Baby just quickened. So relieved and thrilled. Will make appt. to see you soon. Love, Maddie*

THIRTY-TWO

THE FOLLOWING MORNING I GOT OUT OF BED, showered and dressed and was just examining my battered face in the glass when I heard a frantic knocking at the back door. I remember thinking that it was strange that the sound did not set Penn off barking, and realised that it must be someone he knew – certainly not TR.

After a few seconds the knocking came again, more urgent this time. I went to the bathroom window and opened it a crack. It was raining hard and the wind was still high.

"Okay," I called, "I'll be down in a moment. Who is it? "

"You won't remember me, Miss. My name's Roxy Dooley."

"I *do* remember you, Roxy. Just shelter in the woodshed a minute and I'll be down to open the door. I'm just fixing my face."

I applied a little more concealer to my eye socket, wiped it off again and put on dark glasses as I descended the stairs and quickly unbolted the door. Pendragon bounded out and ran straight to the girl who put her arms round him and sobbed silently into his rough fur.

"Why, Roxy, whatever is the matter?" I asked, full of concern and dread.

She raised a tear-stained face to look at me. "Oh Miss, I've run away. It's my dad. Can I hide here with you, please, *please,* Miss?"

"Is your dad ill – or something worse, Roxy?"

"No, no. Miss, he'll look for me and I don't want him to find me. Please, please help me! I broke a window in the van to get away and escaped while he was out in the motor." There was a fresh outburst of noisy sobbing.

"Come into the house and sit down, my dear. I shall make you a hot chocolate drink. Would you like that? Then you can tell me what all this is about, can't you?"

I gave her a brief hug, almost repelled by the rank smell of her hair and clothing. Handing her a box of Kleenex, I busied myself making her a drink, dreading what she might be about to tell me.

"Why did you have to break a window? What's wrong with the door, Roxy?" I asked with a brief laugh as I handed her the drink and joined her at the kitchen table.

"He locked me in, Miss, like he often does."

"Where is your mom, honey? You do have a mom, don't you?"

"She left with the baby, Miss, and promised to come back for me but she never has."

"Is that why your father locks you in, d'you think?"

"He says sex-slaves have to be locked up or they might run away," she sobbed.

Oh my God! I thought. *My initial dread was well-founded; but this disclosure has to run its course, horrific though it is.*

"Sex-slaves, honey?" I tried to keep my voice level.

"He said I had to take my mum's place in every way now she'd gone; that's what daughters are for: cooking, cleaning, washing and all . . . and . . . and . . . no, Miss, I can't say the other thing."

"Roxy, my dear, I'll make it easier for you: just answer yes or no, because I think I understand what this is about. Does he touch you in places that are personal to you?"

"Yes, Miss, and he makes me touch him . . . there." Her sobs had turned into a series of gulping hiccups now.

"And last night he came home with a mate and said, 'I'm going to show you what this is really for, and my mate Vince is going to watch and then he'll show you what his is for, as well.' And they did it, Miss. They *both* did it." By now the girl's wailing was almost a scream. Pendragon stood close to her and tried to lick the tears from her eyes. I overcame my scruples and hugged her again, my mind reeling from the unimaginable horror of what she was telling me. At that very moment there was another signal from my own child; another ripple, almost as if in sympathy for the plight of the child I was trying to comfort. I put a hand on my small bump.

"Was that your baby moving, Miss?" *Could that tiny vibration possibly have transmitted through the hand that held hers?* I wondered.

"That's right honey," I said. "I think he or she was just sending us a little message."

"I remember baby Rory sending a message like that to Mum."

The diversion had caused Roxy's wailing to cease momentarily, but now her crying started again. "I wish I was safely hidden in Mum's tummy," she mourned. "Will you promise to keep me safe, Miss?"

"Dear child, what you have told me is very serious indeed. The police will have to be told and the social workers; a doctor too will have to examine you. What your father and the other guy did is an imprisonable offence."

"Oh no, Miss! Please don't tell anybody, *please!* I only want to stay here with you."

"I shall see that it is all handled very carefully," I promised. "It must never happen again to you – or to anyone else. You must be very badly hurt."

"I do hurt very, very badly. There was a lot of blood and still is. Miss, I feel so dirty after what happened. Do you think I could have a wash?"

"Of course you can, Roxy. Let's get you upstairs right now. A bath would be best, I think with a salt rinse afterwards which will help you to heal. Will you mind me having a look?"

"No, it'll be like Mum looking after me. He was horrible to her too and hurt her lot – and the baby, Rory. That's why she left. She had to protect him."

And left it to somebody else to protect her poor little daughter, I thought.

"Why did you come to me?" I asked gently, having ushered her upstairs to the bathroom. "And how did you find me?" I started to mix hot and cold water to the right temperature and ran it into the bathtub.

"I could tell you were a kind lady when you came about the dog, and I knew you would help me," she answered. "I came looking for you in August when my Mum went, but you were never here. If you weren't here today I would've hid in the woodshed."

I turned off the faucet and tested the temperature of the water to ensure that it was not too hot. Remembering that there was a bottle of Cecilia's lavender water in the closet, I poured some into the water. The sweet-scented, steamy cloud that rose from it made it easier for me gently to peel off Roxy's clothing and drop the offensive garments in a laundry basket. She had stuffed a grimy hand-towel into her panties. I tried not to gag as I eased it slowly away from the source of the bleeding.

When I saw the damage to her innocent little body and the accompanying bruising to her arms, thighs and torso, I was consumed by anger and hatred towards the two disgusting and evil men who had caused such injury. The emotion such a horror triggered in me was so far beyond my own experience that only the most supreme effort enabled me to appear calm and practical for Roxy's sake. I ran a little more cold water into the bath.

"Step in now, honey, and I'll help you to sit down very carefully and slowly. It may sting a bit at first. While you get used to it, I'll just take your clothes down to the washing machine. I'll find you something to wear afterwards till they're dry again. Okay?"

Downstairs I made two quick phone calls: one to the estate agent's to say that I couldn't come in that afternoon because of a family crisis; the other to Sarah's cell phone to ask if she could possibly come to the house if she had a spare moment.

As I stuffed Roxy's foul-smelling clothing into the washing machine, I was suddenly aware that I would be destroying vital forensic evidence of the assault. I could not have denied her request for a bath; in her shoes I would have wanted only to wash away the horror of it all. However, I found a clean plastic bag and dropped in both the towel and the panties, hoping that the evidence contained there would be enough to convict the two monsters and get them banged up for life and know the fear of being 'done over' by other criminals who, for all their own wrong-doings, utterly deplore incestuous, paedophile rapists.

Another awful thought struck me as I returned to the bathroom.

"Roxy, dear, have you started your periods yet? Do you know what I mean?" I thought it unlikely, since there were no signs of approaching puberty on her thin little body.

"I don't think so, Miss, but Mum told me that I would bleed when I was old enough. And I did bleed. Does that mean that it's started?"

"No, sweetheart; you bled because you were injured. How old are you now?"

"I'm eleven and a half."

"Then I expect it'll start in a couple years' time. Time to start washing you now."

I soaped a soft flannel and washed her neck, underarms and back, then asked her to lie back in the water so that her lank hair would be wet. I lathered it with my favourite shampoo, rinsed it, shampooed it again and finally massaged it with conditioner, rinsing it off with jugs full of tepid water. Having squeezed out as much water as I could, I fetched two towels from the airing cupboard and wound the smaller one into a turban on her head.

"Your hair will shine like satin now," I assured her. "Now I want you to get up on your knees and wash the other bit. Only you know how much it hurts, so only you can touch it. After that we'll let out the water and run a little bit more with some salt dissolved in it. I'll just wash your face with clean water – no soap – it dries up your skin too much. Fresh, soft water is best, especially Cornish water. When all that's done, I'll wrap you in this nice big towel which is still warm from being near the hot water tank."

Later, Roxy, wrapped in a fleecy bathrobe, sat in a cane chair next to the Rayburn, holding another mug of hot chocolate as I dried her hair.

"Miss, can I live with you here all the time now?" she asked plaintively.

"Honey, I would be breaking the law myself if I kept you here without informing the police and Social Services. I could be accused of abduction if I just kept you here."

"But Miss, you're a good lady, not a criminal. You're the sort of lady I'd like to grow up to be."

"Look, Roxy dear. You can call me Maddie, if you like. It's short for Madeleine which is my first given name. We must do the right thing and report what happened to you last night. It must never be allowed to happen to you again."

"But Dad said he would kill me if I told anyone. What if they make me go back to him? I think he really meant it. He would kill me – and the other girls."

"Other girls??" My heart gave a lurch.

"I heard him and Vince talking. They are going to get some immigrant refugee girls and lock them in an empty van and make them be sex-slaves. Dad says there's a mint of money to be made. All they have to do is lock them up and feed them, and then men will pay to come and do what they did to me. Vince had to pay Dad last night. He wanted to go first but Dad wouldn't let him. He said it would've cost him ten times as much. 'Anyway, she's my girl,' he said, 'so I have to break her in.'"

"Monster!" I exclaimed, too loudly. "Sorry, Roxy; you should *never* have had to go through this. We must do all we can to stop them. The police must be told."

The girl started sobbing again.

"Honey, I shall be with you every step of the way. I shall insist on being by your side wherever you go, whoever you see. Look, it's Friday lunchtime now. We can lie low over the weekend and I'll arrange for the people who need to know to come here on Monday so we are not out and about for the next two days for other people to notice. I don't want to be seen around, either, looking like I do. Stay here while I make a couple of calls, then I'll make us some lunch."

"Did the baby's father beat you up, Miss Maddie? I didn't like to ask."

"Oh no! He would never do a thing like that. I fell against the dresser and knocked my face."

"That's what people say on the telly when they don't want to tell the truth," she said wisely.

I went upstairs and dialled the number of the local police, determined not to be fobbed off in the same way that I had been when I reported the theft of my hedge cutter.

"This is Madeleine Manning of Foxgloves, Polburran. I have a very serious crime to report and would like to be put through to your superior officer," I said to the desk sergeant.

"Very serious, eh, madam? Another theft from the garden shed?"

"Is the incestuous rape of a child serious enough for you?" I asked angrily.

"Are we being a wee bit over-dramatic here, ma'am?" he said patronisingly.

"I insist on speaking to someone who will take me very seriously. Do you wish to be reported for sexist remarks, while I'm at it? Now, kindly put me through right away."

"You foreigners think you can come into this country and tell me how to do my job."

"*Excuse me?* I suspect that I am a great deal more Cornish than you are. I detect a Scottish accent, so you are just as much a foreigner as you think I am. I shall report you for both sexism *and* racism. Now, PUT ME THROUGH!"

"Calm down and hold the line."

"Okay. But bear in mind that you are a public servant and that it's people like me who pay your wages."

"Humph" he grunted, followed by something inaudible.

THIRTY-THREE

Soon after I had finished my conversation with a more reasonable senior police officer and was down in the kitchen heating some soup for lunch, there was a knock at the door and Sarah walked in.

"I came as soon as I could," she said. "What's happened, Maddie? Is it the baby?" she caught sight of Roxy sitting by the Rayburn and raised her eyebrows.

"I'm so sorry if I got you here under false pretences," I said, "but this is Roxy who is in a very bad way and needs your attention more than I do."

I explained as succinctly as possible what had taken place the previous night. For all the initial shock I had felt when the girl told me, as I said the words, I was still unable to believe that a man could treat his own daughter in such a horrific manner.

Sarah looked appalled. "The police – " she started

"Have been informed," I interrupted. "Two officers will visit later, but perhaps you could take a look anyway?"

"Then I'll examine her now, though I expect they'll want a police doctor to do so as well." Turning to Roxy, she greeted her: "Hello, Roxy, I'm Dr Sarah Grant. Shall we just go upstairs so that I can have a look at your injuries?"

Roxy started to cry again.

"Roxy, dear, please don't cry," I said. "Doctor Sarah is not only my doctor; she's my friend as well. She'll be just as gentle and kind to you as she would be to her own children. Go with her now and I'll just finish heating up this soup and warm some bread rolls in the oven. There'll be enough for all three of us. Take Roxy into my room, Sarah."

"I've given her an injection in case of any infection," Sarah said when they came downstairs. "I also did a little needlework, didn't I, Roxy? She was very brave about it. I explained that it wouldn't hurt badly but was necessary for her to heal properly. It was better to do the stitches right away than to wait for hours at the hospital. Good job I had everything I needed in my bag."

"Great, thanks. Now come and have some lunch, both of you. I bet you're missing yours by coming here, Sarah."

"I must be back by half past," she said, checking her watch. "But thanks. It looks and smells so good – and I bet Roxy hasn't eaten for hours."

"No, just a couple hot drinks and a cookie or two."

Later she asked, "And how's that eye of yours feeling, Maddie? It's a pretty impressive colour."

To my surprise, Roxy answered, "She didn't knock it: she was hit by a nasty man. My Mum used to get black eyes like that from my Dad."

"I can believe that;" said Sarah, "but, Roxy, don't think that all men hit their wives and girlfriends. My husband is as gentle as a kitten and would never do that to me or the children. Nor would the father of Maddie's baby, her fiancé."

"So it must have been the other one, the singer that's on telly, then?" Roxy said. "I told you there would be love trouble when I read your palm, Miss Maddie."

"You did, Roxy," I agreed, "but tell me this: could you not foresee what would happen to you, yourself?"

"No, Miss. The 'sight' doesn't work for the one who 'sees'. I can't 'read' what will happen to my own self."

"Well, you are safe now, my dear, and even if you don't like the idea of talking to the police; at least you will never have to face your father again unless you want to."

"Oh, I never, never want to, ever again. I hate him, I *hate* him!"

"It is so very sad to have to say that about your father," Sarah said. "But one day, my dear, when you're grown up, I hope you'll meet a good man who will look after you and be a wonderful, kind father to your children and help you forget the cruelty you have suffered."

She wiped her mouth with her napkin and stood up. "I must fly. Thank you so much for that. Delish, wasn't it, Roxy? Goodbye for now. We shall meet again after surgery."

I followed her through the door and closed it quietly behind us.

"In all my years in medicine, I have never come across anything like that," she said. "That man deserves to be hung, drawn and quartered – and castrated – in public. Let me know how it all goes, won't you? The girl is lucky to have thrown herself on your mercy. Look after yourself now."

"Of course," I said. "It's not just me now, is it? And Fearghal's due to arrive on Tuesday. How complicated is that going to be?"

"I'm sure you'll work things out together, Maddie. 'Bye now."

"Miss Maddie, I was thinking about your black eye." said Roxy when I went back into the kitchen. "You could try the gypsy cure for bruising that my Mum used to do. Have you got marjoram in the garden?"

"Why, yes, there's some in the herb bed but I expect it's a bit dry and wintry at this time of year. I don't use it as much as parsley and mint and other herbs."

"If you take the leaves – and they're better dried – and pound them into a powder, then mix them into a paste with honey, this can be rubbed on to the bruising and it will ease the pain and take the dark colour away."

"Thank you for that advice, Roxy. The herbal remedies are often the best and I don't want Fearghal, my fiancé, to see me like this, so I'll try it straight away."

"What did the police say?" the girl asked nervously.

"I was told that a family liaison officer and a police woman would come round here later on this afternoon. Friday afternoons are very busy, they said, but they didn't want to leave it till Monday."

"Please, please don't let them take me away," she pleaded. "They might lock me in a cell."

"Of course they won't;" I assured her. "You're not the criminal; you're what is called the *victim* in all of this."

There was no sign of tears now; the girl sat there, her clean, straight hair shining as it had probably never done before, looking relaxed and much less troubled than the poor waif who had begged me to take her in a few hours earlier.

True to their word, the two women police officers arrived in an unmarked, black car, dressed in plain clothes. I saw the car and went out to greet them, closing the door behind me.

"I'm Madeleine Manning," I said. "Thanks for not making my little friend come to the police station."

"I'm DCI Donna Bale," said the taller of the two women, "and this is DI Sadie Colson, the family liaison officer. Looks like you've had a bit of trouble of your own?"

"Hi," I said "Yes, quite impressive, isn't it? I had a bit of a tumble."

"That's what they all say. Nothing reportable then?"

"No," I said. "Nothing that won't mend quickly. I hope you can nail these bastards."

"Language, Miss Manning!" interjected Donna Bale.

"You can imagine the state that poor girl is in," I went on. "Expect copious tears. Before we go in, I must apologise for letting her have a bath. I realise it was premature, but at least I saved the two items which are most likely to be useful as forensic evidence. I'll give you the bag now; it's in the back lobby near the washing machine."

"I'm sorry to report, Miss Manning, that our bird has flown. One of our team went round to the camp-site for a preliminary look-around and found no vans, no dogs, no horses, nothing; nothing but wheel-tracks, broken glass and a few paw-prints in the mud."

"So-o-o," I said, "far from coming to you to report his daughter missing, he does a runner. Isn't that an admission of guilt?"

"We draw our own conclusions, Madeleine, and you draw yours. We've alerted the forces in Devon, Somerset, Dorset and Wiltshire. But now to the matter in hand. Shall we go in?"

"Of course. Please don't mind the dog. He's big, but very friendly – unless I tell him otherwise."

"Well, please don't." The other woman, Sadie, spoke for the first time. "Wow! Makes my pooch look like a pocket toy."

After introductions were made, Donna indicated that Roxy and I should sit together on the other side of the table from them. Sadie Colson opened a notebook and sat, pen poised, to record the interview.

"Now Roxy," Donna began, "Sadie and I are only here to establish the facts of your assault. Please remember that you are in no way to blame for what happened. I expect you've seen dramas on television where the victim has to be interviewed before the criminal can be called in for questioning."

"Yes, I have," the girl replied, her eyes brimming.

"So first, can you give me your full name?"

"Roxanne Lavendi Dooley."

"Would your father be Mick Dooley?"

Roxy shuddered. "Yes, Miss."

"And *your* full name, please, Miss Manning?"

"Madeleine Grace Manning. You have the address, I think."

"And are you willing to act as an appropriate adult in this case?"

"Sure; of course I am." I assured her.

"So, Roxy, do you understand that we need to hear your own account of the event, even though Miss Manning has already told us on your behalf?"

Roxy looked at me with a questioning expression. I nodded encouragingly and took her hand in mine.

"Yes, I do," she said in a faltering voice, "but my Dad said he would kill me if I told."

"He would have said that so that you kept your mouth shut, Roxy."

I pressed her hand reassuringly while she was forced to relive the horrors of the previous night, prompted by Donna's questions, one of which had occurred to me earlier.

"Did you scream loudly while this was taking place?"

"I couldn't, Miss. He tied a bit of old rag tight round my mouth. It smelt of petrol."

There was a fresh outburst of crying. I put my arm round her and drew her close.

"Hold on, Roxy, baby," I said. "This will soon be over. I know how hard it is for you to be reminded."

Another question answered one I had not asked. "How did you get out of the broken window without injuring yourself on the glass?"

"I found an old leather jacket of . . . his . . . to put on while I climbed out."

"And where is it now?"

"I threw it back through the window."

"You could have kept it on to protect you from the heavy rain."

This seemed to me an unnecessary suggestion. Roxy gave a long, deep shudder again.

"I'd rather get wet than wear anything of his." Tears rolled down her cheeks and fell onto the table, the table that had seen so many tears in the history of my family.

When the interview was over, Donna asked if there was another room in which she and I could talk. I showed her into the Music Room, leaving Sadie and Roxy together.

"Has it occurred to you that the girl could have been lying about all this?" Donna asked. "After all, you are a bit of a celebrity, connected to a much bigger one. Could she not have been making up a story to get your attention and, possibly, his?"

"Officer, I have seen the damage with my own eyes. I know she is telling the truth. No girl of that age could make up a story like that unless she had actually experienced it."

"Yes, well, she will need to be examined by one of our doctors, but that will have to wait till Monday."

"My own doctor has already examined her, stitched her and given her an injection. She would gladly corroborate Roxy's story, I'm sure."

"That would carry no weight, I'm afraid. You seem to have jumped the gun in more ways than one in all of this."

"Yes, I'm sorry about that. I thought I was acting for the best."

"Hmm. And just a word of warning," Donna continued. "Affectionate physical gestures are not appropriate for an adult who is not related.

Her remark made me see red. "Bloody political correctness!" I shouted. "What the hell about maternal instinct?" I patted my bump. "I'm soon to become a mother; such behaviour is instinctive. All this bullshit about 'inappropriate'. What the fuck is wrong with this crappy world? 'Inappropriate' is a euphemism for what that filthy bugger did to his daughter. He should have his inappropriate cock and bollocks sawn off and donated to McDonald's."

I don't usually swear, but on this occasion I was so angry that all the words I had not been allowed to utter as a child came tumbling out.

Donna held her hands up. "Okay, okay, chill out now. If you're pregnant, the stress all this is causing could harm both you and the baby. We'll get in touch with Social Services and arrange for the girl to be taken into care."

"No!" I shouted again. "That is not what she wants and not what I want."

"I think you'll both have an issue there. They'll do whatever they think is best."

"Well, they'll have a fight on their hands, then," I said petulantly. "Now, I think if you're finished here, you should go away. I would offer you a cup of tea but it's not fair to hold up your departure at the start of the weekend."

THIRTY-FOUR

ALTHOUGH PHYSICALLY, MENTALLY AND EMOTIONALLY exhausted that night, I lay awake for hours, my mind spinning with the events of the day while striving to turn to more positive thoughts. I tried to focus on Fearghal and think rationally about our own future. Using the metaphor contained in his Purple Shadow painting, I imagined myself standing on one of those sharp mountain peaks, contemplating the next range of mountains and those beyond, stretching into the hazy, greyish-purple distance. There was blue sea and golden sand beyond, I knew, and babies in cradles – the 'happy ever after' scene, but I could not see them from here.

Before going to bed I had checked that Roxy was sleeping peacefully. I always kept the spare room ready for visitors. I had given her a cotton tee-shirt and a pair of snug cotton briefs to wear under the fleecy bathrobe after her bath in the morning. When she got into bed, I sat with her for a while, observing that her situation was, in some ways, the reverse of the ballad 'The Wraggle Taggle Gypsies-O', about the bride who left the luxury and comfort of her castle to join the gypsies on the heath . . . not that my house was any kind of a castle!

"Will you sing it to me?" she asked. So I sang the version that I knew, surprised that I could remember all the words:

Three gypsies stood at the castle gate, they sang so sweet, they sang so low;
The lady sate in her chamber late; her heart it melted away like snow.

They sang so sweet, they sang so low that fast her tears began to flow
And she laid down her silken gown, her golden rings and all her show.

She pluckéd off her high-heeled shoes, all made of Spanish leather-o,
She went in the street with her bare, bare feet, all out in the wind and the weather-o

'Oh saddle to me my milk-white steed, oh go and fetch me my pony-o
That I may ride and seek my bride who is gone with the wraggle-taggle gypsies-o'

Oh he rode high and he rode low, he rode through wind and weather-o
Until he came to a cold open field, and there he espied his a-lady-o.

'What made you leave your house and your land, your golden treasures for to go?
What made you leave your new-wedded lord to follow the wraggle-taggle gypsies-o?'

'What care I for my house and my land, my golden rings and all my show?
What care I for my new-wedded lord? I'm off with the wraggle-taggle gypsies-o.'

'Last night you slept on a goose-feather bed, with the sheets turned down so bravely-o;
But tonight you'll sleep in a cold open field, along with the wraggle-taggle gypsies-o

'What care I for my goose-feather bed, with the sheets turned down so bravely-o?
For tonight I shall sleep in a cold open field along with the wraggle-taggle gypsies-o.'

"I've never heard that before," Roxy said. "Did the lady ever go back to her castle?"

"Who knows? The song doesn't tell us; though sometimes those ballads related to real events."

"It was lovely to hear you sing. I wish I could sing like that."

"Have you ever tried?" I asked.

"I once went to school for a while and we sang a bit but the teacher didn't have a lovely voice like yours."

"Why did you go to school only for a while?"

"Because we're always on the move, I s'pose."

"But you can read and write, can you?"

"Yes, I can, Miss Maddie, but I'm not as good as I should be – as I'd like to be. My mum said it was important but my dad said it was a waste of time. 'It's arithmetic that matters,' he would say. 'Just learn to add up the money and take from the *Giorgio* what he don't need and can well afford to replace.' (*Such as hedge cutters and their like,* I thought). If my dad found Mum helping me to read from a book she'd bought specially for me, he would hit her and hit me as well, so we had to do it whilst he was out and about"

"Oh, you poor baby!" I exclaimed. "I shall help you read tomorrow. There are plenty of children's books on that bookshelf over there from when my younger relatives used to stay here in the summer holidays."

I pulled the duvet round her shoulders and gently kissed her forehead.

"Good night, honey. I shall very soon lock the outside doors and go to bed early, myself."

"You're going to your goose feather bed; not away with the wraggle-taggle gypsies-o?" A faint smile lit up her face.

"Absolutely." I said, smiling. "Sleep well, honey."

I switched off the bedside light. "I'll leave a small light on the landing outside. Penn will look after us both: he sleeps out there."

*

So there I lay on said goose-feather bed; no 'sheets turned down so bravely-o', but a comforter all twisted up by my thrashing around, thinking furious, feminist thoughts about certain men and their Calvinistic attitude towards women. *If they displease you, beat them into submission. They're only good for cooking, cleaning and sex*. I could not even commune with my beloved grandmother, Cecilia. She would not come to me when I was so full of rage and bitterness.

But then, almost as if she had arranged it, my own darling Fearghal came to mind; he who was so gentle and loving; he who had planted this precious little seed within me as a token of our love. A tiny squirm from within seemed to acknowledge this change of direction in my thoughts. My dear man was due to arrive in three days' time. I considered what I would tell him and what would remain untold. I hoped the black eye would have faded by then. I had applied more of Roxy's 'ointment' before going to bed and hoped it was working its magic, in spite of Pendragon's attempt to lick it off. Naturally, I should have to tell Fearghal about Roxy's arrival. I intended to fight any social worker who tried to take her away so it would be likely that she would be with me when he arrived. I rehearsed what I would say if 'they' decided that Roxy should go into Care. By all accounts, she might be just as much at risk in a children's home. Also, she would hate to be in such a place. She felt secure here, I knew, and the fact that she had come to me as a friend must surely count for something. In spite of the girl's nomadic lifestyle, we had encountered each other twice in seven months and who was to know that it had not been more frequently than that?

And where on earth were Roxy's mother and her little brother, and how could they be traced? It would need the co-operation of every police force in the country and maybe further afield. I had no idea how these things worked. When the policewoman, Sadie, came again, I planned to question her on this procedure. She looked more approachable than the more austere Donna. I was still smarting over the latter's 'inappropriate touching' remarks. This thought led to the unwelcome memory of TR's recent assault. A more *inappropriate* gesture I could not imagine! His reaction was more likely to have been motivated by pride than by genuine hurt. The drama of Roxy's arrival the following morning had put his attack and its consequences out of my mind all day, though the physical evidence was there for all to see. It was very important that the news of our 'split' should not break until I looked normal again, so that the two events would not be connected. Roxy's herbal cure would work, she had said, but should have been applied immediately for best results.

*

I must have dozed off for a short while because I awoke from a brief dream in which Fearghal and I were consulting an elderly, white-haired guy in a clerical collar, wearing a black frock-coat and gaiters. His words rang in my ears: "You will both need to examine your consciences very carefully."

Well, yes indeed we would, I thought; *had both already done so.* Once the euphoria of our impending reunion was fading a little, we had seriously to consider what came next – from both a practical and a religious standpoint. I had already consulted the Anglican priest of the parish, a forty-something, trendy, 'call me James', and 'see you down the pub' kind of guy.

"Wow!" he'd exclaimed. "Sounds like one for the Archdeacon of the diocese to sort out for you. I'll arrange a meeting for you once your fiancé has arrived." He had assured me that there would be no problem if Fearghal wished to continue as a priest in the Anglo-Catholic faith. "I look forward to meeting him," he finished. "I suppose it's a matter of changing to another denomination within the same faith – all because of a major disagreement several hundred years ago. I'm glad to have met you, too, something of a celebrity round here, I believe. Rachel, my daughter, has been a huge fan of TR, ever since he was lead singer with *Next Level*. I guess that relationship is in the past now, eh?"

"Very much so," I'd assured him. "That is, if it ever was a relationship. But hush, please: I haven't yet dealt with that particular closure. Not a word to your daughter, *please*."

"I'm cool with that," he'd said. "You must meet my wife, Suzannah – Suzy, for short. She knows you by sight, of course, but I think you two would get along well."

At this point in my nocturnal musings, another positive thought struck me: *had not the Reverend James Harrison told me that his wife was a social worker?* I would try to arrange an unofficial meeting with her as soon as possible and beg her to put in a good word for me when Roxy's case came under review. On that more hopeful note, I must have relaxed sufficiently to spend the rest of the night asleep.

***

THIRTY-FIVE

When I looked in on my young guest in the morning, she was sitting up with the light on, a dozen or more books spread around her on the bed.

"I'm practising my reading," she told me.

"Good idea," I commented. "After we've had some breakfast, I can listen and help you, if you choose a book you especially like."

"I really, really like this one." She held up one of Cecilia's own childhood books, *The Flower Fairies*.

"That was my grandmother's," I told her.

"I've seen some of those fairies in the hedges and fields."

I was unbearably touched. *Here is a child who still believes in fairies*, I thought: *a sweet innocent, violated and sullied by those two evil men . . . and one her own father.*

"Oh, lucky you!" I said. "You must be very special indeed if they let you see them. They must know that they can trust you not to try and catch them."

"Oh yes, they do know that; there may be some in your garden, Miss Maddie,"

"I do hope so," I said. "In June there are lots of foxgloves. They were my gran's favourite flowers . . . and her gran's as well."

"Your gran is, like, your spirit guide, isn't she?"

"Cecilia and I were very close," I agreed, amazed at her perspicacity.

*

I had planned to spend the weekend preparing for Fearghal's arrival: cleaning, chopping firewood, shopping, cooking and generally making sure that there was the same warm welcome apparent in my home as I felt in my heart. Roxy's presence, however, caused me to alter my plans. Fearghal had, after all, been living in primitive conditions, acceptable in warmer, summer weather but, most probably, cold and damp three months later. So a good log fire seemed to be the main priority. There had been a delivery of logs which needed to be sorted and stacked. Also there was kindling to chop. If Roxy felt up to the task, I would ask her to help me.

As for shopping, I had milk, eggs, bread, oats, vegetables and fruit, which would keep my young guest and me going for the weekend. I would leave anything else until Monday.

I noticed in the mirror that the honey and marjoram concoction had worked some of its magic overnight. The bruising was fading to a shade that might make it possible to mask it with concealer and skilfully applied make-up. With this in mind, I devised another little plan for Sunday.

While I was getting breakfast, I checked my emails and found one from Mistletoe asking if she could call by that very afternoon, 'about teatime. Don't start baking, I'll bring a cake. I'll assume it's convenient unless you message me otherwise. Useful news for you.'

The useful news might well concern employment for Fearghal. I had asked Mistletoe to enquire from her friend, Zara, with whom I had stayed on my visit to London for the fateful meeting with Fearghal's fearsome mother, if there might be opportunities for him in the field of commercial art; commissions that he could undertake at home, rather than having to live and work in London or elsewhere. So I welcomed the prospect of positive news in that matter, and could tell my friend about recent happenings in the knowledge that I could absolutely rely on her discretion.

Over a breakfast of porridge with honey, buttered toast and fruit, I told Roxy that we should have a visitor at teatime, assuring her that she was a very discreet and trustworthy friend and that I was sure Roxy would like her.

"But will she like me, d'you think?" she said diffidently. "I had very few friends at school because they said I was 'different'. 'Dirty tinker' and 'Pikey' some boys called me."

"Roxy dear, you have to think of it like this: you are *special* rather than different. You should feel proud that you are a genuine Romany."

"Only half, Miss Maddie. Dad is a *Giorgio*. Mum was in trouble for marrying out of her tribe. So me and Rory are half Romany and half *Giorgio*."

"Nevertheless, you inherited the gift of 'sight' from the Romany side of the family, which I think makes you very special indeed – the genuine article."

"Thank you, Miss," Roxy said, with a wistful smile.

*

We passed the morning doing reading and a little writing. A child so eager to learn is every teacher's dream.

"I'd like to write a story myself," Roxy said. "I once started to write one but my dad caught me and he took away the paper and put a match to it and threw it out of the van."If I write another one, what can I write about?"

"Well, you know that song I sang last night? Why don't you write how you think the story might have begun, continued and ended? Why do you think the lady was willing to leave her life of leisure and luxury, with servants to do all the household chores and wait on her all the time?"

"Okay, I'll try and do that – as long as you don't get cross if I go wrong."

"Do you *think* I would get mad at you?" I asked.

"No, you're too kind and good," she giggled

I thought it would put too great a strain on Roxy's stitches if she were to help me sort out the logs, so I left her to her writing and stacked the logs into the woodshed on my own, afterwards splitting up some of the driest wood with a small hatchet on a firm block to make good kindling for the log-burner. It was too dark in the shed to see through my wrap-around shades and I was dressed in my oldest, dirtiest clothes.

I heard Mistletoe's old jalopy panting down the drive at precisely four o'clock and presented myself at the ramshackle door to greet her.

"As you see, I didn't bake a cake or even wear my best afternoon tea dress," I said.

She stared at me. "Oh – my – God!" she exclaimed. Never mind the dress. What the devil happened to your eye?"

"You guessed! It was the devil who did it. He biffed me one when I told him about Fearghal – and the baby"

"The swine! You'll have him for assault, of course?"

"Now, think about it, Mistletoe. A celebrity gets dumped? I'd be lynched by the fans. I've got to get rid of this eye before the public get to know about the split. It's sensitive stuff. Anyway, that happened on Thursday – and early Friday morning there's another drama". . . And I briefed her on what had happened since. She looked horrified.

"Now come on in and meet Roxy," I invited.

Mistletoe caught sight of Roxy's illustration almost before she noticed the girl herself.

"What a beautiful picture!" she said.

I too was astounded by the girl's artistic talent. I had left plenty of paper for her writing, and some pencils, felt-tip pens and oil pastels in case she felt inclined to illustrate her story. I was amused to see that the lady of the ballad had hair of the same colour as my own. Roxy's depiction of the old-fashioned, dome-headed Romany caravan was spot-on, and she had done a superb job of colouring it in the traditional shades. 'The lady' stood beside the van in her bare feet, wearing nothing but a long white shift, while an old gypsy woman offered her a cloak or blanket of vibrant and intricate design. In the background, in perfect perspective, a man rode a white horse towards a copse of bare-branched trees.

"Mistletoe," I said. "Meet my friend, Roxy. Ms Masters is an artist herself," I explained. "How did you learn to draw and paint so well?"

"Nobody *taught* me," she replied. "It's something you just *do*."

Mistletoe laughed. "Yes, I think you're right, Roxy. It's a gift to be able to put the pictures you see in your imagination onto paper. Some people never develop the skill to draw or paint better than seven-year-olds. You teach yourself by observing from life and studying the work of great artists of the past."

"To do the lady's bare feet, I had to look at my own," Roxy said, "but they weren't the right way round for the picture and they got too cold on the floor." A little smile lit up her face.

"Mistletoe is a professional artist with her own studio in St Ives," I told Roxy. "Maybe one day we could go and look at her pictures."

"That would be really cool — when it's safe for me to go out. Are you *really* called Mistletoe?" she asked.

"No. I have to admit to having a made-up name," Mistletoe answered. "I get more attention because of it so I guess it helps to sell my work."

"The mistletoe is mysterious and kind of holy," said Roxy musingly. "Especially when it grows in an apple tree."

"So how did you get on with writing your story?" I asked.

"I wrote one chapter and then started the picture. I'll need your help to get it right, please."

""Okay," I promised. "We'll work on it together later on."

Over tea, Mistletoe told me that her friend, Zara, had said that it would be perfectly feasible for Fearghal to work from home and that she herself had more work than she could cope with and would be willing to share some commissions with him. It would depend on how *au fait* he was with the computer.

"Probably, not very," I commented.

"Oh well, there are always courses available locally. All in all it sounded pretty encouraging."

"Great," I said. "He'll need something to occupy him – and a way to earn a crust or two for his family. I expect I shall have to spend my remaining capital on building him a studio extension."

"Better get planning permission in early, then."

"On second thoughts, it may be a case of 'bye-bye woodshed'" I laughed, thinking of all the wood I had stacked so neatly. "A simple conversion may be easier, with a lean-to log store, small enough to comply with local building regs."

THIRTY-SIX

ROXY'S STORY WAS VERY REVEALING OF HER STATE OF mind, I found; especially concerning her attitude towards men. True, it was not as well written as it would have been if she had been a regular attendee at school, but what she intended was imaginative and bore evidence that she had listened to many stories, watched many television dramas and had an ear for the familiar phraseology of traditional story-telling.

Rightly or wrongly, I suggested a correction here, a rewording there and, having tweaked it somewhat, I transcribed the final result onto the computer and printed off one or two copies. She particularly liked the words 'however' and 'nevertheless' and wanted to ensure that each was included at least once in the narrative. I decided to leave, for the time being, any 'rude' words in the dialogue.

THE WRAGGLE-TAGGLE GYPSIES-O
by Roxanne Lavendi Dooley

CHAPTER ONE

Once upon a time there lived a beautiful lady who married a handsome lord. He took her to live in his castle and gave her a great chest full of sparkling jewels and a wardrobe full of gowns fashioned of silk and satin and delicate chiffon. Some were for summer and some for winter. These last were edged and trimmed with fine fur, for the castle was very cold, being built of stone. However, there were many fireplaces to keep her warm, looked after by the servants who did the stoking of the fires, the cleaning and the cooking. She even had servants to dress her, look after her gowns and brush her long, red hair at night and do it up in curls by day.

She didn't have to do a stroke of work but could spend her days sitting in her own room in her own turret, just reading books, drawing pictures or doing her needlework. You would think that she was the happiest lady alive, wouldn't you? Nevertheless, there was one great sorrow in her heart: her husband did not love her and treated her cruelly. He wanted her to bear him a son who would be heir to all his estates and be lord of the castle after him. If she refused to have sex with him, he beat her till she was black and blue and she would cry out in pain.

One day, however, she found she was pregnant. In her heart of hearts she knew that the baby was a girl-baby and not the boy that her lord had wanted. She realised that both she and her baby were in great danger. The lord would blame her for having a girl and might harm them both.

Then, one winter's evening, as she sat up late in her beautiful bedchamber, all hung with silken curtains in a delicate shade of rose pink, she heard a haunting melody coming from beneath her window. When she looked out, she saw three gypsies standing in the moonlight just outside the gate. They were singing a song so sweet and sad that it moved her to tears. She put a hand to her belly and whispered to her child, "To save us both from the wrath of your father, I shall run away and follow those gypsies. They will protect us from cruelty and pain; they will teach us the ways of wild Nature and we shall see flower fairies in the hedges along the secret paths." So saying, without calling for help from her maid, she kicked off her high-heeled shoes made of Spanish leather, unfastened her elegant gown and threw it upon the bed; she removed her stays and her stockings of gossamer silk, and stood bare-footed, clad only in her sheer white petticoats. Taking no cloak, even though the night was as cold as charity, she crept down the stone steps of her tower. Silently she went down, round and round and round, each stone stair like ice to her pretty, delicate feet. Carefully she opened the heavy oaken door, closing it behind her as quietly as she could in spite of its creaks and groans. She ran to the gatehouse, managing to give the gate-keeper the slip. He had not yet locked the gate, for Milord had not yet come home. He was either at the local inn or seeing another lady over Bodmin way. She caught up with the gypsies who wrapped a woollen cloak of many colours round her shoulders and helped her quickly into the caravan and said "Walk on" to the trusty black horse who was harnessed to it.

[To be continued]

*

Having carefully applied make-up to my now grey eye (grey being the new black!), I was able to put my Sunday plan into effect.

"I need to go out for a little while, Roxy," I said. "Will you be okay with Penn here to look after you?"

The girl bit her lip and looked doubtful, "I think I would feel safe – but what if my Dad guessed I was here and came looking for me?"

"He won't dare to show his face in Polburran with the police looking for him. I'll give you a spare key then lock you in. You needn't open the door to anyone; anyway, Pendragon would never let anyone near you."

"It's like Snow White, isn't it? She was told not to let anyone in."

"I'll be back as soon as I can," I promised. "You'll be fine."

*

I was not unfamiliar with the Anglican services. As a Music student in San Francisco, I had sung in the special choir of Grace Cathedral and had often attended the sung Eucharist, which was not so different from our own Catholic Mass. Locally also I had attended C of E services with the Byrd Singers.

As I walked into church, the sidesman on duty greeted me with surprise. "Good morning, Miss Manning. I thought you was one of the other lot." He handed me two books.

"They say it's a woman's privilege to change her mind sometimes," I said with a smile. "Now, where shall I sit? Not too near the front, please, so that I can watch how things are done."

He ushered me to a pew about seven rows back.

The vicar registered both surprise and pleasure when he spotted me from the pulpit. His sermon was short and held my attention throughout, being on the subject of religious intolerance. Later, when the time came for Communion, I did not go up to receive the Sacrament but simply observed the rest of the congregation and wondered how Fearghal was going to adjust to this change of procedure and accept the more relaxed doctrine of the Anglo-Catholic Church.

As I left the church, James Harrison shook me by the hand and said how good it was to see me there.

"I must introduce you to Suzy," he said. "Ah, here she comes now." He seized the arm of a smartly-dressed, blonde-haired woman wearing a resigned expression on her face as she was harangued by an older woman with a sharp nose and what Cecilia would have called a 'witchy chin' sprouting several bristly white whiskers. Suzy's expression turned to one of relief.

"Please excuse me, Mrs Trewarren: my husband seems to need me."

"Very good, Mrs Harrison. Vicar comes first. Now don't forget it's W.I. on Thursday, mind. I'll see you there."

"That woman could talk for England," Suzy said, once she was out of earshot. "Thanks for rescuing me, darling."

When James introduced me, she said, "Great to meet you at last, Madeleine. Look, I have to get back to the vicarage and put the lunch on. Why don't you pop in now and have a drink?"

This was working out just as I had hoped it would.

"I have a problem at home so have to get back myself," I hedged, "but if it could be a very quick visit, I'd love to come because there is something I'd like to discuss with you both."

"Of course," said James. "Make it as long or as short as you like. Look, you two go ahead and I'll catch you up. I just have to clear up a few things here."

THIRTY-SEVEN

I WAS NEITHER SURPRISED NOR PLEASED WHEN I GOT home to receive an email from TR; simply relieved that he had a very expensive security system installed on his Wi-Fi devices to protect his private correspondence from being hacked either by fans or the gossip-mongers of the Press.

Hey Maddie,
What can I offer in the way of an apology? Can I expect forgiveness? Do I deserve forgiveness? My life-coach says it was absolutely wrong of me to hit you and that you would be justified in suing me for assault right away. As I have heard nothing from the police and read nothing on social media, I hope it means that you haven't taken that action.

Nate (life-coach) says I should have fought to keep your friendship even if you do not love me. I hope the baby was not harmed. It should have been *my* baby and I would accept it as my own if you would agree to marry me. I guess the other guy won't be able to give the kid what I would — the best toys, clothes, holidays, schools – the very best of everything in life. Think about it Maddie. You would have the best of everything too – something that Irish loser will never be able to give you. Dump him right now so we can take our relationship to the next level (LOL). I promise I would never, ever hit you again. I can't believe I really did that. I was so hurt that I overreacted.

Please reply ASAP that you forgive me and accept my offer. Imagine wearing the biggest sparkling diamond on your ring finger to WOW the whole world – and a designer gold wedding band that would go down in history because it was commissioned by a mega-celebrity for his beautiful bride.

All the love in the world,

TR XX

"Huh!" I grunted as I read his words. *As if all those promises of material wealth would appease me! I have failed to report his assault for my own reasons,* I thought; *for the sake of Fearghal and our unborn child.* I objected to his calling my beloved 'that Irish loser' and referring to the baby as 'it', as if our future daughter was an inanimate object or a spider or an ant, whose gender could not be determined. *I shall ignore his message*, I thought, *and let him wonder for the rest of his life whether I ever read it or considered it.*

*

"What did you do while I was out?" I asked Roxy.

"I wrote chapter two of my story."

"Is it ready for me to read?"

"I'll need some help with the spelling, specially as I've given the people names."

"We'll work on it after lunch, then – and you can do another picture while I type it. It's not fine enough to go for a walk."

It was a typical November day, overcast, damp and dreary. "If we do that first, we can watch *Country File* after tea," I went on.

"Oh yes, and please can we watch *Downton Abbey* too? I always see that. It's about a very posh family who live in a very big castle with lots of servants. Sometimes it makes me want to be a *Giorgio* when I see that." she embarked on a detailed description of 'the family' and the intrigues of the 'below stairs' characters.

"Uh-huh," I interrupted, "I watch it too, so we shall definitely see it as long as you promise to go to bed straight afterwards."

"Promise I will," she agreed

After lunch, as we worked together, I was impressed with Roxy's imaginative narrative with its mixture of traditional expression and more down-to-earth detail. She read me what she had intended to convey while I made suggestions to improve her spelling and punctuation, which was, in fact, non-existent!

"Can we make it into a real book, Maddie?" she begged.

"Sure, we can, Roxy. With your wonderful illustrations it would be a very fine book."

I told her about the Ashford sisters whose stories were published in the 1920s, the best known being *The Young Visiters* by nine-year-old Daisy Ashford, which had a foreword by J.M. Barry of *Peter Pan* fame. "My gran had a reprinted copy of that and also a first edition by Daisy's sisters from the days when you had to separate the pages of a book with a paper knife. They're in my bedroom bookcase. I'll show you them later."

As we worked on the second chapter of Roxy's story, which I organised into sentences, explaining how punctuation helped to make sense of it and make it readable, both aloud and silently, I pointed out that certain expressions would be better rephrased in the final edition, especially if they contained 'rude' words. However, I have left the dialogue in the original at present since it expresses and reveals so much of her own experience.

CHAPTER TWO

The lady's new-wedded husband was a young nobleman, William, Earl of Salisbury in the county of Wiltshire. He had inherited the title and the castle from his father when the old earl died, which he did in a very noble way in his own four-poster bed, lying on white feather pillows under a coverlet of crimson silk. William stood at his bedside and wept one or two tears as his dad breathed his last. But secretly he was thinking aha – now I can have that red eiderdown and the big bed for myself. Not only that: I can have this castle and the gardens and all the lands that go with it. I shall be the one giving orders to Carson, the butler, and every horse in the stables will be mine. I must now find a wife to give orders to the housekeeper and the maids and, most important of all, to give me a baby son to take my place when I either die in battle or fade away with old age.

Within a twelve-month he had found the lovely Lily who came from Somerset and who was as gentle and kind-hearted as she was beautiful. She had thick, shining red hair and skin as white as milk. She will do nicely, he thought to himself; she is worthy to be the mother of my son and heir. He courted her in a most handsome and charming manner and, in a very grand ceremony, entered into the holy estate of matrimony with her.

Nevertheless, I must point out to the reader of this tale that milord William, for all his good looks and charming manners was not a kind and good man; in fact he was secretly a very cruel character.

He forced Lady Lily to have sex with him every single night Even when he was home late from boozing in the local inn, greyhound racing or womanising, he would wake her up and make her do it, which she did not enjoy at all. In the daytime he liked her to wear the finest gowns he had given her, adorn herself with sparkling jewels and have her maid dress her hair in a fancy style. "See my darling, beautiful wife," he would say proudly to his low-life drinking mates. But at night he would rip her nightgown of delicate, white lace and say, "What the fuck d'you think you're *for*? Give me a son and heir or it'll be the worse for you." What could possibly be worse than this? She thought.

On the night in question, (see chapter one) he had been out drinking, betting and chasing skirt. When he mounted the stone stairs to her turret bedchamber, there was no sign of his wife – only her best Spanish leather high-heels and silk stockings lying untidily on the carpet and her stays and gold-trimmed green silk gown flung across the bed. There was no sign of Lily anywhere.

"Where the fuck is my wife?" he demanded of the lady's maid, Annie.

"I do not know, my lord," she answered with a curtsey, "But the young footman says he was looking out the window and he saw her go off with some gypsies."

Lord William was purple-faced with anger. "Well, he's fired and you're fired and the gate-keeper is fired," he shouted. "Now, you imbecile, (spelt imber-seal!), go and tell the groom to saddle the white palfrey so that I can go and find my lady wife."

"My lord, if you have fired me, I don't have to obey your command. And I must say that I don't blame that poor, lovely lady for running away from you. You can huff and puff and go red in the face as much as you like, but if I don't work for you no longer, I refuse to do your bidding."

So he hit her hard in the face, threw her on the bed, tore off her bloomers and raped her. (This resulted, nine months later, in the birth of another MALE bastard . . . but that is another story).

After this brutal act, milord ran down the stone steps again and went to the stables himself to wake the lad and bid him to saddle the white horse at once.

Annie was not the 'imber-seal' she had been called by the boss. Although she was all shook up on account of being hit and raped, she helped herself to all milady's lovely clothes and packed them into a carpet-bag along with all the jewels she could find.

[To be continued].

THIRTY-EIGHT

Reassured somewhat after my visit to the vicarage, I slept much better than I had done the previous night and felt equal to anything that Monday might throw at us.

Suzy had told me that she was temporarily in charge of the Child-Care department at the council because her boss had saved up her holiday allowance so that she could visit her sister in New Zealand. She said that it was in my favour that I was a teacher who had been CRB checked and that there was no good reason why Roxy should be removed into Care at present if I was willing to continue caring for her as a friend; this on the condition that it was not too stressful for me, especially in view of Fearghal's impending visit the following day – in addition to my being in the early months of pregnancy and carrying on with at least three part-time jobs: estate agency, journalism and instrumental teaching. I had assured her that I could – and would – cope.

"Then I shall support you in this," she'd said. "But it's unofficial at the moment. The family liaison police officer will probably come to see you first thing in the morning. That child is extremely vulnerable and what she told you about the father's intention to set up a sex-slave business will be their first priority for investigation."

"I'm sure it will," I had agreed.

I had shown Suzy the first pages of Roxy's story, commenting on how her whole attitude to men had been twisted by her father's treatment of both her and her mother, saying how shocked and shaken I was that such things could happen.

"Oh, believe me, I've come across even worse in my time," she'd said, "such as rape, both incestuous and otherwise, leading to pregnancy and or imprisonment, not to mention STDs and HIV.

I shuddered. "A loving physical relationship is wonderful," I'd observed. "But, conversely, there is a hideous, repellent and thoroughly *evil* aspect to certain sexual behaviour. That child will be damaged for life, I very much fear. Now I must get back to her. Thank you so much for all of that."

"Just let me know how things go, won't you? So good to have met you at last. I'll make an official visit very soon." She had handed me a small card. "Here are my home and work numbers and email addresses."

*

Sadie Colson, the Police Family Liaison Officer, arrived soon after nine thirty on the following morning. I was glad that she came on her own, feeling her to be more approachable than Donna Bale, who had received the rough edge of my tongue. I started by apologising for my outburst of three days ago. "It's just that human feelings and instinctive behaviour don't seem to count any longer, these days," I remarked.

"No," she agreed, "I'm afraid everything has to be done by the book these days. Time was when the word 'appropriate' meant something totally different; it would never have been applied to human relationships back then."

"So I'm forgiven for my language then?"

"Well . . . I would forgive you. Being a mother myself, I know where you're coming from. I'm not sure about my colleague: she's very much the career-girl; says kids are an alien species to her.

However, to get down to the reason I'm here: I had a word with Social Services who say they're short-staffed at the moment and feel it's in Roxy's best interests to stay here with you at present. Someone will probably call later in the week. Now, DCI Bale told me that your fiancé is due to arrive very soon. I'd like a few details about him. Is he going to be living here, for a start?"

"Yes, he arrives tomorrow. I was going to ask you about that. I have to drive to Bristol Airport to pick him up. Should I take Roxy with me or ask someone to look after her here?"

"There's no reason why she shouldn't go with you, if she feels up to it. She might like the ride; she's used to travelling, after all. Now for a few details." She had a ballpoint pen poised above a notebook. "Your fiance's name?"

"Fearghal Gabriel – no relation," I joked, carefully omitting his former title. I noted that she had written 'Mr'. (*Oh, please, please don't Google his name,* I prayed)

"Address?"

" Well, it will be here from tomorrow, but hitherto it has been Inishcoll, Derrybeg, Oughterard , Co. Galway, Eire." I spelled out some of the words as she wrote.

"Lovely part of the world," she commented. "We went there on holiday when the kids were younger. Luckily, we took loads of books and jigsaws because it rained practically *all* the time."

I groaned sympathetically. "I was *much* luckier: I spent the whole of August there and only got a real soaking once." *(Oh, that day of blessed memory!)*

"And what is his occupation?"

"He's an artist now, but was once a Classics teacher," I added quickly.

"So he'll have CRB clearance, then?"

I nodded. "Or whatever the Irish or EU equivalent is."

"Okay; that seems to be in order. We just have to make sure that he's a suitable person to be around a vulnerable girl like Roxy."

"Oh, absolutely!" I assured her, relieved that it seemed unlikely that they would require further information. Even though I had been 'economical with the truth', I had not lied.

"I had a little chat with Roxy when you were talking to Donna Bale. She told me how kind you were: 'the only person I could run to', she said."

"That trust is really important to me," I said. "Poor child, so cruelly maltreated by her father and let down by her mother. I guess the woman is too frightened of that villain to attempt to rescue her daughter. Let's hope he gets caught and banged up for several years."

"The police will do their best," she said. "Unfortunately, the lawyers will do their best as well. Real, dyed-in-the-wool criminals can slither out of our clutches on some technicality. But I must keep quiet on that subject. The Press can play their part in the breakdown of justice, as well." She looked at me with a wry expression.

"Don't worry: I'm not *that* kind of a journalist," I smiled. "If I were, I would use my art to ensure that public fury was thoroughly stirred up towards men who exploit and humiliate women."

Sadie nodded, then looked at her watch. "I have to be somewhere else five minutes ago. Anything you want to ask me?"

"Oh yes – about the doctor. Have I prejudiced the case by arranging for my own doctor to examine and treat Roxy? She'll need her stitches out eventually."

"Only the large city police stations have a permanent doctor. DCI Bale came from one of those. As long as Dr Grant is willing to testify in court, she can continue to treat Roxy. You did right to preserve the forensic evidence."

When we went back into the kitchen, Roxy was hard at work on the final episode of her story. Sadie had read the first two chapters while I was making her coffee, and had commented, "very revealing – and quite amusing, too, in places. And she's quite an artist as well," she had added with a smile.

"Oh yes, there's real talent there; I feel this is helping to take her mind off her horrible ordeal, so I'm encouraging her all I can."

*

Roxy's Story

CHAPTER THREE

The young earl mounted the gentle white mare (who was actually the lady Lily's own horse, Matilda), and clattered over the cobblestones and through the castle gate. Once on the grassy lane, he dug his sharp golden spurs into the poor horse's flanks and made her gallop along, jumping hedges and ditches where the brambles reached out to tear at her legs. Although it was a wild night, the moon lit the way through a large wood where the bare branches of the trees nearly unseated the rider. At last they reached the edge of the wood and emerged into an open field, where William saw his lady wife alighting from a gypsy caravan, helped down by a wise old woman called Lavendi. Lily was very frightened when she beheld her cruel husband and shrank into the coloured woollen shawl, looking to her companion for protection.

"And what the devil do you think you are doing, you stupid bitch?" he asked in a rough, cruel voice.

"I have run away to live with the Gypsies," she answered in her clear, pretty voice.

"Well, I've come to fetch you home to your comfortable goose-feather bed with the smooth linen sheets that you love so much. Get on the horse, NOW!"

"I shall not," said she, bravely. "I care nothing for the goose-feather bed. I intend to sleep here with these good people."

"But what about your silken gowns, your Spanish leather shoes and your sparkling jewels? You stand here in this cold field in only your shift . . . and your lily-white feet look to be cold as ice. And what about your beloved husband, your new-wedded lord?"

"I care nothing for any of those; less than nothing for you, my lord, for you are the very cruellest and most evil of men. I shall stay forever with these good Gypsy folk and my baby will be brought up as one of them."

"But our baby will be a boy. He will be heir to my castle, my lands and all my fortune. You shall not take him away."

"The baby is a girl. This good woman's granddaughter, who is called Roxy, told me so." (They had no other way of telling back in those far-off days because antenatal scans had not yet been invented).

"How could she fucking-well know?" shouted Lord William, red with rage.

"She has 'the sight', Lily answered.

"Pah! Absolute crap!" quoth he.

"Nevertheless, be you gone now, husband," said Lily boldly. "You will never see me again, for I shall never return to you and my former miserable life."

At this, some of the Gypsy men stood forward to threaten the earl with stout clubs and cudgels so he hastened away, cursing and swearing.

On his way back through the wood a large and hungry wolf leapt at him and unseated him from the gentle Matilda who returned to the camp alone. Seeing blood-stains on the mare's flank, Roxy said: "Lady Lily, your husband is no more. A wild beast has killed him and eaten him."

"God be praised!" they all said. "The world is well rid of him."

In due course the baby girl was born. She grew up to be beautiful and good. Her hair was as red as fire and her skin as white as snow. Lily called her Madeleine and she grew up as good as gold. You would never have known that her father was such an evil man for there was never a trace of him in her nature.

That is the end of my story, but one day I shall write another about the baby when she grows up.

*

On a separate sheet of paper, her colourful illustration shows Lily on one side of the page, holding a red-haired baby; the white horse turns her back on a skull and a heap of bloodied bones under a large tree in the forest and returns to the camp. The mare has a 'think' bubble coming out of her head with the caption 'Serv him rite; he got what he dizzervd.'

*

"Do you think you really will write what is called a sequel to your story?" I asked my promising little author.

"I guess every story leads to another story," she said, nodding her head wisely. "Everyone who reads the end of a story must wonder: did they *really* live happily ever after? They can't have been happy all the time. What about divorce? And how do ladies know that their husbands won't beat them after their happy wedding day? Or go after other women? After all, Lily found that her charming, handsome husband didn't care whether she was happy or not. He just thought that giving her a lot of stuff would be enough. He didn't *really* love her, did he?"

"Clearly not," I agreed, impressed with her perception. "Yes, I guess there's another story there already taking shape in your imagination. You have talent, Roxy,-- a gift – not only of being able to draw and paint so well, but as a story-teller too. So don't stop, will you? One thing, though: I think you'll change your ideas about men when you meet Fearghal tomorrow. He is a true gentleman – by which I mean gentle man. We shall be married before the baby is born and I know he will always be a gentle, faithful and loving husband and a kind and responsible father. I can be absolutely sure of it."

THIRTY-NINE

"IT'LL BE A BIT OF A SQUASH IN THE CAR ON THE WAY back," I told Roxy on the morning of Fearghal's arrival. There'll be Fearghal and his luggage as well as you, me and Penn."

She suggested that she should share the trunk space with the dog but I advised against it on account of her stitches. I added one or two plump cushions to the back passenger seat to ensure her comfort and, at her request, gave her a silk scarf to cover her head, 'in case my Dad is watching out for me'.

"Honey," I said, "I don't think he will be looking for you when he realises that the police will be looking for *him*."

She sat in the front passenger seat on the way to the airport and was quite chatty, amusingly so at times.

"So you and Fearghal, do you have sex? I guess you must do if you're pregnant."

I laughed at this, more amused than offended. "That's a very personal question, Roxy – but you could be right."

"Well, is he *definitely* the father?

"Of course he is. I guess you've been watching too much 'Eastenders', if you ask such a question."

She giggled. "All the babies born on there seem to have someone else's dad."

"They're probably all related to each other in ways they don't realise," I said. "Maybe they should bring the 'Corrie' crowd down from Manchester to London to introduce some new blood."

She giggled again. "They would carry on just the same anyway, I expect."

After a short silence, she started again. "Maddie, did you tell Fearghal that my Dad and his mate had sex with me?"

"Roxy, honey," I spoke rather too sharply. "They did not '*have sex*' with you: they *raped* you. Yes, I told him on the phone why you are living with me – but not any details – so he'll be expecting to meet you."

"Are you very excited, Maddie?"

"Very much so," I assured her, "Though with all that has been happening I haven't had much time to think about it till now. The 'butterflies' are doing their fluttering right now, all right."

"Do you think he's having butterflies as well?"

"I wonder. I guess he does. We haven't seen each other for weeks and weeks and he's coming to a strange country as well."

"Did you think it was a strange country when you arrived here from America?"

"I did," I answered. "We speak the same language but, all the same, it's a very different country. However, I do love it, after all this time."

I told her how I had come on my own on the eve of my eighteenth birthday from Dublin where my mother and I were visiting with my Irish grandmother, Moira, to find my English grandmother, Cecilia. I promised I would read her some of Cecilia's memoir one day. She would soon find out that my own origins were every bit as dubious as those of some of the characters in *Eastenders!*

*

I was lucky enough to find a parking place very close to the main entrance at the airport. Leaving Roxy cocooned in a blanket on the back seat with plenty to occupy her in the way of writing and drawing materials and telling Penn to guard both her and the car, I made my way to the greeting area to find that Fearghal's plane was on schedule, joining the small crowd waiting at the barrier for the arriving passengers. Some held notices bearing the names of businesses or tour companies. I exchanged smiles with one or two of them and waited, with the butterflies doing their fluttering, my heart beating at twice its normal speed. The baby intermittently joined in the general physical disturbance.

"You are about to meet your father," I told her, silently, suddenly nervous that Fearghal would take one look at us and regret his decision to leave the priesthood, his country and all his former life. I thought of Cecilia's accounts of meeting – or being met by – my grandfather, her beloved Bruno, at the rail station. Clearly she had shared only the excitement, not the misgivings. Or was it that air-travel seems more serious and momentous than arrival by train?

The first arrivals began to appear. Ridiculously, I found that I had forgotten what Fearghal looked like. What would he be wearing? I wondered; not his clerical garb, I imagined. I myself would be instantly recognisable by my hair. Also, I had done nothing to disguise my pregnancy under my open raincoat, whereas at home I hid my condition under loose tunic tops.

At last, a tall man wearing a long, black overcoat appeared at the back of the emerging line, his eyes searching the waiting group behind the barrier. He did look somewhat clerical, even though there was no 'dog-collar' about his neck. When he spotted me, his face lit up in a way which told me that nothing had changed. He rushed through the barrier, flung down his bags and took me in his arms.

"Maddie, my Madeleine," he said into my hair and, placing his hand on the small mound of my belly, he added, "And hello to you in there, whoever you may be."

"Hello Daddy," I answered in a baby voice on our daughter's behalf.

When we had finished our rapturous greeting, I said, "I don't know about you, darling, but I could use a coffee or a cup of tea before we drive home. There's a cafeteria over there; it would give me a chance to explain more fully about our unexpected house-guest."

"Yes, fine all right," he concurred. "I was intrigued by the little you told me."

"I'm afraid you'll be horribly shocked, rather than intrigued," I warned. "I'll be brief because I don't want to leave her in the car too long."

He was indeed appalled when I told him of Roxy's arrival at my door the previous week and what she had told me.

"How utterly shocking!" he exclaimed, his eyes wide with the horror of it. "I know, in theory, that some depraved individuals are capable of such offences, but oh! I'm shaken to the core to hear of such a thing so close to home. The poor child couldn't have run to a better person than you for help."

"Well, just act normally and say nothing about it unless she raises the subject – which I don't think she will. We shall show her how sweet and loving human relationships can – and *should* – be."

Roxy was asleep when we reached the car, cuddled into the blankets and cushions on the back seat with Penn resting his chin on the back headrest, as if guarding her. At our approach he turned round excitedly, impatient to be let out and greet Fearghal. Roxy sat up and rubbed her eyes and stretched her arms. Fearghal opened the door and said simply, "Hi Roxy, good to meet you. I'm Fearghal." Rather than offer a formal handshake, he held up his hand and invited a 'high five' which set just the right tone for the start of the easy relationship that ensued.

Fearghal's small amount of luggage was stowed in the available space and we set off on the long journey home.

"The countryside gets more interesting when we run out of motorway on the far side of Exeter," I promised, pointing out a glimpse of the Bristol Channel with Wales visible beyond. The afternoon light was already beginning to fade.

"Better this way," I commented. "Driving into the setting sun can be a real trial late in the day at this time of year."

When we eventually reached Foxgloves, we stepped into a kitchen full of the savoury aroma of a casserole I had left in the slow oven of the Rayburn before our departure for Bristol.

"Oh how wonderful that smells!" said Fearghal. "All we had on the plane, as an apology for lunch, was a none-too-fresh bread-roll containing a wafer of rubber ham and half a lettuce leaf."

"You need to tell the stewardess you're a vegetarian: you get better food."

*

After an early evening meal, Roxy went into the Music room to watch television and I showed Fearghal her story. He was full of admiration for both her imagination and her illustrations and smiled several times as he read the narrative.

"This is excellent therapy after her ordeal," he observed. "What a good idea on your part!"

"I'm able to teach her by correcting the spelling and suggesting new words here and there. For the most part I've left it unexpurgated, as you see. Some of the dialogue will need cleaning up if it is ever published. At present it's a rather charming mixture of traditional story-telling and rough language: the heroine all sweet, pretty delicacy, the villain the epitome of the cruel, selfish male, clearly based on the author's own father. I hope that in her next story she will introduce a handsome, courteous prince character, inspired by you, my darling."

"I'll do my best to be a worthy role-model for that character," he promised. "Now . . . we have several matters to discuss while we're alone . . . a future to plan. Also, there is another thing which has been on my mind: something to do with what my mother told you. You said we could only discuss it face to face."

I knew what was coming and clenched my fists by my side, otherwise trying to appear relaxed. This was something I felt reluctant to talk about.

"After I told her I was expecting your baby, thinking I was playing my trump card, she delivered her own by telling me that the ...er...girl who had accused you of ... um ... sexual misconduct had given birth to a baby and that, according to the girl's mother, there was irrefutable DNA proof that the child was yours."

Hard though I tried not to show my emotion, my eyes brimmed with tears; I felt one or two escape and run down my cheeks. He came to me quickly and took me in his arms.

"My love, there can be no such proof. Such an encounter never happened – however much the girl invited it. Mother would go to any lengths to put doubt in your mind. You never questioned it when I first told you about it. I beg you not to doubt me now, my darling."

"I believe and trust you absolutely," I declared. "Sorry to be so emotional; blame my condition."

"I'm sad to say this about my own mother, but she is a possessive and manipulative woman. She is not likely to forgive you for 'leading me astray'. She made life difficult for my poor father towards the end of his life and drove him, not only into the arms of another woman, but to take his own life. I blame her for that tragedy, truly I do."

"Do you feel you've escaped her clutches now you've come over here?" I asked.

“I surely hope and pray that I have,” he said. “I promise to keep you and her grandchild out of her reach. I fear she will never accept that I can give up *her* ambition for me in favour of another woman.”

“I always wondered what it felt like – to be ‘the other woman’.” I laughed to lighten the mood, though I was little comforted by his words. Underlying his promises there was an element of foreboding in my mind. Would she accept defeat and leave it at that . . . or would she fight to the death?

*

That night, like the last one we had spent together in Ireland, was more about mutual comfort and reassurance than a steamy love-scene to celebrate our reunion. We were both tired; he from the journey that would irrevocably change his life; I from the long drive to and from Bristol and from the emotions stirred up, both by our long-awaited reunion and by the events of the past few days since Roxy’s arrival. Fearghal and I simply sank into the comfort of the soft bed, lay in a close embrace and slept like babies.

At around eight o’clock the following morning there was a knock at the bedroom door.

“Yes?” I murmured sleepily.

“It’s Roxy; I’ve brought you a cup of tea. Can I come in?”

“Yes, please do,” I answered. “What a very kind thought.”

The door opened and in bounded Penn, giving me a cursory greeting and going to the far side of the bed to bid good morning to Fearghal who reached out a sleepy hand to pat him.

“Yes, I really am here,” he told the dog. “I haven’t disappeared in the night.”

Roxy followed, carrying a small tray from which she delivered a mug of tea to me and then took the rest of the contents round to Fearghal’s bedside cabinet.

"I didn't know if you like milk and sugar," she said to him, "so I brought those separately in case I got it wrong."

"Thank you so much," he said politely, to which I added, "Roxy, you're a real honey to be so thoughtful."

"Well, I didn't hear you about as usual, so I thought it would be a treat for you both."

"Oh, it is, it is," I said. "I can't think when I was last treated to tea in bed. It must have been in my grandmother's time. We'll get up as soon as we've drunk it. Do get yourself some breakfast; you know where everything is."

It was barely light outside but the day was quiet and the weather forecast had promised sun later. We sat up in bed companionably, sipping our tea and discussing our future plans, after which we got up, showered and dressed. After a breakfast of porridge, toast and coffee, we added warm outer clothing and I took my future husband for a tour of 'the estate'. He seemed much taken with his new home and surroundings. As we came to the dell in which the ashes of Cecilia and Bruno had been scattered, a shaft of sunlight illuminated St Elowen's Well. We lowered our joined hands into the water and Fearghal said, "I remember so clearly Cecilia's description of this well. You know, my darling, I think we should name our daughter Elowen."

I was delighted. "I already call her that in my heart. Are you sure you don't want to call her after one of your family, though?"

"My mother, for instance?" he suggested. "Perish the thought," he scoffed. "Perhaps her second name could be Jane after my favourite aunt, my father's sister?" That would annoy Mother: they could not stand each other.

"Elowen Jane . . . that sounds lovely. Or – Elowen Jane Cecilia Gabriel; how about that?"

"Perfectly well-balanced and elegant," he agreed. "Such a special babe should have at least three Christian names."

"Non-PC, honey. You have to say 'given names' or 'forenames' in these days of religious diversity. You might offend one of another faith – or none."

"I stand corrected," he replied. "You have to be so careful in these times of free speech."

"Indeed. Free speech can become *costly* speech if you say the wrong thing," I warned, and we laughed comfortably.

After lunch we took Penn and walked in fitful sunshine along the cliff path and back through the village, taking a detour up the lane to the common and paying a brief visit to the piece of bare ground where the gypsies usually camped. There was no sign of any vans, just a few wheel marks and a certain amount of detritus swept against the hedge by the prevailing wind. Penn had a good sniff round the place where I had first seen him on that spring day just three seasons ago.

"It seems like years and years since I was here the day that I first met this wonderful guy," I told Fearghal, indicating Pendragon. "So much has happened to change my life in those few months."

"I hope you feel that the change has been for the better," he said.

"What do *you* think?" I asked, laughing and kissing the hand I held.

FORTY

THE EVENTS OF THE FOLLOWING FEW WEEKS CAN BEST be summed up in my early Christmas letter to Bridie and family.

December 2013

My dear Bridie, Declan, Grainne, Colm and all,
I'm sending my Christmas greetings and news update early this year because there's so much going on at present and Christmas itself is going to be more eventful than ever before, and I want to make it all special for my little family.

Our wedding – civil ceremony – is to take place two days before Christmas, Monday, 23rd, with a blessing in Porthwenna (Anglican) Church on Friday, 27th. Both occasions are, of necessity, going to be very quiet affairs with only a few friends and relations at both Registry Office and church. You would all be more than welcome to attend, though I think it would not be at all convenient for you at that time of year. However, maybe we can do more celebrating together at the Big Birthday and family reunion next August? I'm so looking forward to that great event and to introducing Fearghal to you all. Also of course my little 'passenger', who appears to be in good health and spirits and is full of energy, thank God. Are you really sure you can put up with us all in Oirbsean Lodge?

I am still acting in loco parentis to Roxy, about whom I told you in my last email. She may eventually be reunited with her own mother and little brother, especially when the former hears that her evil husband is now in custody awaiting trial for rape / incest / domestic violence and conspiracy to procure and enslave young refugee girls for sexual purposes. Unfortunately, his partner-in-crime has not yet been apprehended and may well be still in the neighbourhood, which is a worrying thought indeed. When it comes to the trial, Roxy will have to testify by video-link, which will be a real ordeal for her, poor child.

She has asked to be my bridesmaid in both ceremonies, but I've explained that it really isn't that kind of a wedding. However, we can compromise and she can wear a pretty dress and be my flower-girl and carry the wedding rings – Best Woman, so to speak!

TR has been conspicuous by his absence, thank goodness. I think he must have gone back to London and abandoned the idea of buying a house round here. I haven't heard a word since his email apology after his assault, which I ignored. As a result of his not being seen in the area, there has been little fodder for the gossip-mongers since the dramatic headlines in the local paper after my 'change of heart' was discovered. It seems that a gossip column starved of either fact or fiction soon fizzles out like the proverbial damp squib!

Fearghal and I are now firm friends with James, the Anglican priest, and his wife, Suzy. They have been very supportive, both about our 'conversion' and forthcoming nuptials and about Roxy's presence in our home. The Church of England services are not so very different from the Catholic rites – just very far from the aggressively Protestant attitudes of the Church of Ireland. It is easier for me than for Fearghal, I guess: The difference lies in the dogma . . . which is the reason we had to change denomination. I don't think that he feels like an outcast. Our discussions with James have helped him a great deal, I'm sure. Celibacy is imposed upon the priesthood as a discipline, not a law. It seems to be all about the dirty business of SEX ... which leads to all sorts of fascinating philosophical discussions. Things will change, we are assured. Priests will one day be allowed to marry and procreate, James thinks – but not soon enough for us, it seems!

Anyway, enough of our concerns. How are you all? I so often take imaginary walks round the house, garden and surrounding countryside and remember my lovely month in Killogan. I can't wait to come back next year.

I look forward to hearing all your news and wish each one of you a blissfully happy Christmas and the best of health, enjoyment and prosperity in the New Year. It will be a year of milestones: Fearghal will be forty and a father; you, Bridie, will be eighty; there's half-a lifetime between you, a mere heartbeat in the context of eternity! I hope you are willing to assume what would have been Cecilia's role: that of great-grandmother to our infant daughter?

Fondest love to you all, and kind regards from Fearghal,

Maddie

FORTY-ONE

OUR FULL AND FRANK DISCUSSIONS WITH JAMES, sometimes with Suzy present, helped both Fearghal and me to come to terms with our adjustment to a change of faith. He found that their own close and easy relationship helped him to see a clerical marriage as a force for good in the community. I found I was able to voice some of the thoughts that Fearghal admitted had occurred to him as he sought to justify his denial of his vow of chastity. After a few such sessions, one evening I felt bold enough to speak of the conclusions I had reached regarding that subject.

"Look," I began, "from childhood I never really questioned the faith into which I was born – not until I fell in love with Fearghal; then I was forced to dispute many aspects of it. It seems to me that S-E-X is the great taboo here. In the whole history of the Christian Church, the dogma, the pronouncements, the laws have all been drawn up, mainly, if not entirely, by *men*, all of whom have come into the world by the same route, namely sexual reproduction. Is this not the natural order? Is this not what the Creator himself designed? All except for one, apparently. We are taught to venerate his holy mother because he was conceived *without spot of sin*; in other words, without SEX. WHY? God was made man, but not in the usual way, my friends. Virginity is purity, therefore no other woman can become a mother without becoming impure and besmirched. Consider Candlemas, the feast of the Purification.

No priest is fit to administer the sacrament if he has had sexual relations with a woman. In all my thirty years as a Catholic, no one has ever bothered to explain this. We are just expected to accept and believe what the superiors of the Church have decreed over centuries and never ask the question: WHY?"

I looked directly at James. "Even in your church you recite in the creed, 'I believe in Jesus Christ our Lord ... born of the Virgin Mary'. Now, how can anyone believe in Virgin birth? Virgin *conception* might be physically and biologically possible but how could a woman give birth to a seven or eight pound baby and still be *virgo in tacta* in that sense? So we are professing to believe in a myth or a metaphor and, in so doing, are denying not only Christ's essential humanity but the joy and delight of human love."

I paused and looked from one to the other.

"Wow!" exclaimed James. "That was quite a spiel of refutation."

Fearghal merely looked somewhat bemused. I had not treated him to such a discourse previously. I drew a piece of paper out of my pocket.

"Furthermore . . . though this may be a *non sequitur*, when I looked this subject up online, I came across this definition, which I copied here: 'Sexual Reproduction,' I read, 'is the root of organisation and semiosis which began to evolve together once Nature had produced a species in which a brood benefits from two parents; thus, with the twofold contribution of nurture and support, the offspring prove able to survive and thrive . . .et cetera, et cetera'. I am probably going off at a tangent here, so I'll soon be finished. I'm just trying to assert that sex is not just an unsavoury and regrettable accident but, rather, part of the grand design. As an expression of love and mutual pleasure it cements the parental relationship, thus providing security and stability for the offspring."

Fearghal smiled. "I'm reminded of the passage in your grandmother's memoir in which she says that the nearest they came to sex education at her girls' school was the reproduction of the brussels sprout."

James joined in the laughter. "No, really? Oh those days of innocence! Now they tell children as young as five about LGBTs."

There was a light knock on the door and Suzy appeared, carrying a tray with a bottle of wine and four glasses.

"Did I miss something amusing?" she asked. "I heard the laughter."

"Thanks for the wine, darling. Yes, you just missed a rather splendid dissertation by Maddie."

"Oh, shame!" she said. "I'll stay now in case I miss any more pearls of wisdom."

"Actually, I'm nearly done," I said. "I'd just like to point out that Jesus Christ's main message to the world was not about sex; it was about peace and harmony and love in its widest sense: love and respect for the whole of Creation – not a bit of nookie in a dark corner." There was laughter all round. "Okay, that's it now. Someone else's turn."

"I'm not sure that either Fearghal or I can follow that," James said, smiling. "Let's leave it for another occasion and enjoy our wine and a few more laughs."

*

On the few occasions Fearghal and I went out together in the evening, we left Penn at home to 'guard' Roxy. She was happy either to watch television or work on her stories and illustrations. On this occasion she was tackling a Math workbook I had bought for her, calling it her 'homework'.

When we got home, however, the poor girl was in a very distressed state. We found her huddled, surrounded by cushions under the harpsichord, crying bitterly.

"Why, Roxy, whatever is wrong?" I asked, alarmed.

"Oh, it was terrible; I was so scared," she sobbed. "That man came knocking at the door and banging on the windows, calling for Miss Manning. I'm sure it was him."

"What man?" I prompted. "Who are you talking about?"

"The man who . . . you know . . . my Dad's mate, Vince." There was a fresh outburst of sobbing.

I pulled her up from the floor and guided her to the sofa to sit close beside me. Fearghal sat opposite us in an armchair, a look of grave concern on his face.

"Now tell us, Roxy, exactly what happened. The shutters were closed, the curtains were drawn. Nobody could possibly have seen you. What did Pendragon do?"

"He went crazy, barking and growling really loudly. The man went right round the house banging on doors and windows and shouting your name."

"But how did you know who it was?"

"By his voice – his hateful, rough voice. I can never forget that – *never*."

"Oh darling, how horrible for you!" I hugged her to me closely. "And you say he was calling my name, not yours?"

"Yes, yours. Oh Maddie, suppose you'd been here without Fearghal and opened the door to him."

"You would have told me who it was, Roxy, and I wouldn't have opened the door. Now I'm going to make you a hot drink and phone the police; then I guess it's your bedtime. You've had a nasty fright but you're safe and sound and no one can hurt you. Things always seem worse in the dark: tomorrow, in the daylight it won't seem so bad."

"I'll make us all hot chocolate," said Fearghal, "while you call the police station."

"This is all very worrying," Fearghal said as we snuggled down in bed. "What d'you think that guy wanted with you?"

"The duty sergeant I spoke to reckons that he may have found out where Roxy is," I replied. "His motive may well have been to silence her as a witness. There is an alert out for his arrest on other charges, though of course Sergeant Pencarrow was not at liberty to discuss it further. They are all on the lookout, knowing that he has been in the area and can't be far away."

"I'm so worried about *you*, my darling. All this anxiety and stress cannot be good for you. Are you sure that there is not somewhere safer that Roxy could go? How about Mistletoe in St Ives?"

"I'm sure she would help if I asked her to," I said, "but Roxy feels safe with us. I can't let her out of our care now. That monster will never dare try again. He must know that he has to lie low after this. The police guy said that they are about to put 'Wanted' notices around, offering a reward for information leading to his arrest."

"Well, we mustn't leave her alone again in the evening. Next time James and Suzy must come to us."

"Agreed. One of us must always be here with her, night and day. Tonight's traumatic episode could undo all the recovery of the past weeks. She was making such good progress."

FORTY-TWO

DECEMBER CAME AND CHRISTMAS LOOMED, WHICH meant our wedding was imminent. As only a small celebration was planned, there were not many invitations to send. There were, however, invitations to design and send for Bridie's eightieth birthday event the following August. I had promised to oversee this and we had decided that they should be sent out with Christmas and New Year greetings.

I enlisted Roxy's help with this task. She was delighted to help and was keen to design the cards herself.

"Will I be invited too?" she asked. "I've never been to a big party like that."

"Of course you will," I replied."If you're still with us then."

Her face fell. "Does that mean that you may send me away? I want to stay with you and Fearghal and Pendragon forever and ever."

"But, honey, your mother may one day come and find you and claim you back again. Wouldn't you want that more than anything?"

"She didn't keep her promise and come back for me before it was too late, did she?"

"But Roxy, both she and your little brother were in mortal danger. She dared not to come back."

"Still, even if she did come back now, I'd want to stay with you. I love it here and even if I do have to go to school after Christmas, I still want to stay."

“What will be will be,” I said. “She has first claim on you. We shall work something out and, if at all possible, we’ll still take you to Ireland in the summer.”

That seemed to mollify her; the worry lines on her forehead disappeared and we started work on the invitations.

Fearghal and I drew up a list of friends and relations who should be invited to the blessing of our marriage.

“Your mother should be invited, even if she refuses to come,” I insisted.

“She *would* refuse. I know that without a shadow of doubt.”

“Even so: it’s only polite to tell her – and show we mean to go ahead, whatever.”

He was reluctant. “Okay, I suppose so,” he said. “She can only refuse – or simply fail to reply. She’ll be in serious denial about the whole thing.”

*

“Who’s Mrs A. Gabriel?” Roxy asked as she addressed envelopes. “Is Fearghal married already – or divorced?”

“It’s his mother,” I explained. “She’s very much against this wedding, but I feel she should know that it *is* going to happen.”

Roxy drew in her breath. “Don’t send it, Maddie. Don’t tell her. It’ll mean nothing but trouble.”

“Oh, she’ll just ignore it,” I said. “There’s nothing she can do to stop it and she knows that already.”

As it turned out, I was wrong, and Roxy’s gut-feeling – or clairvoyance – was right.

It was while we were at this task during that first week of December that we received a visit from Sadie, the Community Support officer. The message she brought was both a surprise and an immense relief.

"I thought you should know, before you hear it on the regional news," she said, "Vincent Colworthy has been arrested, charged and is in police custody in Truro. Obviously I can't tell you too much but he has been charged with rape and other serious crimes. I know how worried you've been since that night-time episode. Now you'll be free to go out and about, Roxy, without looking over your shoulder. You'll be able to start school in January, too. As always, it will be ages before the actual trial begins but there is enough evidence to see him remanded in custody by the Magistrates' Court. Meanwhile, both he and Dooley will be safely out of the way until they are sentenced to a term in prison. There'll be no question of bail."

We both sighed with huge relief at hearing this news.

"When the time comes, Roxy, you will be a key witness, but there will be other girls as well. None of you will have to appear in person: it will all take place on video-link."

I thanked Sadie profusely for imparting this welcome news before we saw it – or even missed it – on television.

As soon as the door had closed behind the police officer, Roxy threw her arms around me.

"This means I can go out and walk around, Maddie. I don't have to hide in the car every time we go to the shops. I don't have to worry anymore that that *horrible* man will kidnap me."

Sure enough, it was there on the regional news that evening: *Vincent Colworthy arrested for rape and imprisonment of immigrant girls being used as sex-slaves. An under-cover police investigation had busted him. He was referred to as a notorious sexual predator. The girls in question, all under-age, had been confined in a freezing cold terrace house and were undernourished and scantily clad when found.*

As we all sat together on the sofa watching this report, Roxy's relief turned to agony as she was forced to relive her own ordeal.

“Don’t cry, honey,” I consoled her. “If you hadn’t run away when you did, you could have been one of those girls. But *you* are free and *they* are free and will be looked after. Those two villains will learn how it is to be imprisoned themselves. They will be put away for a very long time, I guess. Do you have any regrets that one of them is your father?”

“For what he did to me – and my mum – he deserves to be locked up for ever. They should drop the key into the nearest drain. I shall never, *ever*, forgive him. Fearghal is my father now.”

“I think that calls for a group hug,” Fearghal said and we both put our arms around Roxy and each other.

FORTY-THREE

IT WAS JUST A WEEK BEFORE OUR CIVIL WEDDING THAT the call came. Invitations had been sent; acceptances were arriving with Christmas cards, though never a word from Mrs Gabriel. Roxy and I were decorating the cottage and trimming the Christmas tree, an occupation that gave her touching delight. I was on the small step ladder fixing the angel to the top of the tree so that a light shone through her or his diaphanous robe, when the phone rang with what seemed to me afterwards to be a shriller and more demanding tone than usual.

"Answer that, would you please, Roxy," I said. "Put it on speaker so that I can hear who it is."

She picked up the phone and clicked the two buttons. "Hello?"

"Is that Miss Manning?" I heard a frenzied voice say. "I need to speak with Father Gabriel urgently."

Roxy's eyes widened and she looked at me questioningly. "No, it's Roxy, her foster-daughter. Would you hold the line, please and I'll pass you to Maddie while I fetch Fearghal."

"Madeleine Manning here," I announced. "May I ask who's calling?"

"I am Mrs Mary-Claire Quinlan, a close friend of Fr Gabriel's mother; I'm afraid I have bad news for him."

"I'll hand you over right away," I said as Fearghal came into the room. "Mary-Claire Quinlan for you," I said to him, passing him the handset.

"Mrs Quinlan? Fearghal Gabriel speaking."

The woman's voice was loud and clear, her words tumbling out in an urgent stream.

"Oh, Fr Gabriel I'm afraid I have very bad news for you. Your dear mother has been taken very ill with the cancer and is not expected to live more than a few days. She is asking for you, Father, and really needs her only son to be with her at the end. I'm sorry to be the bearer of such bad news but can I have your assurance that you will come right away?"

"I will, of course," Fearghal said. "As soon as arrangements can be made. Is she in hospital?"

"She *was* in hospital," the voice said, "but they could do no more for her and she wants to die in her own home. As a former nurse, I'm looking after her here and the cancer-care nurses visit every day. Oh Father, I'm so relieved to have contacted you. I'll pick you up from Shannon Airport myself if you tell me what time your plane gets in."

The voice was less anxious now that Mrs Quinlan felt she had been able to grant her friend's dying wish.

The conversation ended and Fearghal disconnected. "You heard all that?" he asked. I nodded.

"So you understand that I have to go?"

"You must, of course," I agreed, stifling the uncharitable thought that it would have been better if his mother had actually already died. "She *is* your mother. You cannot refuse. We'd better book you on a flight to Ireland tomorrow."

*

"Why did that woman call Fearghal 'Father'?" Roxy asked as soon as Fearghal had left the room. "He won't be a father till the baby's born . . . although I do think of him as *my* father now, but she wouldn't know that."

This was a question I could have done without having to answer, my mind being in turmoil at this turn of events. Had

I not confidently told Roxy that there was nothing that Mrs Gabriel could do to stop our marriage? She could not have timed her illness and impending death better, I thought, trying to rid my imagination of that death-bed scene: the chalk-white face framed with its bright golden curls lying on a pillow of rose-budded cotton with matching duvet; the dutiful son looking down in grieving regret and immense guilt and taking her small hand, delicate as a butterfly's wings in his firm, capable fingers.

But Roxy's question still hung in the air. "Listen, Roxy dear," I said. "Can I explain all that another time? There are things to see to right now."

"Okay," she said reluctantly, "but you were wrong when you said that there was nothing his ma could do to stop the marriage, weren't you?"

"Not only a clairvoyant but a thought-reader!" I commented. "Just what *I* was thinking. She will see this sudden illness as God's will," I added.

"Well, *I* see it as God's will that you and Fearghal should be married and that baby Elowen should have a properly married mum and dad," she said sagely. "Fearghal's mum may upset your plans for a while by dying now, but the wedding *will* happen before the baby is born."

"I just hope you're right, you wise little bird. Now I must go and look up flights to Shannon online."

*

Later, as Fearghal and I lay in bed, there seemed already to be a distance between us. For the rest of the day, after the phone call, he had seemed withdrawn and bleak. Any conversation that took place had been concerned with practical arrangements for his journey. Now, I could only imagine how he must feel about his mother's illness and inevitable demise. I tried to take him in my arms but he seemed unresponsive to my touch and my words of comfort. Feeling rejected, for the first time ever in our relationship, I was close to tears and needed to sob my heart out, but did not want to burden him further with my own distress. He would be struggling with guilt, I knew, of which our impending marriage was the cause, so it was not my right to make demands.

As soon as I sensed, by the evenness of his breathing, that he was asleep, I gave in to the urgency of my tears until I fell into a fitful and uneasy sleep myself. I had set the alarm for an early start so that I could help him with the departure that I so dreaded.

FORTY-FOUR

We had decided that, as Fearghal had to leave so early for the airport, he should be taken by taxi. I was having to dig deep into my savings anyway to fund his travel, fares being considerably more expensive during the Christmas holiday season. Joe Burrows at Polburran garage had been very helpful the previous afternoon, saying that his son, Grant, was just back from his first term at university and would be glad of the work.

As the car was turning in the drive, Fearghal and I clung together for a moment and he kissed away the tears that ran down my cheeks

"Don't cry, my darling girl." he consoled. "I shall be back, whatever happens. I'm so sorry it will upset all our plans for next week. Just be here for me when I return – and look after our little one." He laid a tender hand on my 'bump'. He hugged Roxy and patted Penn's head. "Look after them for me," he said to them both.

"We will, won't we, Dragon?" Roxy told him. "Maddie has been there for us all this time."

There was a disturbing finality about the sight of the Mercedes' tail-lights disappearing up the lane. I felt at one with all the women of old who wept at seeing their husbands and lovers riding away to war. Would that be the last embrace, the last kiss? The 'enemy' in this case was not one who would threaten his physical life, but one who, alive or dead, sought to control his mind and spirit – his conscience.

Roxy took me by the hand. "Come on in, Maddie, out of the cold. I'll make you some hot chocolate like you did for me when I was in trouble. I'm here for you now like you were on that day. Come on; you too, Penn."

She led me to the rocking chair beside the Rayburn and Penn stood beside me and licked the tears from my cheeks with his great tongue, his whiskery face tickling my skin.

I let Roxy cosset me for a while, which she seemed to enjoy, then gathered myself together and rose from the chair.

"Thank you so much, honey," I said. "Now I suggest that we go and put our clothes on and have our breakfast. After that I have some phone calls to make because our wedding plans will be all up the creek and I must let people know."

"But Fearghal will be back for Christmas, won't he?" she asked anxiously. "Your first Christmas together – *our* first Christmas together: we *can't* miss that."

"It will all depend on Fearghal's mother, sweetheart. Perhaps she'll rally when she sees her son." My heart sank. *This could go on for weeks,* I thought.

*

Somehow I struggled through that long, long day, helped to some degree by an unexpected visit from Mistletoe in the afternoon.

"As soon as I read your email," she said breathlessly as she came through the door, "I knew I must come and offer you my condolence and moral support, you poor darling."

"Oh thank you. You're such a dear friend. I'm so, so worried, Misty: I've heard nothing from Fearghal and he must have arrived hours ago. He promised to phone me as soon as he'd seen his mother. He's not answering his cell phone and I don't feel I can call the house."

"Well, I should do so if you don't hear from him by this evening. It can't be good for you to have this stress – this *dis*tress – in your condition."

"You're right; I'll do that," I promised. "I can't bear another night without sleep."

Roxy offered to make tea. "I promised Fearghal that Penn and I would look after Maddie," she told Mistletoe.

"And so she has, already," I put in quickly. "I wonder how long it will last," I added, jokingly.

"It will last until Fearghal comes home," she said firmly. "*I'm* the boss now; are you cool with that?"

"Cool," I agreed, laughing. "You're a great kid, Roxy and a great comfort to me."

"You've done wonders with that girl," Mistletoe said, as soon as Roxy was out of earshot." It's good to see her repaying you."

Soon Roxy returned, carrying a tray with three cups of tea – a fairly good imitation of rats' piss, my grandmother would have remarked. I winked at Mistletoe. More acceptable were the accompanying slices of malt loaf, spread thickly with butter.

"Good comfort food," Mistletoe remarked.

"That's what I thought," said Roxy. "Actually, it's my favourite. I saw some crumpets in the fridge but I thought they'd take too long."

"We'll keep those for an even colder day and toast them by the fire," I said.

As Mistletoe was leaving, she said, "Look, if things go wrong at Christmas and Fearghal still isn't home, you and Roxy are welcome to come and spend the day with me. Alex will be there for lunch with a rather nice girl he has paired up with, I had high hopes for him and you, as you know . . .

but Chrissie is okay – she'll do, anyway. Oh, and Pendragon is welcome too, of course."

"Bless you," I said, "but I have a strong feeling that he'll get back in time." I spoke much more confidently than I felt.

"Maddie dear, give him a call on the landline ASAP. You've been checking your mobile, your watch or the clock every two minutes since I arrived here."

"Have I really?" I asked, fully aware that I had been acting like a teenager, obsessively looking at my cell phone.

"*Really*," she confirmed, grinning "*Do* it! 'Bye all,"

*

Fearghal's cell went only to message so, my heart pounding, I finally screwed up the courage to dial his mother's number, feeling sure that either Fearghal himself or Mrs. Quinlan would answer. The phone was picked up after about five rings – a woman's voice, not Fearghal's, to my great disappointment.

"Yes?"

"Oh hello; this is Madeleine Manning. Am I speaking to Mrs Quinlan?"

"No, you're speaking to Mrs Aisling Gabriel." The voice bore no trace of weakness or illness. I was completely dumbfounded.

"I ... erm ... I—"

"I suppose you want to speak to my son," she interrupted. "Well that is not at all possible because he has been arrested and is in the custody of the Limerick Gardai."

"Bb...but...

"But you thought I was on my deathbed and you thought there was nothing I could do to stop him from committing the ultimate sin. So I arranged for the guards to be here as soon as he arrived. You'd do well to cancel all those wedding plans, Miss."

I tried to protest but my voice would produce nothing but a feeble squeak. Eventually I managed to lower it, taking a deep breath to support it. "But I don't understand …" I started.

She interrupted again: "Oh, I think you understand all right, madam. Did you really think that I would surrender my son to a scheming strumpet like you?"

Anger overcame my intense shock and my pathetic squeak became a roar. Roxy's eyes widened with horror as she sat at my feet, listening to both sides of the conversation.

"However, you saw fit to trick your *own son* by a monstrous lie and deliver him into the hands of a much worse enemy. How could you risk his good name and his reputation by such a cruel trick?"

"At least I shall keep him out of the clutches of the scarlet woman – the heinous harlot," she shouted back. "He'll be tried and sent to prison, which will stop that woman from having him, and that wretched Mrs Corcoran, from demanding money from me all the time."

"If that is so, you should have told the police straight away. You would do well to remind yourself that I am to be the mother of your son's *child* – your own grandchild – and all you can do is insult me."

"I do not *need* this conversation: it's unnatural and disgusting," she screamed, and there was a firm click as she disconnected the phone.

Roxy reached up and laid a gentle hand on my 'bump'. "Poor baby, Elowen," she murmured. "Your horrible granny doesn't want you. But *we* will make it up to you and we'll get your daddy home for you."

Anger and shock got the better of me and I collapsed in a heap on the hearthrug beside Roxy and cried my heart out.

Roxy put her arms around me and Penn got up and sat as close as he could to both of us. There we sat – a tight-knit little family group – though without its most beloved member.

One day in the future, Roxy was to describe that scene to Fearghal himself: "Wow! I've never heard an adult cry the way Maddie did that day; not even my Ma when Dad beat her up. She couldn't speak for hours after your witchy mother told her what she'd done."

At last I pulled myself together and got to my feet.

"I'm sorry, Roxy. You didn't need to witness my complete disintegration. You heard that whole conversation, didn't you?"

"Every single word," she answered. "Fearghal's mother is an evil witch. How did *he* turn out so well?"

"I guess he took after his father. By all accounts he was a good man and a good dad; but he took his own life when Fearghal was about your age. Probably couldn't stand her any longer. Now Roxy, I must think what to do next – or at least get my head around it."

"But why is Fearghal locked up? I don't understand what he has done wrong. The police can't just lock people up for nothing."

"There was no need for me to tell you this before, but I can see that there is now," I explained. "The reason that he and I met at all was that he was sent away from the parish where he was a priest because a teenage girl said that he had made her pregnant."

"You mean he *raped* her? *Fearghal*?

"No, honey; she is lying, of course. Her boyfriend is most likely the father of her baby, but she had a crush on Fearghal and would have *liked* it to be true. Her mother didn't go to the police but she complained to Fearghal's boss, the bishop, who sent him away to Connemara for two years. When the baby was born, the mother asked Fearghal's mum for money – you heard that? No doubt it was a form of blackmail. You know what that means don't you?"

Roxy nodded. "Oh yes. It means threatening to tell everybody unless you give them money. It happens on telly sometimes, even in *Eastenders*."

"Actually, Roxy, telling you all this has given me an idea, "I said. "Fearghal will need a lawyer. Bridie, in Ireland, has a daughter called Grainne whose husband, Colm, is a barrister; so I'm going to call him right now and ask what can be done. He should be home from work by now. The police can't hold Fearghal for very long without charging him, and if there's no proof, they haven't got a case."

FORTY-FIVE

I THOUGHT I HAD CRIED MYSELF DRY, BUT WHEN I HEARD Grainne's voice, I lost control of my own again, managing only to announce myself in a tearful voice.

"Why, Maddie, whatever is after happening to you over there?" she asked. "Oh, don't tell me it's the baby."

To my surprise, Roxy gently took the phone from me.

"This is Roxy, speaking, Miss Grainne. I guess Maddie has told you about me. No, it's not the baby, but Maddie is very, very upset – we all are, even Pendragon. We badly need the help of your husband: it's about Fearghal."

"Holy Mother! Whatever has happened to him? He hasn't met with an accident, please God?"

"No, he's all right. It's just that the police in Ireland have arrested him. Please may I speak with your husband now and I'll tell him. Maddie is really too upset to speak."

"I'll get him right away, so, Roxy." We heard her shout, "Colm, can you please come here as quick as you can?"

Roxy introduced herself in a high, clear voice as 'Maddie's foster-daughter' and gave a meticulous account of the evening's nightmare news, of my conversation with Fearghal's mother and of the accusations against him. "Maddie has only just explained to me about this," she said. "It's something to do with S-E-X, and it's lies, *all lies*" she finished, indignantly.

"Tell Maddie that I shall make enquiries right away," I heard Colm say. "I may well go to Limerick myself in a day or two. I shall phone her back in an hour or so."

*

"Oh Maddie," Roxy said, turning to me with a devastated expression. "I had such a bad feeling about this when you said you were sending that invitation to Fearghal's mum. I should have stopped you. It's all my fault."

"How could you have stopped me?" I asked, pulling her towards me. "I felt it was the right thing to do at the time. How could a mother do such a thing to her child – have him publicly disgraced as a sexual predator rather than see him renounce his priestly vows to marry the woman he loves?"

"But if he didn't do what she said, he can't be guilty, can he? I'm old enough to understand if you explain it to me, Maddie, and remember: I'm the only one who can look after you now so you must tell me everything."

"Bless you, dear Roxy. Just wait while I phone Fr James. After that we must keep the phone free for Colm's call."

It was Suzy who answered my call. I was pretty sure that I was in command of my voice before dialling the number.

"Why, Maddie – is everything okay? You don't sound too good."

"No, I'm afraid disaster has struck, at the whim of a vengeful matriarch. I need to speak to James, please."

"Sorry, he's out at the moment, my dear. Old Mrs Pencarrow is on her deathbed – not for the first time, I have to add. She rather makes a habit of it."

"Look Suzy, I'll tell you anyway – and probably I should have told you this before. For some reason, our media is not interested in news from the Republic of Ireland, whereas US news often takes precedence over our own." I recounted the events of the afternoon and my exchange with 'the vengeful matriarch'.

"Oh great heavens!" Suzy exclaimed when I finished. "How could any mother do *that?*"

"My thoughts exactly. To think that the honourable estate of matrimony is the greater of two evils in that woman's mind! Look, Suzy, I'm very aware that I should have told you about Fearghal's suspension when you first asked questions about his suitability to be around a child. I have never doubted his word that the girl's boyfriend was responsible for her pregnancy. There has been so much scandal over paedophilia in the Irish Church. It's so unfair that, once accused, a priest is deemed guilty, even if proved innocent. I should get off the phone now in case there's a call from Colm."

"Of course, my dear, I'll tell James as soon as he comes in. He may well want to come round later, though I know he hasn't finished his sermon for tomorrow."

FORTY-SIX

"I'M SO SORRY I COULDN'T SPEAK TO YOU MYSELF", I apologised to Colm when he phoned about two hours later.

"My dear Maddie, I so understand – and young Roxy was an excellent intermediary. You have a real gem there, Maddie. Now, let me tell you what my inquiries have turned up. I've spoken to both Fearghal himself and the Gardai. First and foremost, Fearghal sends you all his love and asks you not to worry about him because he is quietly confident that the case against him will collapse before it comes to Court."

I heaved a sigh of relief. "How long will all this take?" I asked breathlessly.

"Time," he said grimly. "The DPP in their wisdom – or otherwise – have decided to take action and charge him. People in this country have been baying for the blood of paedophile priests for some while now, mainly those who interfere with young boys. But an under-age girl and a resulting pregnancy – indeed, an actual birth . . . Yes, they have decided to make an example of Fearghal, so he has been arrested and charged and will probably be remanded in custody until his case comes to Court next year."

"Oh God help us!" I cried, breaking down in tears yet again.

"Calm yourself, Maddie. I am on the case. Everything will hinge on DNA tests. As long as they prove that Fearghal cannot possibly be the father of the child, there will be no case to answer. This will be done as soon as possible, I assure you. Christmas and New Year will delay matters for a while and your wedding will have to be postponed. But rest assured – it will happen."

"Should I come over, d'you think, Colm? He will need someone to visit him, poor love. I'm quite sure his wretched mother will not be at all welcome. God! I could kill her for what she's done."

"'Tis no more than she deserves. But take my advice and stay put for the moment. You've the baby to think of – and Roxy too. Sure, who'd look after her? Bide your time till after Christmas is done and let's see what happens. I'd only a short talk with Fearghal on the phone, so I shall go down to Limerick tomorrow and try to hasten things on. I shall also make noises about suing the Corcoran girl's family for defamation of character after she has proved to be a liar – and the mother a blackmailer."

"Oh Colm," I sobbed. "I'm so grateful for your help. You must tell me how much we shall owe you for taking on this case. I have savings –a legacy from my grandmother. Also I have a cottage to sell, if necessary. Fearghal himself has yet to get established over here."

"Whisht, Maddie; you're *family.* As the Big Chief in my firm, I answer to nobody except the accountant and the tax-man. Now, see if you can relax a little until I get back from Limerick. Let the admirable Roxy wait on you and cosset you. Just believe that everything will be all right before the baby is born. I'll phone as soon as I get back – promise."

*

Just as I rang off there was a knock at the door. Roxy ran to open it and I heard James greet her.

"Hey Roxy, I've come to see Maddie. I hear you've been a tower of strength."

"I'm doing my best in these difficult circumstances," she answered. "Come in, please, Father. She's in the kitchen."

"The Reverend is here to see you," she announced quaintly as they came through the door. Neither James nor I could suppress a grin.

"My dear Maddie," he said as he came across the room. "No, don't get up." he greeted me with a kiss on each cheek. "Roxy, could you give us a moment, please?"

"Let her stay," I begged. "She knows exactly what's going on here."

Roxy nodded vigorously. "I am speechless, to be honest. How could God let this happen to a good man?"

"How indeed!" James agreed, once again trying to stifle a smile. Roxy's voracious reading of literary classics had resulted in her dialogue containing a quite old-fashioned turn of phrase sometimes.

"Can I offer you something to drink?" she asked. "And let me relieve you of your greatcoat."

"No drink, thank you, Roxy, I've just had supper." He shrugged off his overcoat and sat in the cane chair at the opposite end of the Rayburn. "Now then, Maddie; Suzy told me the gist of it but please recap on what has happened to Fearghal."

James's reassuring presence enabled me to give an account of the day's events without breaking down again. I finished by telling him of Colm's recent phone call.

"Good man," he commented. "Fearghal will be okay with someone like that on his case. Really, the sooner the Pope and the Vatican Council permit their priests to have normal human relationships, the fewer cases of sexual scandal there will be."

At this, Roxy, who had been quietly occupied with her artwork at the table, piped up, "I couldn't agree more! When I'm older I shall start a campaign and march about with a banner saying 'Marriage for Catholic Priests!'"

"I can just picture you doing that," James laughed.

FORTY-SEVEN

THERE WAS NOTHING FOR IT ON THE THURSDAY, TWO days later, but to go to work as usual. The day had to be endured somehow. I would probably hear nothing from Colm until the day after his visit to Limerick. I left Roxy with an English Comprehension exercise and a Math workbook, as always, telling her to open the door to no-one. I had no qualms about leaving her in Pendragon's guardianship. He was very protective of his humans and would be more than a deterrent to any ill-intentioned caller. I was never out of the house for a full working day.

Pandora Bennett, who had left me alone since the end of my 'romance' with TR, sprang out of her chair when she saw me come into the Gazette office.

"Did you *see* in the Sunday papers what TR is up to now?" she asked excitedly.

"I was busy with other things at the weekend," I replied, "so no, I didn't read the paper thoroughly, if at all."

"It was all over the Mail and the Mirror," she continued. "He's having an affair with a WAG – you know that well-fit, dark guy who plays for Chelsea, Robbie someone, his wife – gorgeous blonde, ex-model." She looked at me expectantly.

"Bully for him," I commented nonchalantly, "So you've got plenty to write about again?"

"You bet I have! I shall say how utterly devastated and heartbroken you are at the news."

"Don't feed his vanity, Pandora; he doesn't need it. And it wouldn't be true, either – or doesn't that matter anymore?"

"Well, let's just say that a gossip-columnist has to *bend* the truth now and then."

"Maybe – but not tie it in knots and bows," I laughed for the first time in four days.

"Talking of truth, Maddie, and not wanting to be personal of course, do I detect that there might be a little bun in the oven? Could that be why you were looking a tad peaky a few weeks ago?"

She was looking speculatively at my middle. I had dressed carelessly that morning, pulling on an extra jumper for warmth. I looked down at the small, round bump revealed by the welt. "Oh *that's* what it is, Pandora! I was wondering what on earth it could be. Thanks for pointing it out."

She laughed delightedly. "Now for the real truth: is it TR's?"

"Emphatically not!" I expostulated. "My fiancé is the father and if you suggest otherwise, I shall kill you slowly and painfully. You had your sport when TR and I had our brief dalliance, so please leave it – before real damage is done."

"Okay, okay, we'll say no more. I'm dying to meet this mysterious fiancé of yours. I've not set eyes on him but I've heard tell that he's a bit of a dish, if not as great a dish as TR himself. My source says he has a Scottish accent."

"Western Isles," I said, deliberately vague, yet not untruthful. "No doubt you'll get to meet him one day. Now I must get on with some work."

I sat down and typed up the details of the only property on the market likely to grab attention at this time of year: a pretty, cosy-looking cottage sure to appeal to some well-off visitor or local who wanted to indulge his wife or girlfriend for Christmas, TR maybe, though a bijou residence was not his style . . . and he could hardly give such a present to someone else's wife!

Anyway, my contribution made it sound irresistible and the accompanying photograph had been taken in rare December sunlight, which emphasised its SW facing position.

I rushed home at lunchtime, though I knew that there could be no news yet. The practical Roxy had taken soup and crusty bread out of the freezer. One was in the pan and the other in the oven of the Rayburn.

"Any calls?" I asked.

"Yes, Mistletoe rang," she answered. "I told her you'd heard from Colm who is doing his best for Fearghal and said you'd tell her all about it at the Carol Concert on Sunday."

"Good girl. I don't want to say too much on the phone or email, just in case there are gossip spies listening in."

Her eyes widened. "Do you really think there *could* be? Is his predicament that interesting?"

"It might be . . . to a certain gossip columnist, in view of my past involvement with TR. And remember, any scandal of a sexual nature connected to Fearghal could jeopardise your foster-care here."

"That's a new word to me – jeopardise. I can tell what it means – but can you write it down for me, please?"

I wrote it on a scrap of paper. "Is it anything to do with *leo-pards*?" she asked.

I smiled. "No, I don't think it is, though you might be in je-o-pardy if there were a le-o-pard about. Well spotted!"

We both laughed at my unintentional pun.

"Nevertheless," she said, "I shall use it in my next story. I suppose poor Fearghal is in jeopardy from the police?"

After we had eaten, we went over the work I had set for Roxy to do in the morning. I had consulted my colleagues at school as to the level that might be expected of her when she started in the spring term, and it appeared that she was more than adequate, especially in English. She seemed determined to read and learn from every book in the house, from the classics to my grandmother's memoir. This last was of particular interest to her and she often brought it up for discussion, having noted how very different lifestyle and attitudes were in Cecilia's childhood in this same region of the country. I had read her some of the early chapters until she was sufficiently interested to continue reading it herself.

*

The phone rang just after six o'clock. I grabbed it on its first ring. It was Colm. I greeted him breathlessly.

"Maddie," he said, "I spent a long time with Fearghal himself this afternoon and quite a long time with the Gardai. Fearghal first: he's a grand guy altogether – I like him a lot, and he loves you to *bits*. He swears to you that the next time his mother sends for him from her deathbed he will not go running off back to Ireland. As you know, the girl who made the accusation against him had a massive crush on him and tried to tempt him in every way she could think of."

"I never asked him to explain," I said. "I just trusted him – even when his mother said there was proof."

"Well, *proof* they will have to provide – or the family will be in serious trouble with the law. I have persuaded the detective in charge to require mother, child and boyfriend to have DNA tests before the first Court hearing. Everything will depend on this; as long as there is no match to Fearghal, the girl will be considered to be an unfit witness and her mother will be accused of demanding money with menaces."

I heaved a huge sigh of relief. "So no case can possibly be brought against Fearghal?"

"Only if there were a match – and I know he is telling the truth when he says it would be impossible. I was present when he willingly allowed a saliva specimen to be collected. He was eager to provide the swab and he's more than eager to get back to you."

"Oh Colm, I can't thank you enough for going to Limerick today. Are you home now?"

"No, I'm staying overnight because I had to wait a bit to see the man in charge. I'll go back to Galway in the morning."

"Your visit must have been a great relief to Fearghal, too. Thank you so much."

"I was glad to do it, Maddie. He's a great guy and I look forward to meeting him again at the family reunion in August. By the way, you can expect a letter from him in a day or two. I took him pen, paper and a stamped envelope so that he could write to you while I went to talk to the garda in charge of his case."

"Oh, bless you for being so thoughtful, Colm. What a great idea! I can't wait to read it – I miss him so *much* – so does Roxy."

"Great kid, that. You'll be bringing her to the party, won't you? Bridie would want that. And, by the way, she sends her love and is devastated to hear what is going on."

"Bless her. Send kisses from me too. Yes, I do hope we can bring Roxy. It will depend on whether her mother turns up to claim her before then."

Roxy's face fell and tears gathered in her eyes. "Anyway," I went on, "I know she'll want to come, whatever happens." At this she beamed and nodded vigorously.

Colm promised to call again as soon as there was any further news and we said our goodbyes.

FORTY-EIGHT

Wed. Dec .18 2013

M*y darling beautiful girl,*

Colm has given me both opportunity and materials to write to you while he goes to see the officer in charge of my case.

I think of you every moment that I am awake in this grim cell and dream of you whenever I can get comfortable enough to sleep on the uncompromising 'bed'. It is so hard to be without you – a homesickness that knows no relief – except the hope that all this will be over soon. I miss your loving arms, your kisses, your humour and the presence of that little person safe inside you.

Thank you for sending the admirable Colm to me. What a good friend he is, to be sure – a man you could trust with your life – indeed, I have to do just that. He told me about Roxy taking charge of his phone call, bless her. I feel so guilty that I have brought all this anxiety upon you; so stupid for falling for my mother's wicked deception. If she can do such a thing to her own son, I shall have nothing more to do with her. She drove my father to take his own life; she might have driven her son the same way were it not for the sweet and tender love of his wonderful Madeleine. Forgive me, my dearest and keep our little one warm and safe. Pray for me always; love me forever.

With all the love in the world,

Your Fearghal.

PS Colm has just come back for this letter. He tells me that the Corcoran baby is going to have a DNA test and so shall I.

I devoured the contents of the letter twice and hugged it to my heart, tears of relief pouring from my eyes.

*

The following evening, Sunday, the Byrd Singers were to hold their annual Carol Service in St Breaca Church and, as well as singing, I had agreed to play the clarinet part in the accompaniment to John Rutter's *Shepherds' Pipe Carol*, so I did a little practice in the afternoon. Roxy had begged to come and I had arranged for her to sit with James and Suzy, using the ticket I had obtained for Fearghal.

How I mourned his absence that night. Only James, Suzy and Mistletoe knew the truth of his non-appearance; for everyone else, his mother's terminal illness was the explanation.

My close-fitting black dress revealed a contour that had not been apparent at previous performances. In the interval for mulled wine, mince-pies and general social exchange, there seemed to be a few glances at my abdominal area – or did I imagine them?

It was late when Roxy and I got in and there were two messages on the landline voicemail, the second from Colm. "I have great news for you: please phone me when you get in, however late you are. I'll still be up. I guess you're out partying."

With trembling fingers, I dialled his number.

"Colm, I'm sorry: I was at a Carol Service – not exactly partying."

"Maddie, Fearghal has been released. He'll be home for Christmas after all; I've booked him a flight from Shannon to Exeter tomorrow."

I was ecstatic; my knees turned to jelly and I sat down quickly.

"Oh Colm, how wonderful!"

"It seems that the girl Corcoran took fright at the DNA tests and confessed to her priest that she had lied at the insistence of her mother. He promised her that he could not and would not betray the confidence of the confessional but told her she had a duty to save a good man's reputation by making a full confession to the Gardai. They hurried through the confirmation of the DNA results and told Fearghal that he was free to go."

Tears of joy and relief coursed down my cheeks and my voice was nothing but a croak when I tried to speak.

"Colm, you've been so, so good to us. We shall never be able to thank you enough."

"Why wouldn't I do it, Maddie? You're *family.*"

"Not actually related by blood, as it turns out. However, will you and Grainne do us the honour of being godparents to our baby, please?"

"Strangely enough, Fearghal asked me that very same question. The answer is that we would be delighted to accept, particularly as we have never been blessed with children of our own."

*

It was still very dark when Roxy crept into bed beside me the next morning.

"I've been thinking," she said. "We should have a car to drive us to meet Fearghal this afternoon – not drive yourself.

Could we afford to do that? That way, you and Fearghal could sit on the back seat and cuddle and hold hands while I get to sit in front with Grant or Mr Burrows or whoever."

"Good thinking, you romantic little thing! I think 'we' *should* afford that luxury. I'll phone Joe Burrows just after eight. It's only six-thirty now, you early bird. Even Elowen isn't awake yet."

"Oh Maddie, I'm so excited that Fearghal is coming home – and in time for Christmas, too. I'll go and remind Penn, and bring you a nice cup of tea, shall I?"

"This should have been our wedding day," I said musingly. "Yes, a cup of strong tea would be very welcome, honey; then I must get up, shower, put on my best dress and make a lot of calls."

*

How shall I ever forget the meeting and greeting that afternoon and the joyful ride home in the Burrows's Mercedes? As Fearghal said, it was a homecoming like no other. We had agreed not to mention his erstwhile confinement until we got home. Gossip must not reach the ears of anyone in our neighbourhood. I had warned Roxy to ask no questions of Fearghal until it was just between the three of us behind closed doors, explaining that those accused of a crime may be pronounced 'not guilty', but are never *confirmed* to be innocent, which still leaves doubt in some minds; 'no smoke without fire' being a truism beloved of gossips. Careless talk could result in her being removed from our care, I warned. This was more than enough to keep her quiet. She sat in the front seat beside Grant Burrows, chatting away happily to him about anything (else) that came into her head.

Meanwhile, Fearghal and I sat as close as possible on the luxurious leather back seat, talking little but emitting sighs of relief and contentment and gazing at one another raptly every few seconds, unable to believe that the great ordeal was over at last.

It was almost dark when we arrived back at Foxgloves. I had left a light on in the kitchen and the room was warm and welcoming when we stepped inside, out of the chill of the east wind.

"Ah, *home*!" Fearghal breathed, taking me in his arms after an ecstatic welcome from Pendragon.

"Such a warm welcome," he went on. "At one low point I never thought to see it again."

"But you're here now and justice has been done," Roxy said, hugging us both. "And Maddie can't say anything because she's going to cry again. That's all she has done since you went away, Fearghal. I've hardly been able to get a word out of her."

Fearghal's arms tightened around me. I took a deep breath and said steadily, "Roxy, be a dear and let Penn in and then put the kettle on and some crumpets in the toaster, please."

"Right away, ma'am."

Penn came bounding in as Roxy opened the door and renewed his enthusiastic welcome of Fearghal. I had heard Roxy earnestly telling him before we left for the airport that we were going to fetch Fearghal home and that he must be a good boy and guard the house until we returned.

"The hired car is too posh for you," she had said to him. "However, when we go to Ireland you'll be allowed to come with us. You've been there before, haven't you? Maddie told me you were with her the first time she met Fearghal."

After tea and Fearghal's favourite supper of cottage pie with sautéed leeks, we were ready for an early night. It was then that Fearghal told me what a hard time he been given by one particular police guard.

"He was delighted to have a priest to torment," he said. "He was very anti-Catholic – anti-religion altogether. He forced me to read an article that he was going to contribute to a subversive magazine. It was headed THE REAL CHRISTMAS STORY and went on in bold, 'It's official: Gabriel *was* the Father!! A certain 'man of God', who happens to be called Gabriel, is in custody, accused of fathering a baby on an under-age virgin. Fr Gabriel is typical of the unacceptable face of the priesthood which the Church authorities have been trying to cover up for years. Our sons are not safe; our daughters are not safe ... etc, etc.'"

"Surely he cannot publish what should be confidential information before it comes to Court," I protested.

"That's what I said, but he pointed out that it was for an under-the-counter publication. When I'd read it, I had a sudden thought and asked him if he had suffered abuse by a priest himself. Whereupon he gave me a detailed and very disgusting account of his, indeed, having done so. I could only apologise profusely on behalf of the whole Church, but he dismissed my words contemptuously and was even more furious when I was found not guilty of the original charge against me. His last words as I left were, 'They'll get you in the end, you filthy paedo, even if you got away with it this time.'"

"You poor darling," I said. "To have all that hatred directed at you and have to bear the brunt of such a deep-seated mistrust of everything to do with religion. It's probably a good thing that he didn't know that you had climbed over the wall, so to speak."

We held each other close then and slept like babies, as the saying goes. *(Why? I have since found that babies don't necessarily sleep all that well. 'Like dogs' might be more accurate!)*.

*

The civil wedding had been rescheduled for the morning after Boxing Day (Stephen's Day, as it is known in Ireland), and was to be followed by the Blessing ceremony that same afternoon, as originally planned. Meanwhile, Mistletoe insisted that all four of us should spend Christmas Day with her.

"You won't be at all prepared to put on a traditional dinner with all that's been going on in your lives," she said on Christmas Eve. "Alex and his girl want to change their plans anyway and go to her parents in Dorset, so there'll be just ourselves here and mountains of food to eat. You just concentrate on the wedding tea on Friday: that's more than enough to be thinking about."

I accepted gratefully, being in too much of a daze to complete Christmas preparations of our own. Instead, we just shopped for a few basics and last minute presents. Roxy and I had already baked and frozen the scones and cakes for Friday's tea. They simply needed to be thawed, filled and decorated the previous day. Mrs Annie Watson had agreed to come in and serve tea as she had done at my grandmother's Memorial ceremony, eighteen months earlier.

PART THREE

FORTY-NINE

AND SO DAWNED AT LAST THE DAY THAT WE HAD hardly dared hope to see; and here I was, my pregnancy already apparent, putting on a dress that I had long ago bought for this occasion and adding a matching loose-fitting jacket with a flounced neckline which helped to disguise my condition discreetly. The colour was a flamboyant emerald green. People could say what they liked about green being an unlucky colour for a wedding, but I would point out that Fearghal and I had *had* our bad luck – more than most people knew – and that from now on it was 'happy ever after'. (Not that I'm naive enough to think that there are not bumps along the way in any marriage!). Those jagged mountain peaks of Fearghal's triptych had been scaled and crossed, and we were on the fertile plains of the far side – *together.*

Roxy came into the room just as I was fastening the jacket. She wore a dressing gown over white, lacy tights and green, patent leather shoes with kitten heels.

"Oh "Maddie," she said breathlessly. "You look so beautiful. That colour makes your eyes look even greener. Oh WOW! Can I put my dress on now and then will you do my hair in French braids?"

I took the dress I had made for her out of the wardrobe. We had chosen the material together: it had a white background with spots of the same green as my outfit, mixed with daffodil yellow. She stepped into it and turned her back so that I could fasten the back zipper, then twirled away so that the full skirt swung out, and struck a pretty pose in front of the full-length mirror.

"How do I look?" she asked.

"Like the very essence of spring," I answered. "Absolutely amazing! They'll all be looking at you instead of at me and Fearghal."

"Oh no, Maddie – *you* will be the focus of everyone's gaze; I'm only your attendant."

"Nevertheless and notwithstanding. . ." I began. "You look totally gorgeous, honey, and everybody will love you. I'll do your hair now to add the finishing touch."

Fearghal had taken Penn for a quick walk up the lane and returned just as Flora Bundy drove down with the flowers from the Garden Centre. (Actually, her name is Julie, but she likes to be known as Flora, for obvious reasons). Both Fearghal and she gasped when they saw Roxy and me.

"Oh, Mr Gabriel, what lovely ladies! Which one are you marrying, you lucky man?"

"The green one is my true bride," he said, his eyes shining with pride and admiration; "but the other beauty will delight some young man's heart one day, I know."

Roxy dimpled prettily and did another little pirouette to show off her dress. Flora clapped her hands and unpacked the contents of the box she had brought in. My small bouquet was of white roses and hellebores, framed with green, feathery fern; Roxy's flower-basket was filled with white rosebuds and green ferns and trailing ivy. There was a button-hole for Fearghal and, by my special request, a wide green and white ribbon for Pendragon with a bow mounted with an artificial white rose to fasten round his collar. In addition, there were two spare button-holes, "In case you've forgotten anyone," Flora said.

"Penn is Fearghal's Best Man," announced Roxy. "The trouble is, nobody told him about arranging a stag-night.

Actually, it's a blessing in disguise: Fearghal might have been wasted by today."

"You've been watching too many TV soaps, young lady." Flora said, laughing.

*

No sooner was Flora's car out of earshot than another car pulled up outside; one I didn't recognise. To my utter amazement, causing me to shriek with delight, out stepped my father, Dominic, and Colm O'Riordan.

"I know you said you were dispensing with the usual customs, Maddie love," Colm said, "but a girl needs her Da to give her away and Fearghal needs a Best Man – so we couldn't let this day pass without putting in an appearance. Tell me, is this delightful young lady the famous Roxy?"

Introductions were made and warm hugs were exchanged. I was nearly speechless with surprise and emotion, and tears welled into my eyes.

"Maddie!" Roxy said sternly, "DO NOT CRY! You'll ruin your makeup and your eyes will go all blotchy. *Honestly,*" she said to the two men, "Her hormones are all over the place at the moment; she's just so *emotional*. Tell her a joke or something."

"Okay," Colm said, laughing. "How many Sligo men does it take to milk a cow?"

"I really don't know," Roxy answered. "How many *does* it take?"

"T'irty two,"Colm said, in an exaggerated Irish accent.

"*Thirty two*?" questioned the willing stooge.

"That's what I said, all right: four to each udder and sixteen to lift the cow up and down."

We all laughed at the bizarre picture this conjured up, and my tears returned, unshed, to the well from whence they had sprung.

Fearghal came downstairs, looking extremely un-priest-like in a smart, mid-grey suit which I had bought, almost brand-new, in a charity shop some weeks before. The jacket revealed a sharp white shirt and an emerald green tie which I had made from the same material as that of my dress.

"I heard men's voices," he said, "and feared some rival had come to steal my lovely bride."

He greeted Colm with a warm man-hug and looked questioningly at Dominic.

"Uncle Dom," I said, "may I introduce my husband-to-be, Fearghal. Fearghal, meet my father. You know why I call him 'Uncle', but I shall call him Dad forever after, now."

They greeted one another warmly.

"You have done a very courageous thing, Fearghal," Dom said, "renouncing one lot of vows in favour of another. I do wish you both every possible happiness and am delighted to be here to witness your marriage." He turned to me. "Your mother would love to have been here but she has a houseful of family over from the US for Christmas. She sends much love and looks forward to seeing you all at Killogan in August."

As my father and Fearghal chatted, I kept one ear on their conversation and the other on what Roxy was saying to Colm.

"You don't look at all like your voice on the phone," she was saying earnestly.

"What does my voice look like then?"

"Well . . . I imagined you older, rather bald and much fatter."

He was very amused. "And what do you see in reality?"

"Well . . . much younger, quite slim and fit – and almost handsome, with a good head of hair."

"Flattery will get you a long way, young lady," he said, shaking with laughter. "You, my dear, are a girl of great character, have lovely, shiny hair and are *almost* pretty, with enchanting dimples. You will go far in life."

"I used to be rather quiet and sad, but Maddie has brought me out of my shell and has taught me a lot about life as well as improving my vocabulary."

She lowered her voice so that I had to concentrate hard to hear.

"Uncle Colm, maybe you can tell me this: was Maddie born on the wrong side of the blanket, as the saying goes?"

I saw Colm grip the back of a chair to stop himself shaking with mirth and waited, agog, for his answer.

"What books have you been reading, Roxy? I do assure you that she was born on the *right* side of the blanket – *deffo* – as you kids say. It's just that her father is her mother's *second* husband."

(*True now,* I thought, *but not at the time I was conceived*).

"O...kay," she said, doubtfully. "It's just strange that she called him Uncle Dom."

I looked at the clock. "The car will be here very soon," I announced. "Are we all ready to leave? We'll need coats, Roxy, and don't forget the loo."

"I'll take Fearghal in my car," Colm said, "and the bride, her father and Roxy can travel in the wedding car. Oh, and the other Best Man, Mr Pendragon, as well, I presume."

"You do realise, Uncle Colm," Roxy said, "that *I* am in charge of the rings. They will be in my flower basket, so I shall need you to give them to me before the proceedings."

"I'm cool with that, Roxy. I've got them safely at present but I'll see you have them safely in your pretty basket before we go in."

"I do wish grown-ups wouldn't try to be trendy and use teen-talk like 'cool' and 'sweet' and 'deffo'" Roxy whispered to me, after Fearghal and Colm had left the house. "He is a very agreeable man, however."

"Deffo," I said.

*

By four thirty or so that same afternoon, our small wedding group was assembled in the Music Room of Foxgloves, being refreshed with tea and champagne, sandwiches, scones and fancy cakes, Fearghal and I being married at last with the blessing of both State and Church: Anglican, at least, if not Roman Catholic. Well, Anglo-Catholic, anyway. My beloved husband looked as relaxed and happy as he had sounded as he made his vows before the registrar and our family and close friends.

I had time now to greet these special guests. There was Mistletoe, of course, looking resplendent in a predominantly blue tartan kaftan and knee-high blue suede boots with leather fringes falling from the welt. Although we had requested 'no presents, please' on the invitations, she had presented us with one of her marine artistic creations: a view of the rocky islands out to sea, visible from our bedroom window. She had also given Roxy a miniature seascape to hang in her bedroom.

I introduced Lizzie Penberthy to James and Suzy. "You won't have seen her in church," I said. "She lives in the next parish."

"Afraid I don't *do* church," Lizzie explained. "Result of being a vicar's daughter, maybe."

"Fair enough," James smiled. "Perhaps you had too much of it as a kid?"

"Too right we did! Actually, it was my grandmother, rather than my father. Three times to church every Sunday was hardly enough for her."

Lizzie's husband, Ross, and their son, Petroc, were also with us, and Petroc's girlfriend, Sophie, now his fiancée. They were to be married the following August, they told me.

"Do you think we'll be invited?" Roxy had whispered when she heard this.

"Don't get your hopes up, honey," I'd said. "It might be when we're in Ireland."

"Well then, I shan't mind missing it. I really, really must come to Ireland. So many people would be disappointed if I didn't . . . most of all me."

Sarah, my doctor, and her husband, Rob, both told me how glad they were to be sharing this happy day with us. Sarah said, "You look absolutely blooming, Maddie; but you've been through an awful lot of stress lately. Come for a check-up sooner than planned, will you? I'd like to look you over after all that." I agreed that I would make an appointment in the first week of the new year. She commented also on Roxy's progress and asked if I thought fostering might lead to adoption eventually. I answered that both Fearghal and I regarded her as very much part of the family but that it would depend upon whether Roxy's mother came to lay claim to her. The subject of our exchange was out of earshot at that moment, deep in conversation with my father. I hoped she was not questioning him as to the circumstances of my conception.

The sound of an empty wine-glass being struck with a spoon caused the buzz of conversation to cease. Colm had clearly appointed himself as Master of Ceremonies.

"Ladies and Gentlemen, please be seated, if you can find somewhere to perch. Fearghal, please claim your bride and her attendant and sit here." He indicated three chairs at one end of the room. "And now, pray silence for the bride's father, Mr Dominic Manning."

Dominic stood, facing us at the opposite end of the room.

"The opportunity to surprise my lovely daughter by turning up today to give her away was very much a last-minute thing, so I cannot do her justice in a well-prepared speech. Please excuse this omission and allow me to welcome you all here, old acquaintances and new, and to say how delighted I am to hand my beloved daughter into Fearghal's safe-keeping, care and devotion. Madeleine is my favourite – indeed my only – daughter and, needless to say, I would not part with her to any but the most deserving of her affection. In the very few hours since I met him this morning, I know instinctively that Fearghal is that worthy recipient of her love and trust. I ask you now to raise your glasses and drink the health of the beautiful bride, Madeleine, to her most admirable bridegroom, Fearghal, her sweet and pretty flower-girl, Roxanne . . . and to my future granddaughter yet to be born."

After the toast had been drunk, Colm called upon 'the lucky bridegroom' to reply on behalf of his bride.

Fearghal rose to his feet and, placing his hand affectionately on my shoulder, he began:

"On behalf of my treasured and beautiful bride, I would like to thank my esteemed father-in-law for his kind words and say how very grateful we are for his presence here today – and, indeed, that of my human Best Man, Colm. I say 'human' because we already had the handsome Pendragon expecting to fulfil that role." *(Laughter)*.

"As most of you will realise, I never imagined I would ever give such a speech – *ever*. I thought I was called to one direction in life – and I'm not talking pop-music here." *(More laughter)* "It was because of a chance encounter with this very special lady that my life took a very different turn. She might have landed on another island on that summer's morning, but she chose Inishcoll of all the islands of Lough Corrib. There is at least one for every day of the year, it is said. She and her handsome dog emerged from the dark shadow of the trees into the sunlit green of the grass clearing, as if to out-dazzle the sun itself. Waiting to be collected from Colm's mother-in-law, Bridie, who rescued it from the stone hermitage which was my erstwhile dwelling, is the painting which that arrival inspired. It is entitled 'Beyond the Purple Shadow'. I do not have the gift of clairvoyance as does our dear Roxy here, but the painting accurately represents the difficulties which I knew would lie ahead of us before this happiest of days could dawn. I am not naïf enough to believe that we have overcome everything that could possibly go wrong in life but, thank God, those daunting mountain peaks are behind us now as we look forward to many, many happy years together – till death us do part – and especially to the birth of our baby in a few months' time.

"There are more thank yous: talking of babies, our many thanks to Doctor Sarah for her care of mother and daughter-to-be. I am particularly grateful to James; not only for the blessing of our marriage this afternoon but for his acceptance of our situation and the way in which he has welcomed us into what we were brought up to regard as 'the rival camp'." *(Polite laughter)* "He and Suzy are such an inspiring team that I am more convinced than ever that marriage for the clergy is a good, positive thing. Celibacy means isolation and exclusion from real family life, and therefore a regrettable lack of understanding of the married state.

"Lastly – well, almost lastly – I must thank Mrs Annie Watson for presiding over this excellent tea. Applause is allowed at this point, but I still have someone else to mention." *(Applause)*

"I cannot finish without mentioning our dear Roxy, our provisional foster-daughter. She too came into Maddie's life by chance, seeking refuge in a time of need. She has more than repaid Maddie of late, providing support, comfort and practical help in recent troubles. May I thank you, Roxy, from the bottom of my heart and say how very lovely you look today. I ask all present to drink the health of Roxanne, my bride's lovely flower-girl, and wish her all the very best as she starts again at school in January." *(Cheers and shouts of 'Roxy!')*

Roxy beamed with pleasure and, holding out her full skirt, performed a balletic twirl, ending in a pretty curtsey to the assembled company as they raised their glasses to toast her.

Colm rose to his feet once again.

"As self-appointed Best Man… (human, that is) *(Laughter)*… it behoves me to say a few words at this point. First, let me introduce myself: my name is Colm O'Riordan and I come from Killogan in Co. Galway on the western shores of Lough Corrib and the eastern edge of Connemara. For those familiar with Maddie's convoluted family history, I must emphasise that I am not actually a relative – simply the husband of Grainne, her father's adoptive brother's half-sister . . . if you can work that one out." *(A long ripple of laughter went round the room)*

"What can I say?" Colm continued, looking around the room. "All round good guy, almost handsome, fit, successful and exceptionally clever – with a very credit-worthy golf handicap . . . But I'm not here to talk about myself; I'm meant to be paying tribute to Maddie's lucky bridegroom here. (*Gales of laughter punctuated his speech at this).*

"To tell you the truth," he went on, when it had subsided, "I met Fearghal for the first time only a few days ago, being able to help him over a legal matter when he returned to Ireland briefly. So alas, I cannot tell of a life-long friendship, nor can there be any jaw-dropping anecdotes about his wild adolescence or crazy student days. I do, however, fervently hope that we shall remain the best of friends for the rest of our days.

"Maddie is one of my favourite non-relations. The love and mutual respect that she and Fearghal share have carried them through all sorts of difficulties, and I know you will all join with me in wishing them a safe and trouble-free voyage as they journey together towards their own particular sunset." *(Cheers and applause all round)*

"But before you raise your glasses again, allow me, on Roxy's behalf, to thank Fearghal for his kind words to her. Not only does she look beautiful today, but she is to be commended for her commonsense and practicality in what turned out to be exceptional circumstances recently."*(Applause)*

"Now that was mercifully short, wasn't it? Only the bridegroom knew that he would have to give a speech today . . . so that's why his was the longest – and quite right, too. Now please be upstanding and drink the health once again of Madeleine, Fearghal, their adopted daughter, Roxanne, and their, as-yet, unborn daughter, who, I am told, is to be named Elowen, after her grandfather's tragically stillborn twin sister. In our toast let us not forget the other beloved member of the family, that aristocrat of the canine world, the noble and impressively named, Pendragon."

(The toast was drunk amidst cheering and applause in which Penn joined in with some loud barking)

Departing from customary wedding etiquette, *I* stood.

"I know it is not usually done for the bride to speak. For some reason all that has to be said is left to the male members of the ceremony. But then, haven't they always made the rules for what women should and should not do? *(Laughter)* Nevertheless," *(I paused, looked at Roxy and smiled)* "I feel compelled to depart from tradition – very briefly, you'll be pleased to hear – and say how wonderful it is to have had you all with us today to witness our union – our re-union – and share in a day we shall never forget.

"Colm's mention of Elowen brought the spirit of my beloved grandmother, Cecilia, very close. I'm sure that Dominic, my father, will not be embarrassed when I remind him that he and his sister were conceived in this very room and born of a love that was to survive troubles and separations – worse than those that Fearghal and I have had to undergo. It may sound spooky, but I have felt Cecilia around us all day. May we finish with a toast to Absent Friends – in particular the eternal Cecilia; to Bruno, my grandfather, her life-long love, and of course, my own mother, Frances. Let me also mention my uncle Declan, his mother, Bridie, and her daughters, Grainne, Rosie and Connie." I raised my glass. "To Cecilia and Absent Friends."

FIFTY-ONE

MY FATHER INVITED US TO DINE WITH THEM AT THE Trevelyan Arms. "That was a bountiful tea," he said, "but I don't suppose you three have had much else to eat today?

Except for our two surprise visitors, all the other guests had left and we were all in the kitchen, helping Annie to wash and dry the plates, cups and glasses.

"That sounds like a very good idea to me," Annie said, "if you don't mind me saying so. I'm quite happy to stay here and mind Roxy and watch TV– unless she's invited too, that is. It's not as if I've a husband to go home to, so I can easily stay."

"Actually, I'm quite tired after that wonderful day," Roxy yawned."I want to think all about it and I have an idea for a picture; I'd like to start on that. I never thought I'd refuse an invitation to dinner with two real gentlemen, but maybe there'll be another chance one day."

"Sure, and indeed there will, Roxy," Colm said. "You'll be dining in one of the poshest hotels in Ireland when you come over the water."

"What? Even posher than the Trevelyan Arms? Thank you, Uncle Colm – and, by the way, I don't mean *almost* handsome: I've changed my mind to really handsome... *deffo!*"

We all laughed, while Colm bowed low to Roxy in acknowledgement.

Fearghal and I gladly accepted the invitation. "It'll give us the chance to catch up on all the news," I said. "If only we'd known you were coming, we could have made arrangements for you to stay with one of our friends and family."

"We were fortunate that the hotel had a vacant twin room at this time of year, I guess" Colm said. "There are still quite a few Christmas guests staying. I made a provisional booking for three extra guests for dinner so I'll just call to say we're a party of four. Chef said he was glad to be shot of the Christmas menu and get back to normal, starting tonight."

*

We had a very pleasant, relaxed meal together, exchanging all the news from both sides of the family (clan). Life in Killogan had seemed to jog along as serenely as usual; while here at Foxgloves a succession of dramas had been played out. Dominic told us that he had spent Christmas in Ireland, not only to be with Bridie and Declan (Donal) but to continue the process of buying a house at the northern edge of the lough, which he and my mother, Frances, were renting at present.

"Wonderful!" I exclaimed, delighted. "So the clan will be concentrated in one area. Cecilia would be so pleased to know that her boys were in harmony again. I'd like to think that we could join you over there, but this place has such a strong claim. I feel that we are custodians of a house with a very special and particular history."

"You are, to be sure," said my father. "And speaking of that, before we leave in the morning, I should like to spend a few quiet moments with my parents in the foxglove grove."

"Alone?" I asked.

"No; with you, if you'll accompany me."

"Of course I will. I didn't throw my bouquet today, thinking that I would lay that and Roxy's flowers in the tree above Elowen's well."

"Add my buttonhole to that," Fearghal said, leaning over to give me a kiss.

"They will wither and perish," my father said musingly. "But they will be a worthy offering : an affirmation of a love born of those whose ashes are scattered there."

*

We said our good nights, expressed our thanks and drove home. Fearghal went in to fetch Annie while I turned the car so that I could drive her home.

"Roxy went to bed early," she said, "but she's done a wonderful picture of the wedding. You'll find it on the table when you go in. That girl will be a famous artist one day, I reckon. She was so taken up with it that she didn't even watch *Eastenders*."

"Wow!" I said. "It must be very special."

Sure enough, there it was on the table when I got home again: a picture of Fearghal and me standing in the west doorway of the ancient church. Roxy herself was at Fearghal's side, Pendragon sitting at mine; and the whole group was gathered around us, including James in his surplice and stole, with his arm around Suzy. Roxy had used oil pastels and the colours were faithfully reproduced; the architectural details accurately observed. It was better than any photograph. Fearghal came and stood next to me as I read a note from Roxy written on a piece of card.

Dear Maddie and Fearghal,
Thank you for an amazing day. This is for you with all my love. Please make colour copies tonight so that your dad can have one and Colm can have one to show Grawnya and Bridie. Please do one for me too.
Lots of love and good night,
Roxy XXXX

"That deserves a frame" said Fearghal. "Isn't it brilliant?"

Thrilled, I did as I was asked while Fearghal poured us a port glass each of the previous year's sloe gin.

"To my beautiful bride on the happiest day of my life," he said, lifting his glass of ruby liquid. "Well, perhaps I mean the *second* happiest. Now I am going to take you upstairs for the happiest *night* of our lives." . . . And so it was!

FIFTY-TWO

A REMARK OF ROXY'S CAUSED ME TO RAISE MY VOICE to her. "You did WHAT?" I shouted, about ten days later.

Roxy was due to start school the following day and we were upstairs in her bedroom laying out her uniform.

"I sent that picture to that evil witch and wrote a letter," she answered defiantly.

"Oh Roxy," I exclaimed, appalled. "How could you? I fear the damage that it could do."

"As long as the damage only hurts *her*," she said. "I feel that revenge is needed here."

"Surely the picture said it all. Whatever did you write in the letter? Oh, *why* didn't you discuss it with me first?"

"Because you sometimes need someone to fight your battles for you."

"Not this one, honey. It's over ... and we won."

"As for the letter," she went to a drawer and took out a sheet of paper. "Here is my rough, practice copy."

Un-dear Mrs Gabriel,
As well as wishing you an un-happy New Year, I am sending a picture of THE WEDDING OF THE YEAR *which will probly make you vomet your insides up. Be careful that the sick doesn't fall on the carpet cos all that poysin will make a great hole in it and rot the floor*

under neath. With any luck you will fall thro the hole and dye without the oppertuneity for absolooshun for your sin to your son.

I should tell you that I have gipsey blood. A gipsey kers has fatle consi kwences. For what you did to your son Fearghal who is so good and loving I kers you now and that kers will never be lifted. Next time you pretend to dye, you will dye.

May you rot in hell. Goodbye,

Roxanne Lavendi Dooley

I groaned, both inwardly and outwardly. "Oh Roxy, I so wish you hadn't done that."

"Are you angry at me, Maddie?"

"Yes, I am rather – but more hurt than anything that you should do such a thing without a word to me. Have you actually posted it?"

"Yes, I ran up to the box in the village."

"Did you stamp it?"

"Yes,. First Class."

A faint hope came to me. "Not a special EU one then?"

"No, just a red one." (*Perhaps it won't even be sent*, I thought).

"I didn't mean to hurt you; I just thought you and Fearghal would be pleased."

"Roxy, think about it. Remember that Mrs Gabriel is Fearghal's *mother*, however badly she behaved. I don't know what he would say about it. I'm afraid you're transferring all the hate you feel towards your father onto Fearghal's mother. Fearghal is a good man, Roxy, an ordained priest who preaches forgiveness and love. It would hurt him badly to know of this, and make him very disappointed in you . . . and after all the lovely things that he and other people said about you the other day. Is that what you really want?"

She started to cry. "No, no, NO," she sobbed. "That's the last thing I want to do. I just thought the old witch should be taught a lesson, that's all."

"Come here, baby.," I said, handing her a Kleenex and taking her in my arms. I heard Penn bounding up the stairs as she broke out in sobs once again.

"Look who you've upset now," I said, as he came to sit by her side, concern furrowing his brow. "Look, honey, I know where you're coming from with all this. It's done now and I think we've got to keep it a secret between ourselves and not tell Fearghal; not to deceive him, but to save his feelings."

"Yes, Maddie, thank you. I didn't mean to hurt either of you and make you disappointed in me. Shall I write again to Mrs G, and say the curse is lifted?"

"Let's leave it till the baby's born; then maybe you could send a picture of her and tell her then. We may not be able to forget, but it's important that we forgive."

"I get it," Roxy said, drying her eyes. "But I shall never, *ever,* forgive my Dad."

"That *was* truly unforgivable," I agreed.

To be fair, in all the weeks she had lived with me, this was the very first hint of 'trouble' that I'd encountered. It was never that she was 'too good to be true': her development had been phenomenal in the matter of increased confidence and ability to express herself, but she could on occasion be headstrong and assertive. I welcomed this when I compared her to the poor waif who had come crying to my door. She shared my love of words and had developed, through her voracious reading, an extensive vocabulary, as I have tried to recount in this narrative. I felt that she was more than well-equipped to face school, and she was eagerly excited about the prospect, showing no sign of reluctance or nervousness. I gave her what I hoped was sound advice about the social aspects of this new phase of her life.

"Roxy dear, you've been around adults for weeks now and have lacked the company of children of your own age. You've read a lot and you've written a lot. Listen a great deal and talk much less often. At school don't make your conversation sound too grown-up. Let people come to you, rather than trying to impress them. That way you'll make lots of friends. Smile as often as you can. No-one can resist dimples – and yours are one of your most attractive features – so *use* them!"

She ran to the mirror and smiled at herself. "They're just dents in my face," she laughed.

"No, they are much more than that," I assured her.

I had already told her that I'd registered her in my own surname so she should remember that she was Roxanne Manning now.

"Does that mean I'm adopted now?" she'd asked hopefully.

"Sort of; but we'd have to go through all the official procedure first. If it should happen, that's what you'd be called. I am keeping my maiden surname – for work, at least: it's simpler that way."

"But surely now you're Mrs Gabriel?"

"True; many will call me that, but I shall be like Grainne and keep the family name going."

*

Sarah's daughter, Emily, who was one of my clarinet pupils, had started at upper school in September so I had asked her to look out for Roxy and show her around on her first day. She was a shy girl and Sarah felt that it would be good for her to have a protégée. "She remembers what it was like to be new," she'd said. "Her best friend went away to boarding school, so she was on her own. She'll understand. We'll pick Roxy up at the end of the drive at 8.15 and they can go in together. Then I want to fit you in for a little check-up before surgery. Come at 9 o'clock will you? I'll tell the receptionist."

FIFTY-TWO

I WALKED UP THE DRIVE WITH ROXY TO WAIT FOR SARAH'S car. She was full of excitement and walked confidently beside me, her braided hair glossy and neat. The uniform was 'flexible', as is usual nowadays. She had opted for a grey skirt and black sweatshirt, black tights and matching slip-on shoes.

"We can always change anything that you feel isn't quite right," I'd told her, remembering how important it is for girls to go with the trend and not stand out from the crowd.

To my relief, Emily seemed to be wearing much the same sort of thing. She jumped out of the car, said 'hey' to Roxy and "you get in and I'll get in the other side."

Roxy turned to give me a quick hug. I felt a twinge of sadness and separation, but said cheerfully, "Have a great day. I can't *wait* to hear all about it when you come home. See you later, Sarah."

And off they drove on the day that was so important to Roxy.

*

"I rather think there's a bit of a surprise in here," Sarah said later, as she moved the (cold) stethoscope around on my belly."

"That sounds mysterious; hope it's not a hippo or something."

"That would account for your being rather larger at this stage than is normal. Let me concentrate a few seconds longer."

Moments later she removed the stethoscope, straightened up and looked at me.

"Don't be too shocked . . . but I think I can hear two heartbeats."

"Twins? Wow! I *am* shocked – but I shouldn't be, because they run in the family. My paternal grandmother had twins, though one was stillborn; and her own father was a twin."

"Well, you'll need another scan to be sure. I'll book you an appointment at the hospital. It's as well to be certain. It will make quite a difference in your nest-building."

"Whatever is Fearghal going to say? He'll be even more shocked than I am ... and Roxy! There'll be quite an exchange of news when she comes home. Thanks for taking her, Sarah; did she go into school happily?"

"She and Emily walked through the gates with linked arms. I don't know whose decision that was; hardly Emily's, I think. I can't recognise Roxy as the poor little girl she was when I first met her. Being with you has given her so much confidence."

"I'm really going to miss her now she's started school," I said. "She'll change again now and soon we'll both have those difficult teenage years ahead of us."

"I know. Dread it!"

I walked out to the car and sat in it thoughtfully for a while, not knowing if I was pleased or apprehensive. Both, I supposed.

"It seems you've been keeping a secret from me," I murmured to Elowen. "You've had a little companion in there all along: someone who's been hiding behind you. And I don't even know whether it's a boy or a girl."

*

I drove home, rehearsing what I would say to Fearghal but was greeted only by Penn. It was the first day of Fearghal's IT course, so he would be out all day. He had caught the bus as I was unable to drive him, so I wouldn't see either him or Roxy until I had finished at the estate agents' office. I did a few chores around the house, washing, cleaning and tidying, until it was time to leave for work.

Having promised to pick up the girls from school, I left the office in good time. In future they too would catch the bus from the village. I parked in the lot opposite the school gates and walked to wait for them, feeling like a new girl myself amongst the small group of mothers, most of whom were considerably older than I.

"You new around 'ere?" one woman drawled through the cigarette dangling from her lips. "Ent seen you afore."

"No, I've lived near Polburran for years. My daughter started today so I thought I'd pick her up on her first day."

"Lady of leisure then, are you?"

"No such luck. We all have to work for our living nowadays, don't we?"

"You're kidding me. You're a Yank, aren't you, no' a Cornishwoman?"

I had tried to iron out my transatlantic accent over the years – but unsuccessfully, it seemed.

"My grandmother was Cornish and my mother Irish, but I was raised in the US," I admitted.

"Oh, I like it," she said. "It's like the movies."

Meanwhile, a stream of pupils came through the gates, some in pairs, some in groups, a few alone, communing with their cell phones. There seemed to be hundreds passing me. At last, to my consternation, I saw Emily walking towards me alone.

"Where's Roxy?" I asked her anxiously.

"Don't worry, Miss Manning: the deputy head sent for her. I had to show her the way to his office. He said he wouldn't keep her long."

"I hope she's not in trouble," I said, aware that the deputy head is the member of staff responsible for discipline.

"Oh no, nothing like that. She's had a good day and has been smiling all the time. I wish I felt as happy as she looks to be at school."

"Ah here she is now," I said, relieved, as she came into view, carrying a full bag, her hair loose and blowing in the slight breeze. She came hurrying up to us, still smiling.

"Sorry to keep you, Mum", (it was the first time she had ever called me this). "Mr Jones wanted a word with me."

"All good?"

"All good – really really good."

"Great. Car's over the road. I look forward to hearing all about your day when Fearghal comes home."

As we walked towards the parking lot, I asked her what had happened to her braids.

"The boy sitting behind me in maths pulled the bands off when the teacher wasn't looking."

"Yeah; that's just the sort of thing that boys do," Emily remarked.

"What did you do?"

"Oh ... just ignored him," she said casually. "The plaits came undone so I just shook them out and combed my hair with my fingers. He gave the bands back in Double Art while having a good look at my work. I just smiled at him and said, 'Thanks'."

"Josh Willis is just an attention-seeker," Emily said sagely.

The girls got into the back seat of the car and chatted all the way back to Polburran. I dropped Emily outside her house.

"Thank you for the lift, Miss Manning." she said. "See you tomorrow, Roxy. Keep me a seat on the bus"

"Sure, I will. See you."

*

"Now we want to hear all about your day, Roxy – every detail. Then I might share a bit of news with you both."

Fearghal had arrived home shortly after we did and we were all in the kitchen having tea.

"I have homework to do after that," Roxy said proudly.

"Wow! Already?" said Fearghal. "Talk about throwing you in at the deep end."

"I asked for it, actually. That's why Mr. Jones wanted to see me. He teaches Maths. Also he wanted to know how my first day had been and congratulate me for getting a house point for Art."

She then gave a detailed account of her day and how she'd enjoyed most of it. First there had been an assembly for the whole school. She said that she'd never seen so many people gathered in the same space. "I'll never get to know them all," she said; "anymore than I'll get to find my way around those enormous buildings."

When there was a lull, Fearghal said, "And now, my darling, tell us how you got on at the surgery this morning."

"I think you'd better stay sitting down and brace yourselves," I warned. "Sarah thinks there are two heartbeats going on in there."

"A baby with two hearts?" Roxy gasped.

"Two hearts could mean two babies – twins, couldn't it?" Fearghal suggested.

"It will need another scan to confirm it," I said, "but yes, twins do run in my family. I'm surprised you didn't tell me, Roxy. Couldn't you see this coming?"

"Maybe I've become too much of a *Giorgio* and lost the gift," she mused. "But that's epic news. You'll need my help more than ever now, Maddie."

Fearghal was looking stunned. "I think I'd better go to fatherhood classes instead of on a computer course. Just give me a few days to get my head around this, girls."

"I've hardly got my own head around it yet," I laughed. "Just my body."

"Now calm down, both of you and don't panic," Roxy said, importantly. "I know all about babies and can take charge of the whole situation. You two know how to *make* them, but I've actually handled one."

"Oh, so you'll actually give birth to them for me, will you, Roxy?" I said, laughing. "Now off you go and do that homework while I ask Fearghal about *his* day."

FIFTY-THREE

NOW THAT THE NEW YEAR AND THE NEW TERM HAD begun, life settled back to something like normal for the rest of the winter and early spring. My scan showed that there was indeed another baby sharing Elowen's space, gender unknown because she or he insisted on hiding behind her. So we had to double up on our purchases, besides which we realised that space upstairs at Foxgloves was going to be a problem, there being only two full-sized bedrooms, one of which Roxy was occupying. There was, however, a much smaller box room and we decided to clear it and decorate and refurbish it. Whilst Fearghal and I were discussing this, Roxy said, "Two babies and all their stuff will never fit in there. It would make more sense if they had my room and I moved in to the little one."

"Are you sure you could manage in that little space with all your clothes and books and stuff, hon?" I asked, relieved that she had provided the solution herself.

Fearghal surprised us by showing his practical side. "In a previous life, I was quite good at DIY. How about a kind of bunk bed above a wardrobe-cum-cupboard, a chest of drawers and bookshelves?" he suggested. "I'm sure that could be done."

"Wow! That sounds wicked!" Roxy said. "Could you really do that?"

"With a little help from my friends. I'd have a good go at it – and I could always ask for help and advice."

"Very good idea," I said, "but bang goes your studio until after the babies are born. That will have to be our autumn project, after we return from Ireland. "We'll convert the shed and give you good northern light through a roof window."

Roxy continued to go happily to school each day, devoting herself assiduously to her daily assignment of homework each evening. Even her Math, of which I had been able to teach her only the basics, was showing promise. Gratifyingly, she received nothing but praise for her English – for which I allowed myself some credit!

"Josh Willis actually asked for my help the other day," she told us proudly. "He said, 'Come here, brainy swot, and help me with this'."

"What was your reaction to that?" Fearghal asked.

"I just told him that if he wanted my help he'd have to ask more politely."

"That's the spirit," Fearghal said approvingly. "You show him."

*

We celebrated Roxy's twelfth birthday on a Saturday at the beginning of April, with a lunchtime barbecue. It was a risky time of year to plan it – but then, in the British climate, any time of year for a barbecue is risky! She was very excited about her birthday and told me that it was the first time she'd had a party, or any recognition of the date, other than a greeting and a small present, though she was not about to admit this to her friends, she said.

I managed to make some H-A-P-P-Y B-I-R-T-H-D-A-Y bunting out of scraps of colourful fabric while she was at school, which I hid carefully away before she came home, until it was time to display it along the hedge. She invited Emily and six other friends from school and insisted that Mistletoe should be there as well. James and Suzy's teenage daughter, Rachel, who was in a higher class at school, had angled for an invitation as well – just in case 'your mum's ex-boyfriend' would be there. (*God forbid!* I thought, but said she could come, all the same).

Rain was forecast but we were lucky with the weather; even had some sunshine until we had finished eating, when a large, black cloud loomed up over the sea to the south west. Fearghal took charge of the barbecue. (*Why are men so much better at barbecuing*?). By now my bulk was considerable and Misty helped me on quick trips to the kitchen and back to bring fresh supplies. She remarked on how happy Roxy looked. "When the dimples are *in,* the sun's *out* in her face," she said. I told her that one of the girls, a Polish girl called Katya,, had said to me in a confidential way, "I love Roxy; her smile is like a welcome that's there all the time."

"So sweet," Mistletoe remarked.

We all went indoors when the cloud threatened to empty its contents on us; adults to the Music room to drink coffee; children to the kitchen to cease interacting with each other and communicate with their cell phones instead. Hitherto, Roxy had been using my old one, but we had given her a new one for her birthday and she needed help to set it up. My theory that young people should use them only in emergencies is 'So Not Cool' that I have had to accept that the cell phone is a vital extension of the personality – *of the body, almost* – in all social interaction. Banksy's picture of the embracing couple looking over one another's shoulder at their phones says it all!

*

"You kept that wedding very quiet," Pandora had said accusingly halfway through February. There was nothing in the press, no announcement, no photographs – nothing. I feel cheated, you being a celebrity and all that."

"I was only ever a celebrity through association," I pointed out. "Now I'm back to being the quiet, private individual I always was."

"My theory is that you didn't want TR to know what you were up to; didn't want him driving up in his purple cabriolet and kidnapping you from the very altar steps."

"You've been watching too many romantic movies," I laughed.

"Well, promise me an exclusive after the baby's born, then."

"It's *babies* with an s now, Pandora."

"Twins? Even better. Potential for a special feature. One may be TR's and the other your husband's. That would make a good story. It *is* biologically possible, I'm told."

"The sort of story that would end up in a Court of Law" I said over my shoulder as I walked away.

FIFTY-FOUR

THERE FOLLOWED WEEKS OF SERENE DOMESTICITY. While Fearghal wielded saw and screwdriver, hammer and spirit level in the room that was to be Roxy's, I shopped and sewed or scraped and painted in the soon-to-be nursery, enjoying the task in spite of my bulk. Roxy enjoyed helping us at weekends, taking a great interest in both rooms. It was a companiable and creative period – all three of us preparing the nest for the new arrivals.

During this time I went often to the well, communing silently with the spirits of my grandparents, particularly with Cecilia. The wedding flowers had shed their withered petals over the grass, joining the celandines, buttercups, primroses and cowslips. The grey-green leaves of the foxgloves were already thick and prolific, promising a good display in early summer. I promised that I would bring the babies as soon as they were born.

*

A month before I was due to give birth, I called Sadie, the family liaison support police officer, to inquire whether there was any likelihood of a court case coming up before May, or soon after, explaining that I wanted to support Roxy fully myself, which might be difficult whilst I was coping with two babies.

"*Two* babies?" she exclaimed. "I'll pop round; it'll be easier to talk face-to-face." so we arranged a time when Fearghal and I would both be at home and Roxy at school.

She was pleased to meet Fearghal and we were glad to realise that she seemed to be quite unaware of his days in custody in Ireland.

"My lips are sealed about this case, of course," she started. "All I can tell you is that it's a colossal operation, involving rings of people-traffickers and sex-slave traders all over the southwest – not just Mick Dooley and Vincent Colworthy. It's a slow process rounding them all up and ensuring that all the girls are safe. We don't want it all to go off at half-cock. Sorry, perhaps that was an inappropriate expression; begging your pardon, Padre." Fearghal and I both giggled. "Also, it's racially sensitive as well, which makes it all the more difficult. It will take quite a lot longer before it comes to court. I can really say no more than that."

"Thanks for telling us that much," I said. "Roxy is very different now from the frightened little girl you first met. She is so much more confident now – so the more time that elapses, the better – for her at least. But it is dreadful to think of the poor girls at risk from those monsters still out there."

"Has there been any news at all of Roxy's mother?" Fearghal asked. "We should like to adopt her, if there's no opposition from her birth mother – and it's what Roxy herself seems to want."

"Not a word has there been," Sadie answered. "I reckon she's lying low until she learns that those villains are behind bars for a very long time. She may be well to the north by now. If I were her I'd want to put as much space as possible between that man and myself."

*

I asked Suzy what might happen if Richenda Dooley turned up out of the blue. "Roxy is such a vital part of the family now that it would be really hard for us to part company," I told her.

"I think the court would see it as Roxy's own choice," said Suzy. "She told me how much she loves her life with you and Fearghal and how excited she is about school, the forthcoming birth of the twins and the planned trip to Ireland. She seems to have adapted to the *Giorgio* lifestyle and customs. We shall just have to wait and see, I suppose, how she sees her choices if and when Mrs. Dooley does turn up."

FIFTY-FIVE

In one or more African tribes, it's said, a man announces that his wife is giving birth by going into a public place and feigning the pangs and cries of labour whilst she quietly and privately gets on with the actual birth. Fearghal chose not to proceed thus when my time drew near, but expressed the wish to be involved at every stage, saying that he wanted to support me in every possible way.

"Never did I think that I should partake in such an event," he said wonderingly. "To witness a real birth, rather than simply reading aloud a biblical account in an ecclesiastical building."

He accompanied me to all my ante-natal appointments and took part in childbirth and parenting classes with me in those last few weeks.

As a chilly April yielded to a much warmer May, it was my delight and comfort to walk on the nearest sandy beach, ankle-deep in water where the wavelets creamed onto the sand. The frost-cold water numbed and soothed the ankles which tended to swell as a result of my increased weight. Pendragon would always accompany me and often Fearghal would come too. We learned a great deal more about each other on these walks, comparing our childhood memories; our conversations being often interspersed with easy, companionable periods of silent reflection. They were precious and happy days which we were to look back on fondly when the immediacy of parenthood claimed all our attention.

It was on one such walk in the middle of May that I had the first sign that my time had come: the beginning of the beginning, so to speak. Fearghal had stayed at home finishing a commission for Zara, for which there was an imminent deadline. He had been anxious about my going alone.

"It's all very well having Penn with you," he said, "but he's not a midwife; neither can he drive the car or make a telephone call."

I made light of his concern. "Relax, darling. I'm not due for another ten days. There's nothing going on in there except a fight as to who's going to be born first."

We had been amused at the signs that both babies were jockeying for position.

So there I was, walking along on this quiet beach when I felt a sharp pain at the base of my abdomen; so sharp that I cried out involuntarily and bent over, with both hands clutching at the source of the pain. Penn barked in alarm and a middle-aged woman detached herself from a group of adults and came running towards me.

"Are you all right, dear?" she asked. "I couldn't help noticing that you're pregnant. Do you think your baby's coming?"

"I don't know. I've never done it before. It was just a pain that took me by surprise. I'm two miles from home. I must get back to my husband. I'm expecting twins so I have to go to hospital for the birth."

"Oh wow!" she said. "Would you like me to drive you?"

"You're so kind. Perhaps we should call my husband and prepare him. I think I'd be all right to drive, if you could just see me to my car."

"I think it would be best if I drove you," she said firmly. "Look, you call your hubby while I tell the others what's going on and put some clothes on over my cozzie." It's not as warm as the early morning promised. Your feet must be *frozen*."

I fished for my cell-phone. To my relief, Fearghal picked up almost immediately.

"Darling, it's me. Look, don't panic, as Corporal Jones would say, but I think things may be kicking off. The football team may be about to come out onto the pitch."

"Oh, my darling girl! I should never have let you go alone. Whatever will you do now?"

"There's this kind lady who saw my predicament. She's offered to drive me ... wherever. I don't know whether I should come home or go straight to hospital."

"You'd have to come past the end of the drive anyway, so please come home first and I can drive you. Remember that nurse saying that you often get a false alarm?" Fearghal sounded calmer than I felt. "She's just coming back" I said. "Stay on the line, honey."

Another pain stabbed me and caused me to groan loudly, at which Penn started to bark again, looking vainly around for someone to blame for my discomfort.

"It's all right," the woman said. "My husband is going to follow in our car so that he can bring me back."

"This kind lady is going to bring me home, darling," I told Fearghal. "Just be ready for me. The suitcase of stuff is in the twins' room, all ready. Oh, and would you call the school and ask if they'll tell Roxy to go home with Emily, instead of getting off the bus where she usually does? Sarah will be okay with that, I'm sure."

Janet Lomas and her husband, Bill, were holidaymakers from Essex. They rented a cottage with two other couples every year in May or June, she told me. She kept up non-stop chat during the two-mile journey in an effort, I thought, to keep me from any panic I might be feeling. I feigned interest in everything she said, although the panic was certainly uppermost! I had visions of Fearghal having to act as midwife in a convenient lay-by en route to the hospital.

As we drew up to the back door of the cottage, Janet begged me to give her news of the birth.

"We're here for another week," she said. "We often have dinner at the Trevelyan Arms, so perhaps you'd leave a message there? This is definitely the most dramatic event we've ever been involved in down here."

Fearghal came out of the door and thanked her profusely, helping me out of the car and letting Pendragon out of the back. Bill saluted, shouted "good luck!" and leant over to open the passenger door for his wife.

"I'll just turn the car round," Fearghal said, "while you go in and do what you need to do ... but don't be long. I've spoken to the maternity staff and they say to come in anyway so that they can keep an eye on you. And Roxy will be taken care of . . . so no worries there."

FIFTY-SIX

It can be very boring for listeners or readers to endure a blow-by-blow account of a birth. Certainly, it assumes great importance in the memory of the woman involved; the pain, the anxiety, the effort, the exhaustion, followed, if one is blessed as we were, by the overwhelming joy, the utter delight, of meeting at last those two mysterious little people, the flowers, the fruit of our coming together in a loving union which we were powerless to resist.

So I shall spare you the details and say only that thirty six hours or so after the incident on the beach, with the loving attention of my beloved Fearghal and the expert help and encouragement of a midwife called Maggie, I was delivered first of a baby girl and then of a baby boy who had kept his gender a secret (from me at any rate) until he actually appeared on the scene.

We wept, Fearghal and I, as we heard their cries and protests at being out in the cold world. We wept again when they were handed back to us, having been wiped clean, weighed, measured, tagged and wrapped. Elowen, her name on a tiny wristband, was handed to me; her twin brother, labelled simply 'Baby Gabriel' was given to Fearghal.

"You can swap in a few moments," Maggie said. "They should both be put to the breast as soon as possible for the colostrum. They're born with a strong sucking reflex."

"Some of my tears are for Cecilia," I told Fearghal, trying to steady my voice. "I can't help thinking of how it must have been for her in those days, being treated as a disgrace to her family, having no loving partner to support her, having her lovely hair cut off; going through all of that only to give birth to a dead baby, while the live twin was stolen away and given – *sold* – to strangers. However did she cope for the rest of her life after all that tragedy?"

"She was a very resourceful woman, my love. Her constancy to Bruno sustained her in spite of it all. And then the boys found her and she put all her energy into helping them. Finally, when *you* came into her life the mystery was solved and she knew that Dominic was her and Bruno's son, and you her granddaughter." He smiled through his tears. "Speaking of Bruno, we must give this child a name. How about Bruno as one of them?"

"What was *your* father's name?" I asked.

"Finbarr Eoin – a good Irish saint's name. Finn for short."

"Then how about Finbarr Bruno Trelawney – the latter being Cecilia's beloved grandfather's surname? Trelawney was a famous Cornish hero. If Elowen is to have three names, Finn must have the same; after all, he lost the race to be first on the football pitch."

"Sounds very grand," Fearghal said. "So we're agreed, are we? Elowen Jane Cecilia Gabriel and Finbarr Bruno Trelawney Gabriel. That should equip them for becoming notable academics, politicians or writers . . . or simply ordinary peasant citizens of Cornwall and Ireland."

"Important names for important people," I said. "Time to change babies now, I think. Finn should be first at the bar, I guess; he had to wait the longest. I'm not sure whether one can feed two babies at a time. I think three or four hands would be needed."

Maggie came back to us. "Good to see she has latched on okay. It's great for their immune systems, the colostrum. Also it helps to simulate your real milk supply. I take it you intend to breast-feed?"

"I do, if I can," I declared. "It is the natural way – and what Nature intended must be best, I feel."

"Quite right," Maggie said approvingly. "Apart from being healthier and more convenient, it strengthens the bond between mother and child. She seems to be doing well."

"Actually, I 'm sure it's the boy," Fearghal said. "They are so alike that we may have to unwrap them to find out which is which."

Maggie laughed. "There's one very vital difference to be sure, but for the moment you can dress them in different colours. That will be all part of the fun. Now, Mr. Gabriel, you should go home and have some sleep." She turned to me. "You, Mother Madeleine, need to spend the rest of the night asleep, too."

She took Finn from me and laid him in the cot, and told Fearghal to hand over Elowen for her mini-feed. He kissed me fondly and thanked me touchingly for producing two wonderful babies, promising to phone Roxy, who was staying at Sarah's, and tell her the news in the morning before she left for school.

"Thank you, my darling," I said. "I could not have done any of it without you. I shall always treasure the memory of your close involvement today; of your seeing me through each pain and strain, without showing any panic or discomfort yourself. Bless you always, *Father* Gabriel."

"See you tomorrow," he said, kissing me again. "Well . . . I mean later today: it's three am!"

FIFTY-SEVEN

I WAS TOO EXCITED TO SLEEP MUCH. LITTLE DID I KNOW then that the previous night had been my last undisturbed sleep for quite a while.

After my early alarm on the beach, I had been kept in hospital for observation until I went into labour naturally. Twins and other multiple births were the cause of rather a lot of excitement in the Maternity Department, the Day Sister said, and it would not have been wise to risk a premature delivery on the way from Polburran to the hospital. I was advised to stay put until a feeding routine had been established and realised that I would be very grateful for the help and guidance that I received.

Fearghal turned up at around ten o'clock, saying that he too had been too excited to sleep.

"I had to come as early as possible to prove to myself that it wasn't all a dream," he said. "That we really did have two beautiful babies last night."

He looked at the sleeping babes in the cot, his face wreathed in smiles. "How did we manage to produce such angelic creatures?"

"Every parent thinks their own baby is beautiful, I suppose," I said. "Just look at them! They really *are* beautiful!"

Both babies had fair curls and eyes of dark sapphire blue. Any moment now they would wake up and we could cuddle them again and feel those perfect little fingers curling round our own.

"Roxy was so excited she wanted to take the day off school. I promised to bring her in this evening after school. She said she didn't know *how* she could get through the day until then. I also spoke to Mistletoe and Sarah and to James and Suzy. They all sent their love and congratulations and said they'll demand a viewing very soon."

"Great. Thanks for doing that. I think Bridie and Colm and co. should be told the news ASAP. Perhaps you could delegate that to Roxy; she'd love to be the bearer of that kind of news. Another thing: those kind people who helped drive me home that day asked if we'd leave a message for them at the Trevelyan Arms. Maybe Roxy could write a card to them and leave it on your way this evening. I'm sure she'll want to do all she can to help."

*

Roxy advanced up the ward that evening trying to run on tiptoe.

"I've come to meet my brother and sister," she said bursting with excitement. "This has been the longest day in my whole life."

"Oh, so you haven't come to see me then?" I asked in a mock aggrieved tone.

"Of course I have," she said, hugging me briefly, her eyes on the cot in which the babies lay end to end.

"Oh! They've got their eyes open," she breathed.

Fearghal, coming in her wake, said, "Yes, Roxy; they're not like kittens: they open their eyes straight away when they're awake."

She looked at him witheringly. "Fearghal, I *am* experienced in these matters, you know. Probably more than you are. I did have a baby brother once. When can we pick them up – and how do I tell the difference?"

"That's all sorted now," I said. "The nurses have done colour-coded identity wrist bands for them."

"Can I pick them up now, *please*?"

"Not both at the same time, honey," I said, moving from the chair to sit on the bed. "Sit here and I'll hand you Finn while Elowen has a turn at the bar."

"Oh, this is so *cool*," Roxy enthused, playing with the tiny hands that gripped her fingers. "Totally epic! Fearghal, will you please take a photo? Absolutely everyone in the school wants to see them. Some girls asked me today if they look like TR."

I was appalled and looked anxiously at Fearghal, whose eyes widened slightly.

"I hope you told them where to go. Tell them too, for the record, that your foster-mother never slept with that man and never would have consented to do so *if he was the last man on earth*. In fact, if I had known that my beloved Fearghal was waiting for me on a leafy island in Ireland, I wouldn't even have gone out with TR."

"Okay, okay; I mustn't upset your hormones; mind you, they should get better now you've given birth."

"Don't bank on it," Fearghal said, laughing. "They'll be working overtime on milk production now, what with two mouths to feed."

As I reminded Fearghal the following morning, Roxy's induction into school-life had been eased by my erstwhile celebrity connection. Because of this she had attained instant popularity, it seemed – not that she would divulge anything that her peers wanted to know, she assured me; "like that time he beat you up" she had said. "You wouldn't admit it, but I know that's what happened just before I came to you."

This was news to Fearghal who was very shocked and angry.

"If ever I get my hands on that man . . ." he began.

"Now then, man of God," I warned. "It turns out that 'the Irish loser' is a winner in every sense of the word. Forget TR: he's just a metaphorical wraith, lost in the purple shadow forest."

While we were talking, a small and beautiful arrangement of flowers was delivered to my bedside, bearing a card signed by Janet and Bill Lomas and friends, the message reading, 'Congratulations and every good wish to you both on the birth of your little ones'.

"How really sweet of them," we both said in unison. I detected Flora Bundy's hand in the arrangement of the lovely little basket and, sure enough, there was another little card of congratulation from her, hidden among the foliage.

"Roxy wrote an excellent letter to them," Fearghal told me. "We left it at reception before we came in yesterday. The four of them had booked in for dinner. Between mouthfuls of her tea, she did a picture of you walking along the beach in an advanced state of pregnancy. Then, as soon as we got home from visiting, she started on a large card for you, which she'll bring in this evening."

"Between us, Fearghal and I are coping remarkably well without you," Roxy said when she arrived that evening, having presented me with the card and checked the twins who were still asleep. "But we do miss you and can't wait for you to come home with the rest of the family."

I admired her card – a well-observed picture of the twins in their cot, and me in the chair by the bed. Other beds in the ward were sketched in, with a doctor and a nurse, both female, in the background. Inside Roxy had written:

Welcome to Elowen and Finn

Congratulations to Maddie and Fearghal

Come home soon. I love you all

"It's beautiful, Roxy," I said. "I shall treasure it always."

I stood it on the bedside locker where it could be admired by everyone.

"Another thing," Roxy said, looking anxiously for signs of life from the babies, "nearly everyone in the school, even some of the staff, wants me to put on FaceBook a photo of me holding *both* babies. D'you think we can do that?"

"I think we could do that when they wake up," Fearghal agreed.

"But Roxy," I countered, "I'd rather you didn't put it on FaceBook – just email to friends and ask them to forward it. I just feel it would be safer not to share it in the public domain."

"That's cool with me," she said. "Wow! I think someone's hungry; there are signs of waking. I haven't even heard them cry yet."

"Oh, it's quite a chorus when it gets going," I assured her.

FIFTY-EIGHT

A FEW SLEEPS, FEEDS AND DIAPER CHANGES LATER, I was allowed to go home – just in time to celebrate Fearghal's fortieth birthday, for which I was quite unprepared. I had planned to give a small party to mark the occasion but events had dictated otherwise. As it was, I asked Roxy to phone round and assemble a few friends for afternoon tea that Sunday, the day after my return, so that they could meet the new members of the family at the same time.

An embarrassing incident threatened to spoil the occasion as we sat at our impromptu party – though a loud, confident knock at the door seemed to please one member of the gathering who turned out to have engineered the interruption. Fearghal went out to open the door, followed by Penn who was barking furiously. I called him to my side and held him firmly. *A latecomer?* I wondered, but as I looked round, everyone invited seemed to be present.

"You must be the Irish loser," I heard a very familiar voice say.

"And *you* must be the *English* loser," was Fearghal's riposte. "You are not welcome here, Mr Richmond, so take your flowers and GO – NOW!" Penn pulled away from me and tried to push past Fearghal, barking and growling fiercely.

There were sounds of a struggle and then we heard the door being slammed shut and the bolt being slid across firmly. Fearghal looked like thunder as he came back into the room saying, "I'm just going to check all the doors and locks."

"O-M-G! I didn't even get to see him!" wept Rachel, James's and Suzy's fifteen-year-old daughter. There were raised eyebrows and dropped jaws all round.

"Oh Rach!" James exclaimed, reproachfully. "It was *you*, wasn't it?"

"Well, Roxy told us it wasn't going to be on Face Book so I posted the news on TR's fan page. I thought he ought to know. Oh, I'm totally gutted. I sort of invited him to tea."

"He had two armfuls of red roses," Fearghal said as he sat down again. "So there was no way that he could push past me."

Suzy stared furiously at her daughter. "You'd better apologise *on your knees* to Maddie and Fearghal. Now – stop sniffling and GET OVER IT!"

"Teenage hormones," I heard Roxy whisper to Emily.

"You have much to learn about human relationships, Rachel," James said sternly to his daughter. "Now, if Fearghal will let you out, I think we can do without your company. You can walk home alone. You know where to find the key. With any luck, TR will pick you up and give you a lift."

Once Rachel had gone, the equilibrium was soon restored, and Fearghal was duly congratulated and toasted in Champagne, kindly provided by Mistletoe. The twins, hitherto sleeping through all the kerfuffle, woke up and were handed around and admired by all.

*

The following morning, after Roxy had left for school, I told Fearghal that I would like to take the babes to Elowen's Well for a private baptism in the presence of Cecilia and Bruno, their great-grandparents.

"It wouldn't be sacrilegious, would it?" I asked him. "After all, you're an ordained priest and it is a sacrament."

"It is an honour," he answered. "Let's do it now – though expect screams: that water will be icy-cold. They can have an official baptism at a later date. This will be just between us two, Penn and your grandparents. Am I right in thinking we have a scallop shell in a kitchen cupboard?"

I nodded. "I think maybe Penn should not be a witness," I said. "If there are screams, he'll think we're doing something to hurt them."

I took a shell from the cupboard while Fearghal fetched a purificator from the little case in which he carried the vessels needed to administer the Sacrament to the sick, and the oils for the Last Rites.

We wrapped the babies in their shawls, put them in the pram and pushed them gently down the secret path to the well in the place of the ancestors' spirits. I put my hand into the water; it was indeed icy, however warmly the sun shone into the dell.

"Cecilia, Bruno," I said aloud. "The peace of your last resting place is about to be rudely shattered."

Fearghal laughed and nodded, then, rearranging his expression to suit the solemnity of the occasion, he said a prayer for 'the beloved souls who inhabit this sacred place'.

After he had blessed the water in the stone trough of the Well, I handed Elowen to him. Taking the scallop shell from his pocket and holding her close to the water, he said, " Elowen Cecilia Jane, I baptise you in the name of the Father, the Son and the Holy Spirit . . ." So saying, he poured very little water on her forehead and made the sign of the Cross while I handed him the purificator. Up to this point, we had heard only the grizzling and questing crying of hunger from either twin. The outrage and indignation that issued from that tiny mouth on this occasion was something else! Fearghal dabbed her forehead, kissed her and handed her back to me quickly, picking up Finn as he turned back to the well,

"Finbarr Bruno Trelawney . . ." the words, the water, the cross, the kiss ... not a sound! Finn simply opened his eyes wide in surprise and waved his hands free from the close-wrapped shawl.

"Well, they do say hereabouts that the devil comes out of the baby who cries at his or her baptism," I laughed. "So what do we make of that?"

"Just that it came out of Elowen big-time – but not out of himself," Fearghal observed. "Perhaps we shall have a naughty little boy on our hands."

FIFTY-NINE

EVERY PARENT WILL BE FAMILIAR WITH THE MIRACULOUS joy of a baby being born; but also of the worries and concerns of being new to the experience and responsibility of caring for these tiny creatures, these miniature human beings, so dependent. Are they still breathing? Are they getting enough nourishment? Does that crying indicate colic, hunger, a wet diaper or simply boredom? Having been the youngest of the family, I had no experience of babies whatsoever; neither did Fearghal. Roxy, however, settled happily into the role of nursemaid, her Whitsun half-term holiday conveniently coinciding with my first full week at home.

"You will instinctively do the right thing as a mother," she said wisely and reassuringly. "I can remember how it was with my little brother, Rory, so I can help quite a bit. And remember, you've got far more space and mod cons here than my Mum had in the 'van."

After we had been home a short while, I asked Roxy if she'd had any more thoughts about informing Fearghal's mother about the birth of her grandchildren and of lifting the Gipsy curse that she had put upon her.

"Yes – I've started on it in my *head*," she answered. "I thought I'd just send her a picture of the twins with their names, dates of birth and weights and stuff, and a small piece of card saying that I am prepared to lift the curse, to celebrate the birth of the grandchildren she never thought she'd have."

"That sounds good," I commented. "But just one thing, Roxy dear: run it past me before you send it, will you, please?"

"Sure, I will. I promise."

When she showed me, I was amused to see that she had added, *Maddie is an excellent mother, like she has been to me since she adopted me. You are very fortunate to have this curse lifted, considering the cruel way you treated your own son. Maddie would never do a thing like that. I hope you will come to regret your actions very deeply, before The Grim Reaper comes to take you away. When that day comes you will not be faking like last time, it will be for real.*

P.S. Do not expect any of us to come to your funeral.

"Epic!" I said. Roxy grimaced slightly, as children do when adults use their transiently trendy jargon. "And where did you come across that picturesque expression, *The Grim Reaper*?"

"In one of your books," she answered. "There was a scary picture of him somewhere else; I forget where. Maybe I should add that to the PS?"

"No, I think what you have already written will be enough to make her think – though you might add her to the picture in her witch's garb, about to be swiped off her broomstick by his scythe. No, forget I said that; leave it as it is."

*

And thus the days and weeks of the twins' infancy passed, mercifully without mishap or illness while, with the help of Fearghal and Roxy, I grew more confident and experienced at motherhood, even managing to do a little teaching as well as my work for the local newspaper's property pages. For sure, we needed the income to add to the trickle of funds received by Fearghal for his advertising work and the Council's contribution to Roxy's keep. I had spent a large amount of

Cecilia's legacy on preparing for the birth of the twins so the plans for Fearghal's studio had to be put on hold for a while.

Pandora asked me to write a short article about coping with twins, in which she introduced me thus:

> TR's ex, Maddie Manning, the Madeleine of his famous song, has had twins, a boy and a girl, with her newly-wed husband, an Irish artist. I asked her if she was going to call the boy Thane but she said no, he is called Finbarr after an Irish saint – Finn for short. The little girl is to be called Elowen, an old Cornish name . . .

I ended my brief contribution with a plug for an exhibition of Fearghal's paintings in the Tremayne Gallery in St Ives in September, after we'd had a chance to collect them from Ireland. I promised Pandora and her partner an invitation to the preview.

SIXTY

I AM RACKING MY BRAINS TO RECALL THE SIGNIFICANT events of those early months of the twins' life. Needless to say, every event concerning them was significant, but we all had our eyes fixed on the great event that was to come in August. Roxy was beside herself with excitement as I made the ferry bookings to Rosslare. Meanwhile, I had encouraged her to enter a short story competition for under-thirteens at the County Library. She had cast herself, fairly recognisably, as the young protagonist called Lauren, who had single-handedly assisted the delivery of her stepmother's twins on the roadside before the ambulance arrived. The accompanying illustration was very good – and fortunately, not too graphic! Her entry was praised by the judges for its drama, pathos and turns of phrase, and won her first prize. This was well reported in the Cornish Guardian and the WKG, which sent a reporter along for an interview and photograph. He suggested that she should pose holding one or both of the babies.

"And did it actually happen like that?" he asked.

Roxy bit her lip. "No, unfortunately not. I was at school and didn't even know that Maddie was in labour. However, it was just a fantasy of mine that I might have had to deliver the babies."

"And what do you want to do when you leave school?" he asked.

"As you might guess, I want to be a midwife . . . and an author, as well."

"A really worthy ambition," he commented. "Good luck to you, Roxy."

This exchange was faithfully reported the following week.

*

In July I celebrated my thirty-fourth birthday with a small party for local family and friends.

"That will make up for last year's going virtually unnoticed," I told Fearghal and Roxy. "TR took me out to dinner and tried to give me a diamond ring. But my mind was set on my forthcoming Irish trip, and some whisper of the heart must have told me that there I would meet the man of my dreams."

Roxy sighed. "Suppose you hadn't listened . . . life would have been different for us all. But then, we'd never have known what might have been, would we?"

"*The Road not Taken*," Fearghal said. "A poem by Robert Frost." He turned to me. "Thank you so much for finding me, my darling."

"We all found each other, didn't we?" Roxy said. "That poem, Fearghal: how does it go?"

"I can't quote it all; only the gist of it. It has always fascinated me. See if you can find it, Roxy."

I was clearing up in the kitchen after the guests had left when Roxy rushed in, saying excitedly, "I've found that poem on the internet and I really like it. Robert Frost is an American poet; did you know that? I'd like you to read it in the right accent – though really, it should be in a man's voice. It's really so good. I just *wish* I had written it myself because it says exactly what I was thinking." She held out the iPad towards me. I dried my hands and took it from her.

"Just supposing you had agreed to marry TR last year," she went on. "And gone to America with him on his tour: you might not have been here when I came looking for you; you might have a different baby by now. The twins wouldn't even have been *themselves*! Fearghal would still have been a priest in Ireland. His mother would still have been a witch but maybe not as wicked a witch as she turned out to be. And I – I would have been picked up by the police or Social Services and be in a children's home. Read it, Maddie, and you'll see that you were right not to be tempted by money and celebrity – and right to take the path less trodden."

"You are quite the philosopher, Roxy," I said. "Let's go and join Fearghal in the garden and I'll read it. And yes, I did know Frost was American and have always been fond of his work, particularly *Stopping by Woods on a Snowy Evening*

We sat on the garden bench in the evening sun. Roxy called to Fearghal to join us.

"And this *has* made all the difference," Roxy echoed thoughtfully, as I read the last line. She was sitting between Fearghal and me on the bench. "I'm not sure I believe in God all that much . . . but there must be someone up there to thank for my life right now."

"If your soul tells you that, you believe in God more than you think you do, sweetheart," Fearghal said, giving her a hug.

*

As the school term drew to a close, we were encouraged to go and discuss Roxy's progress with her teachers. Both Fearghal and I attended on the appointed evening and were most gratified to hear from her class teacher that her conduct could be summed up as the three Hs: happy, helpful and hard-working.

"She has such a sunny personality," the teacher told us. "Her sheer enjoyment of life is a lesson to us all. We have all noticed the effect her friendship has had on Emily Grant. She was such a timid little thing when she first came here."

"She's so proud of those twins," her Art teacher told us. "You'd think she'd produced them herself."

"Well, she's a great help when it comes to looking after them," Fearghal said, laughing.

"Does that mean you've a built-in baby-sitter now?"

"She's a little young yet. Tonight there's a local friend sitting in for an hour or two."

"Anyway, about her Artwork," Miss Trethewy went on, "she has real talent – and a great capacity for observation. Even though she has been here only two terms, I have recommended that she should receive the Junior Art prize. Please don't tell her yet, but I suggest you book your baby-sitter again next Thursday evening."

We did exactly that, and were thrilled to witness her gasp of surprise and the grace and delight with which she received her prize from Sir V.I.P. Bigwig who had been invited to present the prizes. Her smile and dimples were lit up by a most attractive blush as she walked back to her seat. I may have imagined it, but I think the applause lasted longer for Roxy than for most of the other prize-winners.

"I was completely gob-smacked," Roxy said as we left afterwards, "Why *me*? I haven't even been there a year yet. "

"Because you're the best," we assured her. "And it didn't take them long to find out. We're very proud of you, honey."

SIXTY-ONE

THE GREAT DAY OF DEPARTURE DAWNED AT LAST. Roxy's excitement was infectious. We were all excited, of course, but the whole business of preparation had her in a state of breathless anticipation.

"I was born a traveller," she said hoarsely, "but I never thought I should ride all that way in a car and cross the ocean, well, the Irish Sea. I can't wait to get on that ferry!"

Shopping had been done, presents for the Irish family bought, clothes washed, dried, ironed and packed; party attire dry-cleaned, covered and hung, dog bedding shaken and vacuumed. Baggage had to be drastically pared-down to allow space in the car for five human passengers and a large dog travelling several hundred miles. Pendragon's own essentials were packed around him, limiting his space in the trunk section of the Yeti somewhat. Roxy had to be wedged in at one end of the Moses basket which held a baby at either end. She had a minute space for her feet and no personal space other than that which her neat frame occupied. She said in her cheerful way that she would have put up with travelling on the roof-rack if necessary. James had lent us a large rack upon which Fearghal had fixed any luggage with a regular shape, such as cases and the stand and wheels for the carrycot. There would need to be a complete reshuffle when the twins needed feeding and a change of diaper at service station stops.

At last we were off. Annie had agreed to come in and tidy the breakfast things, clean up and lock up, as well as keeping an eye on the cottage while we were away. We had left plenty of time to get to the ferry port in Wales so that the babies could be fed and Penn and Roxy allowed some freedom of movement at intervals.

"In my new notebook I'm going to keep a diary of every single, wonderful day of our holiday," Roxy announced as we drove along. "I just haven't got the space to write at the moment."

"That's a great idea," I said. "I can include some of your memories in my next book."

"Cool! When I've got some elbow-room, I'll start it – because it all begins today with this momentous journey."

"You'll have much more space on the boat," Fearghal said." Make sure you bring the book aboard with you."

*

ROXY WRITING

The ferry crossing was EPIC! After all that time squashed up in the back of the car, it was such a relief to have all that space. Maddie and I took the hand baggage and ran up the stairs from the car deck and 'bagged' a long stretch of the continuous bench-seating by the windows in the huge passenger-seating area. Meanwhile, Fearghal brought the twins up by himself, though a kind granny-lady, travelling on her own, gave him a hand, while admiring the babies and making cooing noises at them.

Poor Penn had to be left in the car, of course. Fearghal and I had walked him round a bit while we were waiting in the queue to board.

"Don't worry about him," Fearghal said. "He's done this journey before and will do it again. He'll remember from last time that we'll come back in a few hours' time and find somewhere for him to stretch his legs when we drive off the other side."

The granny-person sat quite near to us. I knelt up on the bench next to her and exclaimed as I saw the port buildings moving past.

"We're off," she told me. "It's a strange sensation when the buildings appear to move, isn't it, when it's really the ship moving past *them*? Is this your first visit to Ireland?" Her accent was a bit like Fearghal's.

"Yes, and I'm feeling ecstatic about it."

"I can see that," she said, laughing. "Your dimples are so deep, I can almost see your back teeth. You haven't stopped smiling since you came aboard."

"Maddie says that if I always keep smiling I'll make friends more easily," I told her.

"Is Maddie your sister?"

My turn to laugh. "No way – she's my *Mum*: that is, I'm actually adopted and those twins are my sister and brother."

"What a lovely family to belong to," she said.

"Yes – I'm a very happy soul."

"Indeed; I can feel that in here." she pointed to the centre of her rather large bosom (*bossom*) which was clad in a stripy mint-coloured tee-shirt.

"Actually," I went on, "Fearghal is Irish. Maddie is too, although she sounds American. They met when she came on holiday here this time last year."

"They haven't wasted any time then, have they?"

"None at all," I assured her. "They only got married a few months ago. She was already pregnant. Here, I'll show you some photos, if you like."

I got out my phone and flicked through till I found the wedding photos.

"That must have been a grand occasion: lovely bride and equally lovely bridesmaid, if I may say so."

“Actually, I was a flower-girl,” I explained.” There were issues around that wedding because Fearghal used to be a priest.”

“Holy Mother Mary and all the saints!” she exclaimed. (I realised then that she was Irish and Catholic because the Brits don’t speak that way). I decided I had said enough. (*Maddie probably won’t include this account*).

To finish our chat I announced, “Actually, I’m rather an Agnostic, myself; but when I’m older I intend to write to the Pope and tell him priests should be allowed to marry: I shall *harangue* him. How can they advise people on family life – you know, sex and stuff – if they can’t do it from experience? What do you yourself think?”

“I think I’m going to read my magazine now, dear. But I shall think about what you said and discuss it with my brother who is himself a priest in Kilkenny.”

I noticed her giving Fearghal interested, sidelong glances as he danced Finn on his knees while Maddie was feeding Elowen. The lady kept her friendly expression but I could tell that she was rather shocked. I took the hint when she opened her magazine, and slid back along the seat to join the others.

“That was a long conversation,” Maddie observed. “Whatever were you talking about?”

“Life; history – that kind of stuff. I’m going to write it down while it’s still fresh in my mind; not that you’ll probably include it in the family archive.”

*

MADDIE WRITING

I have left Roxy’s first contribution unexpurgated – except for correcting her spelling in places; for example, she had difficulty with such words as ‘harangue’ and ‘ecstatic’, although quite aware of their meaning as far as her state of mind is concerned! As for her having told her travelling companion too much: the lady was visiting her brother in Kilkenny which is the opposite side of the country to 'somewhere south of Limerick', so it was unlikely that she had heard anything of Fearghal's defection. In any case, what did it matter now? He is a married man and a father of children. It would give Mrs X and her priestly brother something to talk about, but no harm could be done by it.

Roxy's renewed excitement at seeing the Irish coast soon turned to disappointment as we drove off the ferry.

"But it doesn't look any different from England and Wales," she moaned. "This is my first time abroad and I expect to see something foreign and mysterious."

"Wait until tomorrow when we go further west," Fearghal said. "Then you'll see lakes, mountains and places like Bunratty Castle; *then* you'll notice a difference."

"Can we stop at the castle?" she begged. "Ple-e-e-ase!"

"Just long enough to take a photo," I promised firmly. "We can't be in touring mode with all this luggage on board. We'll have a whole week to explore before the party when we get there, which we need to do as soon as possible."

I had booked a night in a dog-and-child-friendly B and B a few kilometres along our route. I had warned our hostess on the phone that our arrival would be a bit of an invasion, but she and her husband or partner gave us a typical warm Irish welcome and made us aware that they considered it an honour to host 'such a lovely family'.

*

ROXY WRITING

It was a long, long way, though it did get a bit more foreign as we went along – which reminds me: we bypassed a town called Tipperary and I remembered hearing the old marching song in a TV programme about the First World War. I was surprised to find it was a real place!

Sometimes there were mountains in the distance and small lakes visible from the road. When we bypassed Limerick we actually went through a tunnel *under* the River Shannon. We had to pay a toll for this. (There's a girl at school called Shannon). Not long after this, we saw Bunratty Castle which I s o-o want to visit another time. We stopped just long enough for me to take a pic of it. We left the motorway to go into the town of Ennis to get a late lunch. (And there's a boy at school with that name too, but neither of them is Irish). When we'd parked, we found a nice restaurant the other side of a footbridge over the River Fergus (not Fearghal!) and had a burger and chips with ketchup at a table on the balcony overlooking the river. It was warm enough but quite windy (the weather I mean, not the burger – joke!). Maddie said not to eat too much because Bridie had said that there would be a hot meal for us in the evening. The waiters and waitresses were very welcoming and friendly. That was all exciting enough but there was more to come . . .

I knew that when we reached Galway, our journey was nearly at an end. Both Maddie and Fearghal said what a lovely city it was – and very special to them. They promised that we would go there again on one of our days out but that now we must bypass it and push on because the road beyond was a tricky one with many bends and wonderful scenery. The road at Oughterard was very close to the lake (Lough Corrib) but then we turned away from it again for a few kilometres and there ahead of us were the real mountains: the twelve Bens of Connemara and wild, wild country which made me want to gallop along on a wild horse, singing at the top of my voice. Just as I was thinking this, we turned down a narrow road towards the lough and then into the back entrance of the huge house, Oirbsean House Hotel, on along the drive and finally pulled up at Oirbsean Lodge, a smaller version of the big house itself, with a beautiful garden stretching down to the waterside. Before we were all out of the car, the front door opened and a lovely old lady with silvery white hair came out, a beaming smile of welcome lighting up her face. If old ladies can be called pretty, she is the prettiest in the world. She hugged Maddie and shook Fearghal's hand (because she hadn't met him before). When I scrambled out of my tight seat she opened her arms, saying, "This must be the Roxy I've heard so much about," and she hugged me as if I was her favourite grandchild. (When the time is right I'll ask her if I may call her 'Grandma'). Fearghal let Penn out of the back and he went bounding off down to the water's edge, then came straight back to greet Bridie. Of course, he remembers everything from last year.

"There are still two more little people for me to greet," Bridie said. "How your family has increased since your last visit, Maddie!"

Maddie and I hauled the carry-cot out of the car between us while Fearghal untied the stand and wheel section from the roof-rack. Finn and Elowen had woken up when the car stopped and, as Bridie looked at them, they both smiled their gummy smiles at her.

"You'd think they'd be fretful after that long journey," she said. "I've a fleecy baby-rug laid on the floor inside and I bet they're dying for a good kick-around while we all have a cup of tea."

SIXTY-TWO

MADDIE WRITING

WHAT A WELCOME – AND WHAT AN INVASION OF Bridie's quiet and elegant household! After that very special cup of tea, I went upstairs to feed the twins while Fearghal and Roxy unpacked the car. I suggested to Bridie that she should hide away and not witness the distribution of our clutter to all corners of the house.

She laughed; " Declan, Colm and Grainne will be home very soon and we can all meet for a drink before dinner, once the children are settled. Your mam and dad will drive over from Cong as well."

"Do I count as a child or an adult?" Roxy asked anxiously.

"Oh, an adult, to be sure," Bridie said. "You're almost a teen; but don't grow up too quickly."

"Well, Maddie thinks I'm a wee bit precocious." At this, Bridie and I exchanged wide smiles.

"I heard all about you from Colm and Dominic when they returned after the wedding," said Bridie. "They said you were quite a character; a great personality. That will get you everywhere you want to be in life."

"I can't wait to see Uncle Colm again. I've got lots of jokes and riddles for him – and I haven't even met Maddie's mum yet."

"I bet Colm's dying to see you again, too – and Maddie and Fearghal and these new little arrivals too. They're all coming back from Galway together. Declan had business there today and the other two work there anyway."

Meanwhile the babies, unwrapped from their clothing and diapers, were enjoying the freedom of their limbs on the fleecy rug Bridie had put down for them. They kicked their legs and punched the air with their little fists, chortling and gurgling with delight all the while.

*

ROXY WRITING

The difference between Maddie and me writing is that I'm doing it *now*, like a diary. She has started the book this will be in but, by the time she finishes it, it will be in the past; especially now she's got the babies to keep her so busy. The trouble is that when anyone reads it, this wonderful holiday visit will be over – except in my memory, where it will stay forever. Nevertheless, I haven't written anything for nearly a week because we've been on the go the whole time. At first I was content just to stay around the garden and the lake; it was all such an adventure. Fearghal has taught me to row in the smallest of the three boats, and we've been over to Inishcoll, *his* island – or maybe I should say *his and her* island because that's where they first met. It's also where the twins were made. (How my friend Emily laughed when I told her that they were born with MADE IN IRELAND stamped on their bottoms in green letters!)

They won't let me take the boat out on my own. "One day," they say, "but not until you're older and more experienced." I can picture myself in a few years' time, taking Elowen and Finn out in the middle-sized boat. How epic will that be for them – and for me!

On our third day it rained all day. It seems a silly thing to say but some rain storms seem to be wetter than others.

That was the wettest I've ever known . . . and I speak as a country girl. The mist came down from the mountains and wrapped itself around the garden and house like a cold, wet, grey blanket. So we stayed indoors and worked on a table-plan for the lunch party. Bridie then produced some old family photographs to go with the ones Maddie had brought with us, both her own and her grandmother's. I helped them to make a montage to display at the party.

"Some of these were taken sixty or seventy years ago," Bridie told me. "Now those young people will be positively geriatric, like me," she laughed. "In fact, it'll be a real Oldies' party.

"You don't seem old to me," I said reassuringly. "Anyway, it's an eightieth birthday party so some guests are bound to be a bit old."

"What a sweet, tactful girl you are, to be sure!" Bridie said, smiling her lovely, warm smile.

"I have had the benefit of good parental guidance," I said.

Anyway, the next day the sun came out with a sort of smile, as if that rain had never happened; so we left Bridie looking after the little ones and Penn, and drove through the beautiful scenery of Connemara as far as Croagh Patrick. The mountain stands on its own, quite close to the sea, some miles away from the Twelve Bens further to the south. Last year the top had been in cloud so Maddie had not climbed it, but today we knew that there would be a glorious view from the top so we ate our picnic in the car park, put on our walking shoes, and set out along the stony trail which wound up the north side. Fearghal told us we had just missed the 'Reek Sunday' pilgrimage, when some pilgrims climb the mountain barefooted.

"They will do it again on the Feast of the Assumption, August 15th," he said. "So we are between the two. This is the holiest mountain in Ireland because St Patrick spent forty days and nights fasting at the summit."

Nevertheless, there were still crowds of people making the ascent. The first point of interest was a large statue of St Patrick himself. I wondered how he had survived on top of this mountain for more than a month. The path was very stony indeed and I shuddered at the idea of going all that way with bare feet. Fearghal explained the subject of Penance but I argued that I couldn't see the point of it. Surely it was a punishment for the really bad people, not for those who said that they loved God and worshipped him every day.

"Yes, well religion and the doctrine thereof are a complicated subject."

"Too complicated for me," I answered. "I'm just doing this for the climb and the view from the top. God made this mountain for us to enjoy. Believe me: I know."

"Direct line to Himself up there?" Maddie asked.

"That's about it," I said.

Anyway, after about two hours, we reached the top and the view was simply *epic*: blue, sparkling sea crowded with large and small islands within Clew Bay and further out; mountains, towns, villages and roads and boreens through all the wildness of Connemara spread out below us. I couldn't stop gasping. There is a chapel at the top and a railed, stony enclosure labelled ST PATRICK'S BED. Oh wow! Poor man! Imagine sleeping there for all those nights, especially when the cold, grey blanket of cloud descended and the wild wind swept the summit. Apparently he didn't die of exposure, however. In the chapel, I prayed all sorts of private prayers to St Patrick . . . mainly that all my worries would go away.

Anyone would think I was a tour guide, going into all that detail; nevertheless, perhaps that visit was the highlight of all our outings. I can't wait to tell Emily and my other friends about it. I had a vision up there, I shall tell them; a vision of joy and delight and the wonders of nature . . . and a sense of achievement that I had climbed so far to experience it. If you are reading this, you must go there before you die. (But go on a fine, clear day, otherwise it *will* be a penance to climb all that way only to be wrapped in cold, wet cloud – even if you have got your shoes on!).

When we got back, I had a serious conversation with Bridie. We were in the kitchen and I was helping her with the vegetables for the evening meal, while Maddie was upstairs feeding the twins and Fearghal was out walking with Uncle Colm and Penn.

"Mrs O'Malley – Bridie – Can I ask you something?" I started.

"Of course you can, my dear."

"Please may I call you Grandma – even if you aren't really? I know you have lots of other grandchildren."

"Yes, of course you may, *a cushla*. I should be honoured."

"I do have a nana somewhere in England, but I never used to see her much; my birth-mum's mother. Did Maddie tell you why my mother left home – and me?"

"She did, darling. It was a terrible, terrible thing altogether that happened to you both, my pet; especially *you*."

"I knew you'd understand, Grandma, because of what happened to you. Maddie let me read her grandmother's story and your own."

"But what happened to you was far worse, my love. Your own *daddy*!"

I tried to fight back the tears I could feel coming but they had already escaped and were running down my cheeks.

"I don't want to talk about it … or even think about it," I sobbed. "I haven't even mentioned it to Maddie for months now. I just try never to think about it. I know that one day I shall have to go to court and stuff; but I dread that so much. I feel so safe here with you – not that I don't have a great life with Maddie and Fearghal and the twins."

"I know you do – and those two villains are in prison so cannot harm you. I understand that the *Gardai* – police you call them – have a massive operation going on to arrest several more individuals who are part of the same criminal ring. It all takes a very long time so it may be some while yet."

I nodded. "And then there's the fear that my real mother will try to find me and take me away so that Maddie and Fearghal won't be able to adopt me."

"Sweetheart, it's your choice, I believe. The Family Court would rule in your favour, I guess, now you're old enough to know your own mind."

"Grandma, please don't tell anyone we've talked about this, not even Maddie; I don't want anyone to pity me, EVER!"

My new gran made a zipping action across her mouth. "I didn't hear a word of it." She smiled her lovely smile and gave me a hug and a kiss. "Now, how are those carrots coming along?"

"This one will be coming along on its own." I held up a carrot that seemed to have two legs.

"A bit rude, that one," she laughed. "He's got a little willy as well."

So when Maddie came down into the kitchen, we were laughing so much that she thought I had laughed till I cried.

SIXTY-THREE

MADDIE WRITING

I THINK ROXY HAD FORGOTTEN THAT CONFIDENTIAL chat with Bridie when I asked her for her notebook, a year or two later. She said that it was in a box with all the mementoes of that first visit to Ireland: a small piece of stone from Croagh Patrick, a piece of green Connemara marble, a few postcards and photos of the Oirbsean Lodge family. Absorbed in some other pursuit, she simply ran up to her room, fetched the box and handed it to me. She was right when she wrote that I would take a long time to finish this archive!

As the Croagh Patrick 'pilgrimage' was clearly for her the highlight of our expeditions around Connemara, she wrote no more on the subject: our visits to Kylemore Abbey, the Connemara Heritage and History Centre, Cong Abbey ruins and gardens and a day in Galway City itself – even having tea in the café where, the previous year, Fearghal had been recognised by one of his former parishioners. We certainly made use of the week we spent at Oirbsean Lodge before the reason that we were all assembled there at all: the long-awaited gathering of the O'Malley/Manning clans in honour of Bridie's special birthday.

The eve of the great day, August 9th, dawned at last, with its arrivals from all over Ireland, from England, from America. I felt rather guilty that my considerably extended family had taken up the whole of Bridie's available space at Oirbsean

Lodge, leaving no room for her own family. However, Grainne reassured me that her sisters, Rosie and Connie and their families were all going to fit into her and Colm's house, Green Lake Cottage; the two pairs of cousins, Jack and Niamh, Aoife and Cahal, were going to have 'enormous fun' camping in the garden. Nearly all of the other guests were booked into the hotel, in the Orangery of which the lunchtime party was to take place the following day. I had arranged to meet some of them in the bar before dinner and introduce Fearghal. Some of the invited guests I had not even met, myself, despite my having written of them in my previous archives. Cecilia's dear friend and confidante, William (Wat) Tyler was one of these, attending with his long-term partner, Dimitrios. They had not been able to come to Cecilia's memorial gathering, being on an extended visit to Greece at the time. Another I had not met before were Bridie's old friend from her London days, Jenny Webb. Now eighty one and recently widowed, she had flown over from England and Declan had driven to Ireland West Airport to meet her and drive her back to Killogan. It was hoped that Robert Gray and his sister, Sarah, the friends of Cecilia's childhood days in Porthwenna would be on the same flight. Also, due to drive from Dublin, was Bridie's god-daughter, Deirdre-Clare, the daughter of Patty Doyle, whose birth Bridie had witnessed in the Kilburn Magdalene home back in 1954. She and Patty had managed to keep in touch, in spite of the rules of the establishment which decreed that there should be no attachments or friendships formed during the girls' incarceration there. Bridie had hinted that Declan and Deirdre Clare seemed to have 'clicked' when they met for the first time and that there was every possibility that their mutual attraction might be cemented during this visit.

"I shall not make my grand entrance until tomorrow," Bridie announced. "So, while I babysit, you and Fearghal go over and greet the guests. They've had strict directions from

Reception to meet in the bar at 7.15 before dinner at 8-ish. Don't forget, it's your wedding party as well, this reunion. You'll be very much in demand, you and Fearghal. Roxy can stay here with me and make *her* grand entrance tomorrow with me and the two youngest adopted grandchildren. If you feel inclined, stay to dinner with them all. I'm only having a cold, salad supper here and they'll all want to see as much of you as possible. And don't worry: all the guests' costs are courtesy of the Hotel.

So Fearghal and I showered, tidied ourselves up, changed into something more formal and walked hand-in-hand over to the Hotel to greet old acquaintances and form new ones. One arrival that I had been keeping as a surprise for 'the boys', was that of the attendance of the Manning's former maid, Cathleen, who had been driven up from Limerick by Katie, their adoptive sister, and her husband, Will Sullivan. It was Cathleen, you may remember, who had been instrumental in re-establishing the boys' connection with their adoptive sisters after their enforced imprisonment in their infamous Industrial Schools.

Gradually the party assembled; my father and mother, Dominic and Frances were already sitting at a table with Grainne and Colm when we arrived. It was easier for me to think of them as 'Mom and Dad' now that they were finally living together – in a house a few miles away in Co Mayo. Mom embraced me fondly and said she was dying to see her new grandchildren.

"What happened to Bridget and Liam?" I asked, referring to my elder (half) siblings who still lived in America.

"They stayed behind to settle the kids after their long flight; but they'll all be here tomorrow," my mother explained. "And your grandmother (*Moira, now 96*) is saving her strength for tomorrow, too."

At that moment Dominic jumped to his feet to greet the party coming through the arched entrance to the Bar:

"Cathleen!" he shouted in delight. "How wonderful to see you! Someone kept this very quiet . . . and Katie! Did you all come together?" There were hugs all round and resounding kisses. "Come and sit down and meet the others. What can I get you to drink?"

Next to appear were Dominic's old mentor, Tom Fahy from Derry. . . with Aunt Isobel *(or Izzy, Cecilia's stepchildren's aunt)*. These two had formed an attachment at the 'Ashes Ceremony' and were, in their early eighties, living together over the border.

Hard on their heels came Declan and Deirdre-Clare, arm-in-arm, looking as if they might already have been 'cementing' their relationship in her hotel bedroom. She was an attractive woman, still slim and blonde at sixty, well-dressed and graceful. In spite of her 'unfortunate' beginnings in the Magdalene home and the struggle that Patty had had in keeping her from adoption and bringing her up single-handed, she had made quite a name for herself in political circles. There was no doubt that she and Declan made a handsome couple.

In all the ensuing confusion of introductions and greetings, I kept a keen look-out for Bridie's old friend, Jenny Webb-Moore, as Bridie had asked me to do. ("It may be daunting to walk alone into a crowd of people who all seem to know each other," she'd advised.). As it was, Jenny came in with Rob and Sarah whom she had already met, being on the same flight from London.

The 'pre-party' was completed with the arrival of two white-haired and white-bearded gentlemen in their mid-eighties, Wat Tyler and his civil partner, Dimitrios. Looking at all the white heads in the assembled company, I murmured to Fearghal, "It's a good thing there'll be some young people at the main party tomorrow. It's quite a geriatric crowd so far."

He smiled. "Well neither you nor I can boast a single grey hair yet . . . but they will come, as they come to us all in the end. By the time the babes reach middle age, we'll be as grey as Pendragon – if we're fortunate enough to see that day

SIXTY-FOUR

Roxy and I wore our wedding outfits to the main party, as did Fearghal too. This time I had no bump to disguise, no flowers to carry. Elowen and Finn were dressed in their best outfits, the old cliché of pink or blue to denote their gender. We were aware that we were a well-presented family but, as I explained to Roxy, this day was not about us but was, first and foremost, in honour of Bridie's special birthday. She was the belle of the ball, just as she had been at the Christmas Ball sixty years ago. She emerged from her bedroom looking touchingly beautiful and elegant in a lace dress and jacket in a vibrant cobalt blue which set off the silvery-whiteness of her softly curled hair. Roxy gasped when she saw her. "Wow! You look absolutely stunning, Grandma."

"As do you all, my dears," she said, smiling. "Shall we walk over now so that we're ready to greet everyone? Declan didn't come home last night: he must be there already."

Fearghal and I exchanged a knowing look and smiled. "Bit more cementing going on," he murmured to me with a broad grin as the others walked together towards the stairs. We each took a handle of the carrycot and followed them down. The four of us left the house together, Fearghal pushing the pram and I leading Penn.

*

For old-time's sake, Bridie had been allotted the Garden Suite for her private use during the party. It was the suite in which she had met her long-lost son, Declan, after fifty-eight years of silence; it was also the suite in which she had stayed the night after the Christmas Ball of 1954 when her beloved Charles had first proposed to her. Both Roxy and I had suggested that she should make her entrance down the magnificent staircase of Oirbsean House, just as she had done on that occasion, to greet her guests. Grainne had agreed that this would be a good plan.

"Grainne and I will meet and greet the guests," I said, "and phone up when it's time for you to make your grand entrance."

She agreed to this plan rather reluctantly but, when the time came, her appearance was really spectacular. A deafening cheer went up from the guests who had assembled in the hall below with welcoming glasses of Champagne to watch her poised and graceful descent. She paused three steps from the bottom of the stairs and a sudden hush fell.

"How wonderful to see you all!" she said. "The first time I descended these stairs, nearly sixty years ago, I was wearing an emerald green ball-gown, and the man who became my beloved husband came forward with hands outstretched to welcome me. I was almost happy for the first time in weeks after being forced to leave my four-month-old first-born son and his adoptive brother in the care of their new parents. You see them before you now, soon to celebrate their own sixtieth birthdays – Declan, known to some of you as Donal." She held out a hand and he stepped forward to take it in his; "and Dominic, the other child of my heart." He too took her outstretched hand and we all clapped and cheered.

"You all know the story," she went on. "You would not be here otherwise – all the special people whom I know and love. Welcome, welcome, to my other beloved children and grandchildren and to all those of you who have come from far and wide. I wish you all a very happy day and know that this will be one of the happiest days in all my eighty years. I may be persuaded to say a little more later on but I do tend to be over-emotional on these occasions. If so, I know you'll understand and forgive me. Meanwhile please make sure that your glass is full and that you introduce yourselves to anyone you've not met before today."

*

After enough time for drinks, reunions, renewals of acquaintance and introductions, we were all called into the Orangery, which was elegantly laid for the luncheon party with four large, round tables, each of eight or nine places, there being thirty-four guests other than two babies and a dog. Bridie and I had designed a table-plan and Roxy had made the place-names on a rainy day. Bridie had wanted Fearghal and me at her table but I had pointed out that her own family should be with her, so we compromised with a Birthday table and a Wedding table. Roxy was happy to sit with the cousins at a table close by. "After all, they'll be *my* cousins too, so I'd better get to know them," she had declared. She thought it would be a good idea to have Pendragon under their table so that he could clean up anything the younger children might drop. "I'll make sure he doesn't frighten any of them, I promise," she'd said, sensibly.

*

After we had finished our most delicious lunch and were drinking our coffee, our glasses were refilled with Champagne, and Declan stood to pay tribute to his mother.

"It is with such great pleasure that I welcome you all here today, ladies and gentlemen. It is hard to believe that, in view of the religious and social attitudes of the 1950s, this eightieth birthday of my dear mother is the first I have been able to share with her since the day I was born, nearly sixty years ago. As Mother pointed out, everyone present here today knows the story, except the latest sweet additions to the clan. (*He indicates the twins, now on their parents' laps*). They, no doubt, will learn of it all in good time.

"I never was one for public speaking, so you will be spared a long discourse, (*Cheers*) but today of all days there must be exceptions to my rule: Mother – Bridie – it gives me the greatest pleasure to wish you the very happiest of birthdays, and to say, in front of witnesses, that finding you has made all the difference to my life. You have tamed the wild, headstrong character I once was, as I'm sure those who know me will have observed. (*Laughter and cries of 'hear, hear!'*). I know that, in spite of your absence in my life, you were always there for me . . . and to have found you and my sisters at long last is the greatest pleasure I could ever have wished for.

I ask you all now to be upstanding and drink a toast to the Birthday girl – my lovely mother – Bridie. Long may she live and may we all be here again for her hundredth!"

After the toast, Bridie stands, dabbing her eyes with a delicate lace handkerchief.

"As you see, I'm already overwhelmed, surrounded as I am on this very special day by all the people I love most in the world. Thank you, Declan, for your sweet words. Yes, we found each other at last – and we have to thank your sister, Katie, for spotting the coincidence that brought us together. As for your other sisters, my three beloved daughters, thank you, all of you, especially Grainne, for making this celebration happen today. The Hotel has done us proud, I'm sure you'll all agree. When we have finished in here, after a short comfort break, I have arranged for a group photograph on the steps outside so that we can all have a record of this long-awaited event.

"I'm not sure about my hundredth – cannot even be sure of reaching ninety – so let's do it again in 2019 when, God willing, I reach eighty-five. I have to admit that some of us here today are quite old, even if eighty *is* the new sixty. It's grand altogether to see old friends again and to welcome new ones. It's also great to see so many young ones as well – my grandchildren and great grandchildren, both natural and adoptive. My dearest wish is that you young ones will keep this family connection going in the years to come and pass it down through the generations. This reminds me that we have Maddie to thank for being the lynch-pin holding us all together, starting with the remarkable memoir of her lovely other grandmother, Cecily, recording the way in which she was found by Declan and her dear son, Dominic. If anything good came out of that disgraceful Magdalene home, it was the boys themselves and the connection that brings us all here today.

Today is also about Maddie's marriage to Fearghal at the end of last year. My family's present to them is one of Fearghal's paintings framed in three sections, which you may have noticed in its temporary position in the entrance hall. Please join me in a toast to Maddie, Fearghal and their delightful family."

Toasting and applause, after which Fearghal stands.

"May I speak in response to Bridie's kind words? I promise it will not be lengthy. (*A friendly cheer from Colm*). I must say how proud and honoured I am to be welcomed and accepted into this amazing family or clan. Thank you so very much for your hospitality today and for your support and encouragement throughout our courtship and marriage so far. Also for rescuing and framing the purple shadow painting, the story of which you will read in Maddie's book, which I am told will bear the same title. We are now nearly three quarters of the way through 2014. Maddie has already begun the archive that would bring us up to date; but I think you may like to take a bet on when it will be completed. You see before you a very busy lady, with both arms full of babies, not to mention our talented about-to-be teenager, Roxy. Moreover, Maddie is a working mum as well.

"We had a very quiet wedding, for reasons that will become apparent in that story. I hope those of you who may not yet know will not be shocked when I tell you that I used to be a Catholic priest. There is no guarantee when a priest takes his vows that he will not fall in love. My chance meeting with my lovely wife seemed like a gift from Heaven to me and I chose to follow my heart and not my vocation. The Catholic Church closed its doors to me . . . I have however been accepted to bat for the other team. (*Laughter*). There will come a time when priests are allowed to marry, but it will come too late for us. Roxy, our adopted daughter, plans to take this matter up with His Holiness, Pope Francis, as soon as she is old enough. Bless her!

"May God bless you all – and do please make yourselves known to me during the short break that I'm told is to follow. Those of you who will still be here tomorrow are warmly invited to the baptism of Elowen and Finn at 3 o'clock in the church where Fr Michael Power has agreed to receive them into the Church. It sounds as if our young ones are ready for *their* lunch. (*Impatient grizzling*).

A toast, please, to our gracious hosts and the entire Magdalene Clan – not forgetting absent members, especially Cecilia herself, who would be delighted indeed to know of our gathering here today."

Everyone stood up and glasses were raised as Fearghal's words were repeated to cheers and applause.

SIXTY-FIVE

As I write, I see before me the framed photograph taken by a professional photographer on that day of such happy memory. It hangs above my desk in our bedroom next to Roxy's own picture of our wedding. Roxy, too, has her own copy hanging above her bed.

Indeed, it has taken me four years to finish our story, as many so rightly predicted! However, whatever has happened since that day, I feel that that ever-to-be-remembered occasion is the 'appropriate' place to end our family story for the moment, with the assurance that the Magdalene Clan is very much alive and flourishing, judging by the appreciative messages from old and young that poured in to greet us on our arrival back in Cornwall, many of which affirmed that the Magdalene Connection would be kept alive for as long as there is life in its members.

The triptych, Fearghal's painting, thoughtfully framed so that it will fit together without a break, and entitled BEYOND THE PURPLE SHADOW, hangs in the sitting room, above the mantelpiece on the broad chimney breast of the fireplace at the far end, so anyone who enters the room is sure to see it and be reminded of the rocky journey to that place of safety where we are now. With such a metaphor to remind us, we feel truly blessed, and look forward to a life of easy contentment, surrounded by our precious children: they in whose guardianship the great legacy of The Magdalene Connection will live on.

AUTHOR'S NOTE *and* ACKNOWLEDGEMENTS

My thanks, as always, to Jo Vernon in whose tranquil French garden I remember writing several pages of this book. Loving thanks also to Isaac who gave me the idea of introducing an extra character with problems that had to be addressed by Maddie. Once again, I am indebted to Saliha for her painstaking editing and pertinent assessment of my work; also to Charlie for his help with computer matters and formatting. In the book I mention (the fictional) Bruno Sabra's own musical setting of Yeats's poem *The Lake Isle of Innisfree*. Others have set it to music but, rather than refer to a fictional setting, I composed a melody myself and, being too idle to write a piano accompaniment, I asked my friend, David Moss, a much more accomplished musician than I, to compose one. My many thanks to him for so readily complying with my request.

I started the penultimate chapter on location, as it were: in the sunny garden of a lovely B&B overlooking Lough Corrib, when I accompanied Isaac to a conference at the National University of Ireland in Galway in June, 2017. My many thanks to Bernadette Feerick for a most comfortable and enjoyable weekend in the lovely Lakeshore House, An Fhairche, which we can wholeheartedly recommend.